THE LAST OPERATIVE

**Center Point
Large Print**

Also by Jerry B. Jenkins
and available from Center Point Large Print:

Riven

THE LAST OPERATIVE

Jerry B. Jenkins

CENTER POINT PUBLISHING
THORNDIKE, MAINE

This Center Point Large Print edition
is published in the year 2010 by arrangement with
Tyndale House Publishers, Inc.

The text of this Large Print edition is unabridged.
In other aspects, this book may vary
from the original edition.
Printed in the United States of America
on permanent paper.
Set in 16-point Times New Roman type.

ISBN: 978-1-60285-877-0

Library of Congress Cataloging-in-Publication Data

Jenkins, Jerry B.
  The last operative / Jerry B. Jenkins. — Center Point large print ed.
    p. cm.
  Originally published: Carol Stream, Ill. : Tyndale House Publishers, 2010.
  ISBN 978-1-60285-877-0 (library binding : alk. paper)
  1. Intelligence officers—Fiction. 2. Large type books. I. Title.
PS3560.E485L37 2010
813'.54—dc22
                                                              2010019982

To the memory of my mother,
Bonita Grace Thompson Jenkins

Author's Note

I URGE YOUNG novelists to resist the temptation to intrude on the fictional construct with extensive front matter. Write a simple dedication, I say, then get on with your story.

I violate my own rule here under special circumstances. You see, *The Last Operative* is a thorough retelling of my very first stand-alone novel. In its original incarnation more than twenty years ago, it was titled *The Operative*, and it marked what I considered a major step in my writing journey.

My first novels consisted of a thirteen-book series called The Margo Mysteries, and they caught the eye of a veteran Harper & Row editor named Roy Carlisle. Roy was intrigued by those early efforts and encouraged me to keep growing and stretching. I had long secretly dreamed of one day publishing with Harper & Row, so it became my goal to land a contract with them.

Every chance I got in the late 1970s and early 1980s, I pitched Roy on the idea of an international spy thriller. He listened but urged me to keep learning my chops in series fiction. I still remember the day Roy finally called to offer a contract on *The Operative*. I felt I was graduating to a new level of publishing.

The original novel garnered a loyal cadre of fans, including some on the staff of Tyndale

House. I couldn't have been happier last year when they asked me to do a complete rewrite and resurrect the story for today's readers. It became a labor of love to dive back into it and write it the way I would today after twenty-plus years' more experience.

Students of the genre may be intrigued by what I consider a successful experiment in the treatment of dialogue in this novel. Much is made today over how to make dialogue taut and realistic and how best to attribute it to various characters with variations on "he said" or "she said." In the original version—and this one—I took what I considered a thoroughly innovative approach by having no such language, and not one reader told me they were confused about who was speaking.

I attempted to make each speaker obvious without attributing any dialogue to anyone. See what you think, and let me know if you agree it works.

And the dedication should come as no surprise.

Jerry B. Jenkins
COLORADO SPRINGS
JUNE 2010

Bad guys look like bad guys

only in the movies.

1

JORDAN KIRKWOOD COULDN'T push the ghastly secret from his mind. Nothing in more than twenty years as an international operative for the National Security Agency had prepared him for this. What would he tell his wife, due to arrive soon from the States? Nothing. How could he? He could tell no one yet, even inside the NSA.

Heathrow didn't slow to a crawl late at night the way the world's other least-favorite airport (Chicago O'Hare) did. Though the evening peak was past, several international flights were scheduled to arrive around the same time, and crowds were beginning to build again.

Closed-circuit monitors told Jordan that Rosemary's flight would arrive at midnight in Terminal Two, which surprised him. Terminal Two was limited almost entirely to European traffic. One of his decoy flights from Frankfurt had arrived there.

Rosemary had been extraordinarily patient for two decades, given that Jordan had been largely an absentee husband and father. Why did this have to arise on the cusp of an overdue vacation? He had promised to set work aside for ten late-October days.

Jordan could hardly believe he had borne such

awful news for just more than twenty-four hours. It seemed a career ago. That assignment in Frankfurt—though it had called for a disguise— consisted of mere information gathering. A walk in the park.

But, oh, the information that came later.

Jordan should have suspected something. Why would the NSA take a senior operative out of Washington just days before his vacation and assign him an essentially menial task in Germany? When the assignment was over and he had asked an executive assistant at Joint Operations Support Activity Frankfurt (JOSAF) to book his flight to London, she had stalled. "Chief Stuart would like to see you first, sir."

"*Stu's* here?"

Stanley Stuart was a jowly man Jordan hadn't seen in more than fifteen years. They bear-hugged, but there was no small talk, no bringing Jordan up to date. Stuart clearly had something on his mind.

"Sorry to bring you all the way over here on a trivial assignment, but the man I trust most in the agency once told me you were honest to a fault."

Jordan shrugged. His Midwestern upbringing— including a whipping for lying at age eight— contributed to an overdeveloped conscience.

Stuart scowled. "True or not, Kirkwood? Chuck

Wallington told me you wouldn't so much as tell a white lie outside the line of duty."

Jordan cocked his head. "It's true, sir." He was sure he didn't want to know—just before his vacation—where this was leading.

"Jordan, I'm sixty-six years old. I retire this year."

"I hope you're not looking for a successor, because I—"

Stuart glared. "C'mon, you know we don't pick our own replacements. And I certainly wouldn't wish *this* job on anyone, least of all you. I just need to know: can I trust you?"

Was Jordan still idealistic? No. Did he still serve his country for the same reasons as when he started? No. Had he become cynical? Sure. But had his integrity been compromised?

"I'm as jaded as anyone who's been in this business this long, but if I was worthy of that comment from Chuck years ago, it still holds."

The older man seemed to study him, then leaned forward and spoke in a whisper. "You know Altstadt, Jordan?"

"Old Town? Sure. Bordering the river."

Stuart nodded. "In the medieval section with the craftsmen's shops is one called Jurgen Glaswerks. Meet me there tonight at eight."

Now in London, eager to rendezvous with Rosemary, Jordan wished he'd told Stanley Stuart

13

he was not a candidate for whatever the man wanted to tell him. Now it all lay on his shoulders, and he'd had to come to the airport in disguise: dyed hair, hat, glasses over dark contact lenses, phony name, documents, the whole bit. He even carried a wooden pistol that had slipped through the security scan. Tonight, as in Germany the day before, Jordan was P. Gaston Blanc, a Frenchman.

On his way to Terminal Two, Jordan noticed a Scotland Yard antiterrorist commander he'd worked with three years before on an al-Qaeda plot. He and Huck Williamsby knew each other well. To test himself, he stepped up to the freckly, red-haired detective.

"*S'il vous plaît*, why would American flight arrive in Terminal Two?"

"Security, I suspect. Wouldn't make too much of it."

"*Merci.*"

Williamsby had manifested not the slightest suspicion. Jordan felt a tingle at the base of his spine. There were days when he enjoyed doing his job well. But not tonight. Maybe never again. Not since Frankfurt.

Finding the Jurgen Glaswerks the night before had been easy. Jordan was greeted in broken English by the owner, who thrust out his hand. "Jurgen Hasse! You are welcome, Mr. Blanc."

With barely a moment to notice the beautiful

blown-glass objects gracing the shelves, Jordan followed Herr Hasse to the back. There his host left him with Stanley Stuart. Stuart sat stiffly with his hands deep in his pockets, hat still on. The room was cold, despite a few remaining glowing coals from the central furnace, where the craftsmen plied their trade by day. Jordan kept his coat on too, hat in his hands.

Stuart nodded toward the departing Hasse. "An old, trusted friend. I wish he had your gifts. Okay, listen. The place is not bugged. Hasse has never seen or heard of either of us." He rose wearily and dragged a heavy, wood chair next to Jordan's. "Wife died four years back."

"I heard. Sorry."

Stuart waved. "Lost the drive after that. Never gave her enough time. Never loved her as much as the agency, she always said. But when she was gone, I knew I'd been showing off for her all those years. The change in my performance showed, Jordan, and quick. I was reassigned here so fast, it took me two years to get over the jet lag."

At least Rosemary had never leveled such a charge at Jordan. She had, however, challenged him about letting her raise the kids, in essence alone.

"I lost track of you, Stu. Didn't even know you were here."

The older man stared deep into Jordan's eyes, as if searching for whether he was doing the right thing. His voice came thick. "I can't even tell Chuck this, Jordan. And there's no one else I trust."

"Why can't you tell Chuck, Stu? You know you can trust him."

"He trusts you. That'll have to be good enough for me."

"But it's not. I can tell. Why don't you tell Chuck and let him bring me into it if he wants?" Jordan knew the JOSAF chief had brought him to Germany for this conversation alone. "It's not that I'm not willing."

Stuart glowered. "Wallington is no longer in a position to do any good. And this is big, Jordan, bigger than anything I've been involved with. Ever. I've been offered money."

"From whom? For what?"

Stuart leaned and looked to the front of the shop, then over his shoulder to the dark alley. He pulled from his breast pocket a fat manila envelope folded vertically and carefully pressed it flat against his thigh.

From it he produced three eight-by-ten photographs. The first showed a rolling hillside with a huge dark opening cut into one end. Stuart pointed with his thumb. "That's maybe two hundred feet across."

The second showed two corrugated metal doors recessed beneath the earthen overhang of the hill, set in about thirty feet.

"What's that look like to you, Jordan?"

"A Quonset hut."

"Bigger. Remember the relative size of all this."

"A hangar."

"Exactly."

The third photo had been taken inside the hangar. Jordan pursed his lips. "MiGs?"

Stuart nodded.

Jordan held the photograph up to the dim light. "Russian MiG-23s, but no markings. I don't get it."

Stuart reached for the picture and placed it gently atop the others, as if he had been perusing family photos.

"Pure white. The naked eye can hardly find them in the sky on a clear day. And this shows only a handful. Actually, there are nearly two dozen in that one double hangar built into the hill-side."

"Cuba?"

"Don't get ahead of me."

"Sorry."

"It's just that now that I've shown you these, I have to tell you, and you have to believe me. I'm not a crazy old man, though you'll be tempted to think so. Your job, your life, will never be the same."

It had been too late to opt out. And now Jordan owned the information as he found himself among

17

the first at the thick, Plexiglas window that separated the waiting from the arriving at Heathrow's Terminal Two. The customs desks had been hastily assembled, as if the arrival here was a late change. The glass partition, however, was permanent.

As midnight neared, Jordan felt the heat of the murmuring crowd stacked several deep behind him. The long line of more than four hundred that began emerging from the Boeing 747 was being divided into rows, and the tedious customs process began.

Jordan felt a nagging in the pit of his stomach. Was it only coincidence that he had run into Williamsby, that the overseas flight was arriving at Terminal Two, and that the customs officers had apparently been instructed to search all hand luggage?

The process would take more than an hour, and it simply wasn't standard. As he watched for Rosemary, he steeled himself against giving anything away. He would have to explain the disguise, of course, and she would be disappointed. But he couldn't tell her the truth, regardless of how much he wanted to. He wished he could tell her the whole story, how Stan Stuart looked when he slowly rose and paced that cold room.

The last ember had died, and the only light came from a couple of weak bulbs. "The hangar is not in Cuba, Jordan, though the planes came from there, yes. Actually, they came from Russia first, of course."

Jordan squinted at him. "Stu, we both know Russia is no longer our enemy. We've known of Russian MiGs in Cuba for years. If we found these in Iraq or Iran—"

Stuart held up a hand. "These are not *in* Cuba, and I didn't say I thought the Russians knew where they'd wind up when they sold them or traded them. This hangar is set back into the earth, invisible from the sky, but it lies in the middle of four other hangars that hold crop-dusting planes. Radar or aerial photography merely confirms the existence of crop dusters and a landing strip in the middle of thousands of acres of farm country."

Jordan was afraid to ask where.

Stuart continued. "You're aware, of course, of the radar gap along the southern border of the U.S."

Jordan nodded. "Biggest headache is drug traffic."

"Until now. These MiGs were shipped from Cuba to Central America, trucked north into Mexico, and then flown—get this, *flown*—into the United States, either between El Paso and Laredo, Texas, or through the Yucatán Channel via the Gulf of Mexico."

Jordan felt the blood drain from his face.

"You're telling me Russian MiGs are hangared in the States?"

"Alabama."

After about twenty minutes, Rosemary appeared in the line about forty feet away and directly in front of Jordan.

Her queue moved particularly slowly, but she appeared in good spirits, youthful and radiant. Jordan more than ever regretted the necessity of his charade. If only he could pop out the lenses and take off the hat and wave at Rosemary, smiling in a way she would recognize.

But she had apparently already studied the crowd behind the glass and decided he wasn't there yet. She struck up a conversation with the passenger behind her, a well-dressed man of average height and blond hair. Jordan watched as they seemed to notice the lightning from the north windows. The man's eyes widened, and she laughed. From her huge shoulder bag, Rosemary dug out a pair of rubber boots and her cell phone.

The man extended his hand to help her balance on one foot as she put them on. Then she studied the crowd behind the glass again, speaking to the man. Jordan assumed she was talking about him.

Opening lines ran through his mind as he fixed his eyes on her. If she recognized him before he spoke, good for her. But as her line slowly advanced, Rosemary looked at him, behind him,

20

next to him, and at him again. He made no attempt to hide or look away. She looked through him as if he weren't there.

As excited as Jordan was to welcome the love of his life to London, the previous night's conversation reverberated in his mind.

Jordan had stood in the Glaswerks. "I don't believe it."

"You'll believe it if they launch a nuclear attack from within our own borders."

"These are warhead equipped?"

"That's the next step."

"How did you get this, Stu? Who else knows?"

"The one who wants to pay me to help him mislead the agency and to let him know if anyone outside his circle catches wind of this."

"Who?"

"Jordan! If I knew that, I wouldn't be talking to you. But the source is highly placed at headquarters."

"*Our* headquarters? How do you know that?"

"How long have I been around? I can tell from what he knows."

"Is he al-Qaeda counterintelligence?"

"Nah. He's new to them, I'm sure. In it for the dough."

"And how does he contact you?"

"Through a local mouthpiece. I've been sitting on this, Jordan, trying to decide whom to tell."

"Stu! This can't wait!"

"You think I don't know that? Who was I supposed to tell? I could go to the top, but what if it's him?"

"Don't be silly."

"Silly! Whoever this is knows all about me, Jordan. Things no one but an insider would know. I had to tell somebody who can check it out before making any moves. I'm not sure Chuck can do that anymore."

"So, your deal is what?"

"If I help, big dollars. If I don't, I'm dead."

Jordan closed his eyes. "You've been threatened before, Stu. We all have."

"The message goes like this: I've got what, fifteen, twenty more years on this earth? So what's it matter who's making threats or carrying out attacks if I'm taken care of, and handsomely?"

"Like you'd be for sale."

"It makes me sick, Jordan, and don't even imply otherwise."

"But why you?"

"Why not me? This guy says he knows I have to hate the agency for reassigning me after my wife's death. I don't, but if that's what he wants to think . . . I'm just glad he started with me instead of somebody who might have been tempted."

"What are you going to do?"

"I'm doing it, Jordan. I'm telling you. Somebody big is helping al-Qaeda put planes in our backyard. And if I forget that at least one of our own people is involved and just send the Defense Department in shooting, how do I know that won't make things worse? We could be talking World War III here."

Rosemary looked troubled that she had been unable to spot Jordan, so he pulled out his cell and called her.

"Hey, babe, I'm here but in disguise. Tell you why later."

"Oh, Jordan!"

"Sorry."

"Listen, my seatmate reminded me so much of you. He and his wife live in—"

Suddenly, from just above Jordan's head and to his right came rapid-fire explosions that drove everyone to the floor. Even as he went down, Jordan's trained ear told him that the weapon tearing into the Plexiglas—weakening it, cracking it, shattering it, then cutting down the passengers as they scattered, screaming—was an American-made M16.

Jordan turned to get a look at the gunman. But a thick, middle-aged woman had tumbled onto his legs and an infant had been dropped on his back. As the others behind the now-fragmented glass moaned and wailed and hid their faces, Jordan knew the attacker was long gone. He drew himself up to his knees, carefully reaching back to set the baby on the floor.

Jordan studied the damage. The M16 carried a thirty-shot magazine the shooter had apparently spent in a single burst of nearly two and a half seconds. The first dozen shots had obliterated the Plexiglas except for a three-foot mountain-shaped shard that could now be pushed over with a finger.

Once the glass barrier had been eliminated, the next twenty or so rounds had been sprayed over a fifteen-foot area, leveling customs agents, disintegrating their wood partitions, and dropping passengers forty feet away with 5.56-millimeter ammunition that had kill power from five hundred yards.

Uniformed police and military personnel appeared from all directions, shouting instructions, securing doors and corridors. Plainclothesmen, including Huck Williamsby, arrived seconds later, producing badges and displaying them from breast pockets.

Passengers who had miraculously survived huddled behind their baggage, plainly terrified of the weapons they saw in several hands. Directly in front of Jordan, a customs agent bled from the head and neck. He crawled toward Jordan, expressionless, eyes vacant, but his nervous system soon surrendered, his elbows quit, and his forehead thudded on the floor. Beyond him and his splintered workstation, Jordan saw the central target of the shooting, the line in which his wife had been standing, bantering with a stranger who had the misfortune to look like her husband.

The man had taken at least four rounds and had flipped backward, his metal attaché case sent sliding. Rosemary's shoulder bag had been ripped from her by the fusillade, dropping in front of her to provide a macabre cushion for her petite body after she had spun, ankles crossing and tripping her.

She had landed with her back on the bag, her head hanging over it, facing Jordan. Not sixty seconds had passed since the deafening *brack* of gunfire, and now Jordan cursed himself for his disguise. Bile rose in his throat, and he fought emotion that threatened the levelheadedness he had always possessed in the face of carnage.

He whipped off his hat and glasses and squinted hard as he pressed fingers to the sides of his eyelids, popping out the dark lenses. He stared into Rosemary's unblinking eyes, willing her to see him, to recognize him despite the dark hair, brows, and lashes, showing her his teeth in a half-sobbing smile, praying she would recognize him.

Jordan knelt transfixed before the image of her there. As officials scurried among the dead and the dying, he caught and lost and caught again a view of her face. No expression. No response. He would learn later that a bullet had entered her neck from the left, nicked a jugular vein, destroyed a carotid artery, pierced a parathyroid gland, and severed her spinal cord on its way toward the heart of the man behind her.

Rosemary Kirkwood had been dead before she hit the floor.

2

DURING THE SPECTRAL silence between the thirty shots and the shrieking that still carried on, Jordan realized his beloved was gone. Still, he stared at Rosemary, wanted to go to her, to pull her from her awkward repose.

With contact lenses, hat, and glasses in his hands, he slowly rose. Law enforcement officers tried to calm the survivors, and people all around him tried to tell the authorities what had happened. They imagined the gunfire had come from all angles and concocted a band of male and female terrorists with grenades and pistols.

Jordan was tempted to break his cover, to assure the authorities that all the bullets had come from the same weapon. But he knew this would be determined soon enough by ballistics experts and a thorough study of the scene. If, as he expected, everyone was detained, he would get his chance to tell what he saw. The weapon seemed to have been trained on his wife and her companion, and the deadly arc of coverage had not expanded until the two of them, and many in front of and behind them, lay twisted in death.

His breath came short as he and others were herded to the south wall. Jordan strained to keep his wife in sight. His thoughts were jumbled. How ironic that he had worked on forcing the job from his mind when he was home in Maryland. But he and Rosemary had long dreamed of the day Christa and Ken would be in college and Rosemary could occasionally travel with him. That time was now, and while Europe had long since lost its novelty for Jordan, he had planned to make the most of it for her sake. Rosemary said she would rather he find some uninterrupted time for the kids, but she also told him that, short of that, she looked forward to this trip the way she looked forward to Christmas. Or heaven.

It had been just an expression.

Physicians and paramedics descended, first frantically trying to determine who was beyond help. Williamsby and an assistant directed them to the line with the most damage. With index fingers and thumbs pressed deep under victims' jaws to check for pulses, they began realigning the bodies.

The man behind Rosemary Kirkwood was quickly outlined in charcoal marker on the light-colored floor. One of Williamsby's men also withdrew identifying papers from the body and scribbled on a notepad. The dead man was then gently turned onto his back, feet drawn together at the ankles, hands draped across his midsection. A metallic covering, like a survival blanket, was pulled over his head. In a few minutes, a second wave of medical personnel lifted him onto a stretcher and transported him to the makeshift morgue under the windows on the opposite wall.

As more and more bodies were traced and their identification secured, someone from the grieving line would cry out:

"There's my husband!"

"That's Jenny!"

"Oh!"

Now it seemed there were more uniformed policemen than passengers and relatives, most busy keeping the grieving from disturbing the scene of terror. They spoke softly, trying to soothe the mourners while keeping the area uncontaminated. "You must understand. You are safe, and we are doing everything possible."

When his wife was examined by a young paramedic, Jordan was stricken with a feeling of invaded privacy of the most intimate sort. The check for her pulse was cursory, and the medic merely pointed to an officer, who traced her, fished through her bag for identification, and wrote on his pad.

It was all Jordan could do to suppress a sob as a man and a woman gently lifted Rosemary so the bag could be removed from beneath her. He wanted to run to her, to embrace her, to comfort her, to speak to her. Now they laid her flat, uncrossed her ankles, and covered her. When her face was no longer visible, Jordan felt as if his own breath had been stolen. He knew the same procedure was being performed on a dozen others, but his eyes were riveted on Rosemary until someone came with a stretcher and moved her away. Her life's blood, which had poured from several wounds, already looked as black as the tracing of her body on the floor.

Jordan had the presence of mind to reinsert his contact lenses and put on his glasses and cap. Unless Williamsby recognized him or someone searched him, he planned to maintain his alias. The ruse was futile, he knew, senseless. He would be asked why he was at the airport, for whom he was waiting, and what his business was. It would be easier to state his real name and tell of his relationship to one of the slain passengers, but how would he explain his bogus papers? And what would he say he did for a living?

Jordan was so shaken that he could react only from instinct. And his instinct was to mislead. For now he was P. Gaston Blanc from La Havre, France. He might be arrested on suspicion of terrorism, of being an accomplice to murder, but as long as he kept Williamsby in sight, he would have an ally.

Certainly this was one occasion when it was permissible to break the code of silence and fully identify oneself. Who could fault him? Jordan's reserves were gone, and when he looked deep inside for the strength to do what was right, all he found were the automatic reactions that had been drilled into him.

He would keep his head, keep his emotions intact, use panic as a signal to trigger calmness. What scared him was that his conditioned responses confused him. He had never imagined this situation, the way he had preformulated so many other crises. Had he been attacked or kidnapped, he would have responded in an instant with immediate, logical, life-preserving actions. He'd have been prepared.

For the first time, Jordan resented his own training. He envied others their grief and fear. Such open, honest, human, unchecked emotions. Why couldn't he cry out, "That's Rosemary! That's my wife! Oh, God, how could You let this happen to her? To me?"

But his orderly, disciplined mind traced overlapping thoughts that wouldn't untangle, wouldn't focus, wouldn't free him to pray, to cry, to shout, to fear, to show anger, to grieve. Second after second, hour after hour, week after week, year after year with every repetition of every physical exercise, every jogged step, every idle moment, Jordan had followed the advice of his first mentor. Chuck Wallington had immersed him in what he called opposite-trigger mode. Jordan had trained his mind to react opposite to its natural inclinations.

The results of that training had stunned Rosemary, who said she noticed the effects at home. She had suffered the usual battles against anger and sometimes found herself shouting at Christa and Ken when they were incorrigible preschoolers. At first she thought Jordan had simply not been around enough for them to get on his nerves. Later she saw he didn't fail even when he had been home all day every day for a couple of weeks and even when the children were at their most irritating. One of them would do something so inciting, so spiteful, so worthy of an angry response that she felt certain he would explode. Yet he did the opposite. In perfect calmness and dignity, he firmly and clearly disciplined the child.

He tried to educate Rosemary in the art of the trained mind, the science of opposite triggers, but it wasn't for everyone. Even in Jordan's profession, only a handful of operatives had mastered the technique. It was more refined even than the tranquility of Eastern mystics who claimed to have found peace by becoming one with the cosmos. Jordan found those types pliable in the face of death, neither rational nor able to defend themselves.

Such training had saved his life more than once, but now Jordan hated the result. His natural mind wanted to panic, to fall apart, to break down, to unravel. Yet the signal that triggered the opposite told him to separate himself from the trauma, to actually become bored with it, take deep breaths, relax, look away, concentrate on the confrontation ahead.

If only God would allow him to be human, able to vent, even if that meant anger directed at God Himself. As he tried to force his natural mind to override his trained response, he felt he might go mad. That seemed sweet relief. *Yes, God, let me go crazy, right here, right now.*

Jordan suffered from sensory overload. Everything acted as a trigger. He wavered between rationality and insanity, and even that pushed him to a heightened awareness.

It appeared that at least eleven passengers and customs agents had been killed. Four others had been wounded, three seriously. The savage power of the weapon was all too apparent. It didn't maim, as a rule. If it got you, you were dead. That confirmed his M16 theory. It also convinced him that not even the second five shots, which had been instrumental in eliminating the Plexiglas barrier, had been slowed enough to diminish their killing force. Murdering people from forty feet with a weapon that powerful was like raising a tricycle with a hydraulic jack.

Indeed, as Jordan looked to the far west end of the terminal, his suspicion was borne out. More than a dozen deep, black pockmarks marred the white wall. So, of the thirty rounds fired in two and a half seconds, maybe five had damaged only Plexiglas. The rest had wounded and killed and passed through bodies and still carried hundreds of feet before they lodged in the concrete block walls.

And why should I care about that?

His wife lay dead, her blood spilled and the form of her body traced in charcoal by a cop who never knew her. Yet Jordan couldn't break out of character long enough to face this. Why had he never prepared for such an eventuality?

A pale, quivering, uniformed young woman from the airline hurried in with a computerized printout of the passenger list. She appeared determined to keep her eyes from the horror. Jordan heard Williamsby instruct one of his aides to first match the names of the deceased with the passenger list, then the wounded, then the unhurt.

"Consult the airline about any discrepancies, any cancellations. Let me know immediately of anyone missing. About a hundred have already passed through customs."

The young woman told Williamsby that the airline preferred the waiting people be sequestered and questioned elsewhere. The veteran looked at her sharply and moved close until his nose was within inches of hers. "I will make those decisions. Do you understand?" She nodded. "No one is going anywhere until everyone has been questioned and searched and we have determined their reason for being here. Is that clear?"

She nodded again and hurried away.

Jordan wondered if Williamsby had determined yet whether the gunman had worked alone. A study of the bullets would prove whether they had all spiraled from the same barrel, but that would take hours.

As the waiting group was finally funneled into single file, Jordan found himself seventh in line. The first woman, who spoke English with an Italian accent, was the one who had tumbled onto him at the first sound of gunfire. When she gave her name, she tearfully asked if her husband was lying by the wall.

She had to know he was, of course, but until it was official, she apparently held out some hope. Her identification was checked, and she was teamed with a priest and a medical worker. She collapsed as her husband's face was revealed to her.

By the time Jordan's turn came and he sat across from a Scotland Yard agent, he was nearly exploding with conflicting emotions. He wanted to be with his wife, to care for her body, to know what they would do with her, where they would take her, how she would be transported back to the States. He wanted to call Christa and Ken, to cry with them over the phone. He wanted to fly to them, to let them comfort him and each other. But as he sat, he spoke in a perfectly calm voice with a decidedly French accent.

"A horrible mess, isn't it?" He casually pulled his identification out of his shoulder bag. "Actually, I was lost. Meeting another plane, a friend from Paris. Wrong terminal. I thought this was where European flights came in."

The agent's grim expression softened. "It usually is." He put Jordan's phony, dog-eared papers back together, tapped them on the table to straighten them, and handed them back. But Gaston Blanc reached for them too quickly, too jerkily, and Jordan was strangely relieved that he was not perfect in the face of this crisis. Indeed, the loss of a wife could affect even the best-trained mind.

The agent stared deeply into his eyes, and through two misleading pairs of lenses, Jordan returned the look. Just before he stood to leave, Huck Williamsby approached. "Get him matched up with a passenger, did you?"

The agent scratched his cheek. "No, sir, wrong terminal. Wrong plane."

Williamsby squinted at Jordan. "Search him."

"Sir?"

"You heard me. Earlier he asked me about this very flight. He knew good and well which plane was coming in. And you, Inspector, know that anyone who cannot be linked to a passenger on this list is a suspect."

"This way, Mr. Blanc."

Jordan faced the wall and leaned against it, palms out, surprising the agent. "Been through this before, have we?"

Jordan shook his head. *Not from this angle.*

The agent started at the ankles and patted him up and under the jacket all the way to the armpits. Then he backed down to the bottom of the jacket and started up again, flinching when he encountered the bulge in the right pocket.

"Commander! Believe we have a weapon here, sir."

Williamsby hurried over and felt for himself. "Call Reynolds over, and don't make a scene. Do we indeed have a pistol here, Mr. Blanc? And how did we get it past security?"

Jordan didn't answer.

"We'll see soon enough. I hope for your sake you're not involved in this."

Reynolds, a forensics expert, arrived with a small plastic bag and a long metal rod about a quarter inch in diameter. He felt the pocket himself, then used both hands to nearly turn it inside out. The original agent gave a low whistle when the wooden gun appeared, and Reynolds dug into the pocket with the rod, snagging the trigger ring and working the entire weapon out.

He let the gun slide into the plastic bag and ceremoniously handed it to Commander Williamsby. He signaled his colleagues both back to work with a nod and led Jordan out of the terminal.

Fifty feet down the corridor, Williamsby unlocked a door and ushered Jordan into a small room, where they sat opposite one another at a gray metal table. The commander sighed deeply. "Do I know you?"

Jordan nodded.

"Who are you with?"

Jordan dropped the accent. "The United States."

"CIA?"

Jordan shook his head.

"Who else has this kind of weapon? Oh, don't tell me. CIA's thorn in the flesh."

The realization that he could stop playacting opened the floodgates, and Jordan nearly burst into tears.

"So who are you? Where do I know you from, and how did the NSA know Lister was here?"

Lister! Jordan couldn't believe it. An American-born international terrorist, Richard Lister was nothing more than a gun for hire, a specialist in political hit jobs that paid big money. Jordan's voice was unsteady. "Who was the target?"

"I have an unanswered question on the table, friend."

Jordan took off his glasses and popped out the contact lenses. He dragged the cap off his head and pointed to his hair. "Think yellow."

"Kirkwood?" The older man looked incredulous. "You're on this one?"

"I'm not, Huck. My wife was on that plane."

"Oh, Jordan, there was a Kirkwood on the, uh, list of . . ." Williamsby ran a hand over his mouth and looked away. "I'm bloody sorry, man. What a horrible coincidence! We got a call about ten thirty from one of our guys out here. Said he saw a tall man wearing all brown, fit the description of Lister without his beard. We got right over. Couldn't put it together. Diverted as much international traffic as we could into Terminal Two, but then we lost him. Thought we had him covered, but for some reason it seemed he might be up to something with a plane coming in from Algiers. Had that one scheduled in Terminal Five. I was heading there when I ran into you the first time. You got me good there. I never gave you a second thought till I saw you in line."

Jordan slammed both fists on the table, startling Williamsby and breaking free of his own captive mind. "What was Lister doing here and why would he kill my *wife?*"

"We don't know yet, Jordan, but he's dead, if that makes you feel any better."

"He is?"

Williamsby nodded. "He went racing out, and we were close behind. When he tried to reload, we opened fire."

Jordan trembled. "I still don't get it."

"I don't either, but I have to ask: were you booked on that flight?"

Jordan nodded.

"You know what that means."

He nodded again.

"The question, then, is not why Lister would kill your wife. It's why he would kill you."

Jordan stood and paced. "My only consolation is that whoever was behind this will soon know Lister blew it. Then I might get to face him."

"Or, more likely, just another hit man."

Jordan nodded. *I'll get to the main guy somehow.* He dropped his head and his shoulders heaved. "I'm going to have to quit."

"This is the worst time to be making any decisions, Kirkwood. You need friends right now."

"I need to be alone."

"You have to ID her, man. I'm sorry."

"I want her flown back home as soon as possible."

"You know the airline will oblige. We'll have the autopsy done before dawn."

The airline was as accommodating as Williamsby had predicted, but it was late afternoon by the time Jordan had identified the body, filled out all the forms, and been cleared through Scotland Yard; he was so bone-weary he could hardly walk to the car Williamsby assigned to run him back to his hotel.

Neither of the young agents spoke during the drive back into London proper. The rain had stopped, but the streetlights glistened in the dampness. It was the kind of evening Rosemary would have enjoyed on the East Coast. What would she have thought of it in London? Perhaps she had discussed that with the kind stranger, the man in the wrong place at the worst possible time.

The car pulled up in front of the Carriage House, a dingy dive Jordan had thought was perfect for his purposes. He was moved when both agents stepped out and walked him into the lobby, waited until he got his key, then flanked him as he trudged up the stairs. They waited in silence as he opened his door and glanced at each other as he disengaged a portable hydraulic security system he had installed himself.

As he stepped inside, they bade him good night, and he nodded.

Jordan knew he should call his daughter and son. Christa was a pre-law sophomore at Salisbury University. Kenneth was in California, a freshman on a tennis scholarship at Stanford. It was midday Maryland and three hours earlier on the West Coast. But Jordan couldn't call them right then. He just couldn't. He'd do it before takeoff the next afternoon.

How he had failed his kids. Jordan had used all the clichéd excuses, saying he was doing his best to give them the best kind of life he could afford. And while Rosemary had continued to urge him to carve out more time for them, Christa and Ken had seemed to accept his remoteness. Now, when they would need each other more than ever, they would see each other as strangers.

He collapsed onto the creaky bed and buried his sobs in the pillow. He was consumed with Rosemary, but flirting at the periphery were thoughts of his future without her, the bankruptcy of his spiritual life, and his resolve to quit the agency, to spare his family the danger that had never come close to them before. And having Russian-provided al-Qaeda planes in the United States was like knowing a murderer hid under your bed and not knowing which side to look under first.

Fitful sleep finally came, but there was really no rest the whole night. And when he rose at last, Jordan stood in the shower like a zombie, scrubbing his hair in a futile attempt to erase the dye he would hate until it grew out.

Lurching down the stairs with his heavy trunk, he reached the tiny lobby and was surprised to see a familiar form dozing in an overstuffed chair by the door. Could it be? He paid his bill quietly, ignoring the clerk's banter about shortening his stay, and tiptoed to the sleeping man. The lanky, swarthy fifty-year-old with the generous lips and the shock of black hair was Felix Granger, a good old boy from Hattiesburg, Mississippi, and now deputy director of the NSA's UKUSA, the U.K.–U.S.A. Security Agreement.

Jordan was touched that Felix had come. He put

a hand on the big man's shoulder. Felix jumped. "Oh, Jordan! Do I have bad news for you!" His drawl hadn't been affected by six years in the United Kingdom, and he was quickly in tears.

Jordan settled onto his trunk next to Granger. "You think I don't know?"

"You don't know this." The tall man straightened and pulled his coat tighter around his neck. "Our man at JOSAF was found dead at his home in Oberursel this morning. Stanley Stuart. You knew him, didn't you?"

3

JORDAN HESITATED AND his voice came in a whisper. "I met him years ago, Felix. Friend of Chuck's. How'd it happen?"

"Suicide, I'm afraid. Never got over the death of his wife, ya know. That's why he was reassigned administrative, they say. Met him a coupla times. Understand he was a heck of a nice guy. Pity."

Jordan hung his head. He fought the urge to tell what he knew. Who would believe Stu's death wasn't a suicide? And what if he told the wrong person? Would he too wind up mysteriously "committing suicide"?

"Jordan, I'm sorry. That news coulda waited. I didn't mean to be insensitive. Listen, headquarters has informed your kids. Ken is flyin' in from the

West Coast, and Christa is coming in from Boston, so they'll both be there when you get back. You wanna call 'em, or you wanna just get home?"

Jordan, the man of action, Jordan, the decisive, started to speak several times and gave up. Could this get worse? The agency that had robbed his kids of their father for most of their lives gave them the awful news that should have come from only him.

Felix Granger was an incessant talker. The mere mention of his name elicited raised eyebrows from Jordan's colleagues. But Jordan had always been fascinated by Felix, a child prodigy who had graduated from high school at fourteen and become the youngest code man in the agency. Jordan always enjoyed talking with the man, but he never appreciated him more than now. Felix told Jordan without blinking that he just happened to have been called back to headquarters and would be able to accompany Jordan on the flight to the States. "If that would be all right with you. If it is, then my advice is to forget calling and just fly home."

Jordan was staggered by the offer. He knew it was his bosses' way to get his mind off leaving the agency. He wished they truly cared for him or believed he was so good they couldn't get along without him. The fact was he had been with them too long, knew too much, was a walking time bomb of information, a target for too many international lowlifes. They couldn't afford his resigning.

Barely ten years his senior, Felix fathered Jordan until they boarded the plane. The veteran lugged Jordan's heavy trunk to his car, drove to the airport, then insisted on carrying it into the terminal. "Nothin's goin' out of Two today, as you can imagine. We're already cleared through British intelligence, so there won't be any delays."

That proved an understatement. Jordan soon found himself outside the entrance to the classified cargo section.

Granger leaned close. "You just tell me what you want. If you want to see her again, we can arrange that. If you want to give them any special instructions, just let me know. In fact, if you would rather a gub'ment plane come over here and git her and you and me, we can do it. Understand what I'm sayin'?"

"I just want to get on that plane and know she's in the cargo hold."

"Done. Wanna board early?"

"Don't mind if I do."

Felix got them on the wide-bodied craft nearly an hour before anyone else and promised to leave Jordan alone during the trip. Jordan knew Felix couldn't remain silent long, and he didn't really want him to anyway.

When Felix told him the flight would be full except for the seat between them, Jordan shook

44

his head. "There are probably ten people in the terminal wishing for that seat, but I appreciate it."

"It ain't for you anyway, Jordan. It's for me. Big man needs room, baby."

The UKUSA deputy director tried to settle in with a newspaper, but it was clear he wasn't reading it. He gazed at one page for several minutes, then engaged in a complicated folding operation to expose another section to his blank stare. Finally he leaned across the empty seat.

"I'm sorry to bother you, I really am, but I feel I got to express myself. I learned a long time ago that there's nothing anyone can say at a time like this and that the best thing to do is to say nothing and let your actions do the talking. I been trying to do that, but, Jordan, I just feel so rotten for you, I want to tell you how awful sorry I am. You know, I never knew Rosemary well, but I never heard you say a thing about her that wasn't special, and I just know she was a wonderful woman and a good wife. I hope you don't mind my saying that."

Jordan's eyes filled. He couldn't look at Felix, but he thrust out his hand when he noticed Felix had extended his. He found himself on the receiving end of a down-home pumper and was reminded that the Mississippian could never shake hands without talking throughout the exercise.

"I'm gonna offer all the help we can in London to find out who was behind this, man, 'cause I know as well as you and Williamsby do that you were the target. Fact is, I'll be working on it during the flight, making notes, trying some theories, but don't feel obligated to be involved. You know they won't let you in on this one anyway, and I know you got other things on your mind."

The things on Jordan's mind might have surprised Felix. As the plane started to fill and the temperature to rise, Jordan was finally able to let drowsiness take over. Sitting straight up, unable to really sleep, he closed his eyes and let his mind take him back to high school, even before he met Rosemary Holub.

During the summer of 1983, just before Jordan's senior year, he had joined a dozen other high school and college students from his church in a short-term missionary trip into Southeast Asia. The focal point was a missionary air base in Sentani on the Irian Jaya–Papua New Guinea border in eastern Indonesia. The group was to consider the internal strife of the country irrelevant, avoid discussing politics, and concentrate on assisting the pilots and missionaries in the area. The Christian endeavor in the country was tenuous, and those responsible didn't want to alienate either Suharto's forces or those who would attempt to overthrow him.

But Jordan had been fascinated by the political situation and was thrilled when the return trip to the United States was delayed in Jakarta. While most of the others were shopping and sightseeing, he went off by himself to explore the unusual sights and smells and sounds of the noisy capital city. He even hired an interpreter and interviewed locals about their views of the government.

On the last day of the trip, six days after the students had been scheduled to leave, two American men in business suits showed up at the mission guesthouse where the group had been staying. The men wanted to see Jordan Jefferson Kirkwood.

The sponsor was protective. "May I ask why?"

They flashed U.S. government business cards identifying them as Stanley Stuart and Chuck Wallington of the National Security Agency. Jordan had never heard of the NSA. The agents told him privately that they had been investigating charges that the CIA had attempted to enlist Peace Corps and missionary personnel in its activities in Indonesia.

It hadn't taken long to convince the investigators that he had not been approached by the CIA. The agent who did most of the talking was Chuck Wallington, a black-haired, brush-cut, stocky, military type. He gave Jordan his card. "Show this to no one. If anyone asks what we wanted, tell them you can't say. If they ask if we were CIA, tell them you can't say. If they mention NSA, tell them you can't say, but call me when you get home and let me know."

"And if no one mentions NSA, I shouldn't call you at all?"

Wallington hesitated. "Tell me something. You jog every day like you did this morning, no matter where you are?"

"Yes, sir."

"Any particular reason?"

"I'm on the track and cross-country teams at Muskegon Central."

"Michigan, eh? You any good?"

"Twelfth in the state in cross-country. Fourth in the four hundred."

"No kidding. What's your best time in the four hundred?"

"Forty-eight flat."

Wallington smiled wryly. "That bother you—not sneaking into the forty-sevens, I mean?"

"Like everything."

"Any other sports or activities?"

"Basketball."

"Guard?"

"Uh-huh."

"You start?"

Jordan nodded.

"Average?"

"Eleven something."

"What else?"

"Class officer."

"President?"

"Vice."

Wallington seemed to study him. "Would you call yourself a patriot?"

"I guess. Sure."

"Not good enough."

"Sorry?"

"We're a little gung ho is all. We see ourselves as throwbacks to when people said things like 'Give me liberty or give me death' and 'I only regret that I have but one life to give for my country.' Can you identify with that?"

Jordan nodded slowly. "My dad was wounded in Nam. Wouldn't have had to work another day in his life, but he wouldn't take charity. Been working more than twenty years. He always said he would have given an arm and a leg to be able to raise his boys as free men. So I guess I'm a throwback too."

Wallington glanced at Stuart, the fleshier of the two, who was sweating and clearly uncomfortable, yet smiling. Then he turned back to Jordan. "Tell you what, Kirkwood. Call me on Christmas Day."

"Even if no one mentions NSA?"

"If they do that, you call me right away. But they won't. Nobody knows us. You call me at Christmas if you've run every day from now to then, if you finish in the top five in the state in cross-country this fall, and if you're averaging over fifteen points a game in basketball."

"What for?"

"You don't have to if you don't want to. And only call me if you've kept our confidence. You tell no one about our conversation, including your family. Let's see what you're made of."

Nearly dozing, Jordan felt Felix Granger's knuckly hand on his arm. "Don't open your eyes, partner. Just tell me if you want a drink or not. Juice or a Coke or something?" Grateful to not have to speak, Jordan shook his head.

Within seconds Jordan was back to his senior year of high school. He had finished eighth in the state cross-country meet and was averaging almost seventeen points a game in basketball. He had been named Most Valuable Player in an early tournament, and he had run every day, even twice with a cold. Christmas approached. His team would be in another tournament in Detroit over the holidays, much to the disappointment of his parents. The family squabbled over it, and Jordan's parents refused to come. Jordan was angry enough not to care. Except for his finish in the cross-country meet, he had satisfied every condition Chuck Wallington had laid out.

"You've run every day?" Wallington sounded cold.
"Yes."
"But you finished eighth in cross-country."
"How did you know?"

"Am I to understand that you didn't mention to anyone your contact with me?"

"Yes, and my season average in basketball is—"

"Seventeen points, and so you thought that made up for the eighth place."

"Eighth in the state isn't bad, you know."

"You going to get straight A's this year?"

"I think so."

"You're getting a B in sociology."

"What else do you know?"

"I know you're only seventeen."

"Anything wrong with that?"

"Only that I can't talk to you about what I wanted to talk to you about until you're eighteen."

"Great."

"Call me April fourteenth, after your birthday party, but only if you've made all-conference in basketball, are still running, get straight A's, score in the high twenties on the ACT and over six fifty on both ends of the SAT. And I want to see that four hundred under forty-seven-point-five before the state meet."

"And I still can't tell anyone what this is all about?"

"What *is* it about, son?"

"I don't know."

"Well, then . . ."

"And you still want me to call, even though you'll know everything already?"

"One thing I won't know is whether you'll call."

51

• • •

Jordan was startled awake again by the gentle touch of his colleague. "I should let you sleep, Jordan. I'm sorry. Just wondered if you wanted some dinner. You ought to eat. You can get dehydrated real quick on these flights. Well, hey, you know that well enough."

Jordan only picked at his meal but drank juice, decaffeinated coffee, and water. Years before, he had collapsed on his first ever overseas flight, only to discover he hadn't stayed sufficiently hydrated.

Felix ate quickly, glancing at his charge. "Up to talking?"

Jordan shook his head apologetically.

"You all right?"

Jordan nodded. "Just thinking."

"I understand. Can you sleep?"

"Dozing a little, I think."

"Good to rest your eyes, anyway. Hectic days comin'."

Jordan nodded again. When the dishes were cleared and his tray table back up, he lifted the armrest and drew his right leg up underneath him. He was soon alone again with his memories.

In April of 1984, Jordan called Chuck Wallington, who did most of the talking.

"Okay, we've got a twenty-seven on the ACT, a six seventy and a six eighty-eight on the SAT, third in the state in the quarter with a forty-seven-point-nine but you had a forty-seven-point-six in the districts. All-conference, straight A's, class officer, and everything else still in order. You called, so you're still curious. You applied to Central Michigan. How serious are you about that?"

"It's a free ride."

"Besides that."

"What's the option?"

"If you're open to talking about putting off college for a year and then letting us put you through International in Washington, I'll come visit you."

"International University?"

"In history and poli-sci."

"Wow."

"Is that high school–ese for 'Come and see me'?"

The meeting with Chuck Wallington at a Win Schuler's restaurant on Interstate 94 would change Jordan's life. He was to tell no one—not his parents, none of his many female friends, none of his few buddies, and neither of his brothers, each of whom he had been glad to see leave home during the previous two years.

The assignment, if he wanted it, was to work undercover for the National Security Agency as a Peace Corps volunteer in Indonesia. "You find out if the CIA makes any forays into corps personnel and keep us posted. You do a good job, we look for something full-time for you, put you through school, and go from there."

"I'd be working *for* my government *against* my government?"

Wallington carefully dabbed at his mouth. "Checks and balances keep a country great."

"I thought you had to be a college grad to be in the Peace Corps."

"I can arrange whatever history is necessary, Jordan. It may be many years before you fully realize the resources at our disposal. One of the things I want to do soon is to get you to Washington to see the facilities."

"Why me?"

Wallington shrugged. "I was impressed when I met you. Stu and I both were. The more I learned, the more I liked. The Eagle Scouts, the church, the civic service. The grades. Of course, the physical stuff. Most of all, you're a bit of a loner and you can keep a confidence. You've got a temper we can work on, but the same thing that gives you the temper is what can make you a highly motivated achiever. Often our weaknesses are also our strengths."

"The same thing that gives me my temper? You know the cause of it?"

"Sure. It's your place in the family, son. Third born in thirty-five months. Lots of competition. Strong father, passive mother, highly religious home. You need challenges; you're disciplined. At least, you think you are. You'll find out what discipline is if you join us."

54

"This doesn't wash. I can't believe a secret government agency would recruit someone my age."

"A legitimate doubt. But we can't grow all of our people through the armed forces. They develop a militarist bearing, an age about them. We're looking for a long-term man we can cultivate slowly. Each of us in recruitment agreed to find a beginner and personally nurture him. Maybe you're not the guy."

"Do I get paid?"

"Just expenses the first year. The reward is college."

"My parents will never go for it. They want me to work over the summer and go to Central."

"I can phony up a scholarship to International that starts next year."

"I don't know. I don't lie to them. Probably I'll just have to go against their will. I've been waiting to do that for years."

"Oh, you can't do that. The first time classified information is traced to you—whether through you or your family or whoever—you're finished."

"I'm going to have to think about this."

"Of course. But how does it hit you at first blush?"

Jordan leaned forward and rested both elbows on the table. "Like a dream, like something I was made for. The order, the structure, the responsibility. I do my job; you take care of me. I don't think I'd ever forgive myself if I passed it up, or if I let my parents forbid it."

"When you get back from your Peace Corps thing in Indonesia, you'll work directly with me while you're at International. I'll tutor you, work out with you, check in on you. I'll be stationed in Washington during those three years."

"*Three* years?"

"You think we'd let you have summers off when we're footing the bill? And listen, very few even within the NSA will know about you, because if it works out, much of what you would do will involve surveillance of U.S. agencies. It might even include surveillance within the NSA itself. But how you do in Indonesia will make you or break you. Think it over and let me know."

Jordan knew his decision would cost him his parents' blessing, in his family no small issue.

His father had come home late, as usual, from the paper mill, smelling of the place. His mother was already crying. Raymond Kirkwood put his lunch box atop the refrigerator and dropped into a chair at the kitchen table. "I'm hungry, but I'm listening. What now?"

Jordan shook his head. "What am I supposed to say when you talk to me like that?"

"I come home to a crying wife, and you think I'm gonna be easy to talk to?" He crossed his bad leg over his good one and began untying his work shoes.

"I want to join the Peace Corps, that's all."

Raymond Kirkwood let his shoe drop and ignored the other. "That's *all?* What about college?"

"I can always go to college."

"You think those scholarships will just be sitting there waiting for you? How long is the Peace Corps?"

"Normal term is two years."

"Two years!"

"I think I can get out after one."

"So then you'll be a quitter. You know, Ray-Ray may not have been the hotshot jock you are, and Walter may not have had your brains, but those boys were never quitters. If they'd had the chance to go to college, you can bet they would have taken it."

"Does that mean I have to?"

"You ought to. Where do you think you wanna go in the Peace Corps? Are those people Christians or just a bunch of bleeding-heart liberals?"

"I'm sure there are plenty of Christians in the corps. And I liked Indonesia. I want to go back."

Mr. Kirkwood shook his head. "Now either my memory's gone or you're lying, 'cause all I remember you saying was that the place was a smelly hole and you didn't care if you ever went back."

Jordan's guilt hit him before the second lie was

even out of his mouth, but he was losing ground and needed a stopper. "Maybe God did a work in my heart about the people over there."

He couldn't look at his father. He knew he'd pierced the man's armor. Mr. Kirkwood stared at him. "Is that it, then? You feel that's where God wants you?"

Jordan nodded.

"You don't seem sure."

"I'm sure."

"You've prayed about it?"

Jordan reddened.

"I don't think you have."

"I don't care what you think! I'm going, and that's it."

His father slammed his fist on the table. "Well, when you come back, don't come here!"

His mother flushed. "Raymond!"

But the old man stormed out.

When Jordan roused, the cabin was dark and a movie was showing. Felix had earphones on but was sound asleep. And Rosemary was gone. Sweet, innocent, lovely Rosemary, Jordan's lifelong love. His melancholy memories were racing headlong toward their first meeting, and he had been protecting himself by thinking of things pre-Rosemary. Now, he wondered when he had exhausted his early memories, should he skip ahead to Christa and Ken?

What had he done, letting them hear the awful news from bureaucrats? Did they know the whole story? Would they want to hear it or not want to hear it? And what about Rosemary's parents? and his own mother? Who would be there when he arrived? Surely not his brothers. Both worked at mills in Indiana and barely scratched out a living.

That the memories of his father were so fresh after so many years reminded him of why he fought against coming across as an authoritarian to his own kids. Maybe they had played him, manipulated him, he didn't know. They seemed to be turning out all right, no thanks to Jordan. Rosemary said she sensed that Christa and Ken sometimes tried to provoke Jordan, just to see if he would put his foot down, set some boundaries, be the dad.

Jordan fought two painful memories from his abbreviated second stay in Indonesia, memories that resurrected a ton of adolescent guilt. He tried to relive his beginnings with the NSA so as to skirt two issues he had never really faced.

But his mind was not working correctly, and those issues were lying in wait.

4

IN THE FALL of 1985, Jordan had been standing in line during freshman registration at International University in Washington, eavesdropping on an amusing conversation behind him.

"I'll be all right, Daddy. Now please, I love you and appreciate you and need you to go."

"What if one of your classes is full?"

"I'll either flirt with the registrar or choose another one."

"Rosemary!"

The young woman finally coaxed her father into leaving, and Jordan casually turned to get a peek. He almost missed her, a head shorter than him and wonderfully trim. Dark hair, dark eyes, and full, rosy cheeks.

He nodded and smiled, and it must have been obvious he had overheard.

"The Reverend Holub forgets I'll see him this afternoon. I'm living at home."

Jordan laughed and introduced himself. She impressed him as refined and at peace with herself. Rosemary told him her father was a Presbyterian pastor and she an only child. Jordan avoided his own church background. In fact, he said little other than that International University had not been his first choice.

"I didn't know you could get in at the last minute."

"I was fortunate. I was going to go to Central Michigan, only because it was cheap and close to home. Muskegon, Michigan, heart of the boring Midwest."

"Don't say that. I visited Chicago once. It was fascinating."

"Muskegon is a long way from Chicago. It's even farther from Detroit."

Rosemary responded to Jordan's every dark comment with something cheery. "How does one get you out of a cynical mood?"

He flinched. "Sorry. Tough year, that's all. Spent time overseas, lost my father, that kind of stuff."

"Forgive me. Of course, I didn't know about your father—"

"No. I'm sorry, Rosemary. I'm not usually like this."

As they parted and wished each other luck, Jordan detected sadness in her eyes. He hoped it wasn't pity for him because there was more to his father's death than he could have ever told a stranger. In fact, the timing of that death and the circumstances surrounding the woman he was in love with at the time were things he never fully revealed to Rosemary, even during their two decades of marriage.

The young Jordan Kirkwood had his own tiny apartment in Washington, and he was lonely. The capital was a strange place in 1985. Ronald Reagan had just begun a wildly popular but controversial second term, and Democrats were already bemoaning the prospect of Vice President George H. W. Bush succeeding him and giving the Republicans at least twelve straight years in the White House. There was much to debate, much to talk about, but Jordan had hardly anyone to talk to. He had only one real acquaintance in Washington. Admittedly, his entire future was linked to the man, but he had been sworn to secrecy about having ever even met him.

He wondered what Chuck Wallington would think of his preoccupation with Rosemary. Since no whistles or bells had gone off during their chat, he remembered only the first initial of her last name. After all, he had another woman on his mind—the love of his life.

Three days later, after Jordan had sat through a few history and political science classes and spent the rest of his time studying, working out, eating, and sleeping, Chuck came over to check on him. He always asked about Jordan's studies, his menu, and his conditioning. Jordan found these visits inspiring, and their Saturday and Sunday afternoon workouts invigorating, but Chuck rarely stayed long.

Jordan wanted—needed—someone to talk to, to share his life with. Maybe that was why the girl in the registration line kept invading his thoughts.

He was irritated when no one in the admissions office could come up with her name in the records. All he wanted was to know what she was studying so he could hang around the right building and run into her again. Maybe something more would come of it this time. And if it didn't, then it didn't.

When he mistakenly thought he saw her three different times in one day, he knew he had it bad. He went back to Admissions and asked for "any sane person, maybe someone who's been here awhile." That sufficiently offended the woman who'd tried to help him before and won him the assistance of a stern, middle-aged supervisor.

"The first name is Rosemary and the last name is Holcomb or Holden or something like that. It just seems there wouldn't be that many freshmen named Rosemary H. and that it wouldn't take too terribly long to look her up."

The supervisor gave him a bored look. "On campus or off?"

"Off."

The first woman, who had been sitting with her back to them, swiveled in her chair. "You never told me *that!*"

The supervisor shushed her. "The name's Holub. But we're not, of course, at liberty to provide addresses or phone numbers."

How many Reverend Holubs could there be?

Finding the number proved easy.

"I'm the one you met in line the other day."

"Oh yes, hi, um—"

"Jordan Kirkwood. I was wondering if I could see you, like for dinner or something."

"Would a lunch be all right, Jordan? Say, next Tuesday?"

"Great!"

"Jordan?"

"Yeah?"

"Where?"

"Oh yeah. Um, same place we met. At noon."

During the week Jordan looked for Rosemary everywhere, but the campus was too large and there were too many students. By the time the weekend arrived and Chuck showed up for their discussions and workouts, Jordan was in a frenzy. Chuck had never seen him run a mile on the beach—barefoot in the sand—in less than five and a half minutes.

After they'd endured a hard, ten-minute swim out and about a seven-and-a-half-minute swim back, they cooled off in Jordan's government-paid apartment with tall glasses of fresh-squeezed orange juice. Usually Jordan stretched out on the floor while Chuck took the couch, but now Jordan paced.

Finally Chuck sat up and ran both hands through his brush cut. "What is it with you today? You worked out like you actually want this job."

"I've always wanted it."

"Yeah, but c'mon, kid! You were unconscious today. Tell me."

Jordan shrugged. "Got a date Tuesday, that's all." He smiled. Chuck didn't.

"Hmm." Chuck rolled onto his back again and covered his eyes with his forearm. "Wives don't mix with this business, you know. Not at this level."

"I'm not marrying anybody. I hardly know the girl."

"I need to check her out."

"Even my acquaintances?"

"You don't date your acquaintances. Now who is she?"

Jordan told him. "When do I know if she qualifies?"

"Wednesday."

"I told you I was seeing her Tuesday."

"Okay, I'll shoot for the end of the day, but don't—"

"*Noon,* Tuesday."

"That doesn't give me enough time, Jordan."

"You can't totally mess up my private life!"

Chuck sat up and studied him with a closed-mouth smile. "If you want this job, I can."

"Then maybe I'd better think about it some more."

Chuck narrowed his eyes. "Have I misjudged you, or do we call it quits right here?"

Jordan looked at the floor and shook his head. "Just call me Tuesday as early as you can."

"Will do. But before I leave, there's something we need to discuss."

Jordan had never seen Chuck like this.

"What?"

"While we're talking about women, I've got to ask you about Cydya LeMonde."

Jordan's eyes popped open when Felix put a hand on his shoulder. "You're sweating, pal. You okay?" Jordan leaned forward and hid his face in his hands. He felt like sobbing. Felix massaged his back. "That's all right, partner. Let it out."

But this wasn't grief. It was humiliation, guilt. It was the memory of Cydya. How could he possibly think of her at a time like this?

And how many times had he asked himself that question over the years? Memories of Cydya had teased him early in his marriage whenever he had been away from home. That he could rationalize and maybe understand. But today? Now? He'd tried to avoid thinking of her by skipping the memories of his second Indonesian trip. But here she was.

Even thinking of her felt like a betrayal of Rosemary. He wished he had been the one gunned down. Jordan knew that if he allowed it, he would think of little other than his and Cydya's first few months together. He had long since quit denying that she was his first true love.

Oh, he'd enjoyed the usual high school romances. There had been cheerleaders and even a homecoming queen. He'd even gone steady twice. Thought he was in love. Until he met Cydya.

He learned that love was more than a faster pulse, more than just wanting to be with someone all the time, more than spending so much time on the phone that your parents threatened to make you pay for your own line.

Jordan blamed the place. The heat. The humidity. The nearly ten thousand miles between Jakarta and Muskegon. The fact that Cydya was of French extraction. Ultimately, the reasons didn't matter. He loved her so deeply that her image burned itself onto his soul.

But he didn't want to think about her now! He forced himself to open his eyes, to work up a smile for Felix so the older man would quit rubbing his back. Jordan lowered his head to his chest and put his hand over his eyes, pretending to sleep. He felt like a schoolboy, his eyes still open, surveying as much as his limited vision would allow.

In the seat across the aisle from him, a woman removed her shoes and dragged a travel bag closer so she could rest her feet on it. A flight attendant walked by. There was grime on the plastic twist-lock holding Jordan's tray table. He didn't want to think; he just wanted to look.

If his mind had been empty, save for thoughts of his wife, he'd have shut his eyes again. If he could sleep without dreaming . . . Could he peek at his watch without Felix noticing? Why did he care? Anything, anything to occupy his mind. Could he push Cydya from his thoughts at least until after Rosemary's funeral?

You will soon face your children, and already you're planning what to think about after your wife's funeral!

Through the sliver between his fingers, he saw Felix wave at a fly. The man's legs were crossed, a bony knee pressing against the back of the seat in front of him.

Anything for a distraction. Jordan continued to spy on Felix, letting the irony of that play on his tortured mind. He pressed his fingers harder to his forehead, as if he could somehow slow the thoughts, the emotions. Guilt. Vengeance. Rabid curiosity. Dread. Fear. Remorse. Love. And a memory he couldn't face until it beat down his every last defense.

Felix fumbled for a button in the armrest and Jordan heard the loud tone. An attendant arrived.

"Could I get a coffee with one packet of sugar, honey?"

Felix flexed his thumb and middle finger in a way that reminded Jordan of how he shot marbles as a child. When his coffee came, Felix lowered the tray table from the seat between the two men and ignored the coffee. He tore open the sugar packet, licked his finger, and dipped it into the granules. He rubbed the sticky stuff between his finger and thumb and wiped it on his left knee. He rested the heel of his hand near it and resumed the cocked, marble-shooting pose. Within seconds, the fly landed on the sugar. Jordan's eyes widened.

Amazingly, Felix didn't immediately flick at the fly. Jordan decided that he must have some knowledge of when a sugar-sucking fly was most vulnerable. Perhaps when it's rubbing those appendages against each other like a wino near a trash-can fire.

Felix finally pulled the trigger and the fly caromed off the seat ahead of him. The fly landed in Felix's lap. It staggered in circles before Felix closed a loose fist around it. With his other hand, he snagged the fly by one wing under his fingernail.

He removed the right wing with a quick motion. Then the left. The fly crawled quickly around his hand. He transferred the insect to his left palm and got his right hand ready to shoot again. When the fly stopped, Felix flicked it against the seat once more, caught it between his thumb and finger, and crushed it.

Casually Felix deposited the creature in his

napkin, guzzled the coffee without a breath, and dropped the napkin into the cup. He turned off his light and folded his hands in his lap, head on his chest.

The trick had been impressive, but Felix had clearly not done it for effect. It simply wasn't something one did for the benefit of the bereaved.

Jordan sat forward and rested his head in his hands, elbows on his knees. Within seconds he might as well have been dreaming, for the picture in his mind was as clear and three-dimensional as life, and it wiped all other reality from his senses.

The sounds of the plane, his revulsion at Felix's execution of the fly, the attendant who leaned over Jordan to retrieve the coffee cup and replace the tray, Jordan's fatigue, his longing to be with his kids, even his festering, angry grief faded into some insulated, subconscious pocket while the image of Cydya LeMonde dominated his mind's eye.

To Jordan, she never aged. Forever locked in his memory during the prime of her youth, she fit every description he had ever heard in sappy love songs. A green-eyed goddess. A blonde vision. A gift from heaven. Perfect.

He met her after having flown from Muskegon to Los Angeles, and from Los Angeles thirty-six hours through South Pacific islands and Australia before landing in Jakarta in the middle of the night.

He had been told there would be just one stop, in Hawaii, and that the next stop would be Jakarta. The six layovers ranged from forty-five minutes to five hours, yet no one was given the opportunity to shave or shower. And Jordan had not thought to carry on a change of clothes.

Besides feeling gamy, Jordan was already homesick. His fear of the unknown vied with remorse over the difficult farewell with his parents. Plus he doubted his own ability to carry out the assignment.

All that and his three-day growth of beard made him feel like a sight when he finally reached Indonesia. He stood like a zombie in a customs line for more than half an hour, staring blankly out the window until something caught his eye. In the window of a tiny, white Japanese station wagon was a hand-lettered message: *Welcome, Jordan! We've only been waiting since nine!*

He scanned the area and found two women waving. One was thick, open-faced, and friendly looking with a jaunty cap, a terry-cloth top, and khaki shorts to her knees. She wore sandals and had a key ring around her finger. Jordan guessed she was about forty.

Next to her was a girl who looked half that age. She wore sandals, faded blue denim short shorts, and a sleeveless, pink pullover blouse. Her sun-streaked hair was pulled back behind her ears. Jordan wondered if he could sneak a splash of Old Spice before he met them. Could the lithe, leggy one be a Peace Corps volunteer? How would anyone get any work done?

When he finally made his way through customs and got his baggage, he was immediately met by the older woman, a talker. "I'm Michelle." She grabbed his largest suitcase. "But I hate that name, so call me Mickey like everyone else does. This is Cydya, and we know who you are, Jordan."

He set down his other suitcase and extended his hand. Mickey shook it. Then Jordan shook the younger woman's hand. "Cindy?"

Mickey laughed. "That's what everybody says when they meet Cydya. You wanna give him your stock line?"

Cydya winked and he felt short of breath. "C-Y-D-Y-A. Think of the word *insidious*. Take off the first syllable and the last letter."

Up close she was almost too much to bear. Her huge eyes were pale green. She wore no makeup, not even lipstick or nail polish, and she didn't look as if she would ever need to. Her deeply tanned arms and legs had the ever-present sheen of perspiration common in that climate, but it made Cydya look luminescent.

They filled the back of the wagon with his things. "Sorry I'm so grundy."

The women laughed. Mickey looked at Cydya.

"Michigan, right? Every region, every state has its own word for the way its natives look when they finally get here. Don't worry about how you look, smell, or sound. Believe me, we understand."

Mickey drove, Jordan sat next to her, and Cydya sat behind them. To be polite, he kept telling himself, he turned in the seat so he could speak to both at once. It was small talk—welcome to Indonesia, a shower is waiting (cold, you know; he knew), and all that—but it afforded Jordan opportunities to glance at Cydya. It was all he could do to look away. He tried to tell himself anyone who looked that good had to be dumb or lazy or cantankerous.

He asked about assignments.

Mickey chortled. "You're wondering how we got stuck with escort duty."

"No, it's not that. I—"

"The newcomer's group leader—that's me—gets to pick him up. We always travel in twos, and Cydya drew the short straw because she's going to train you. You're replacing her."

Jordan was amazed at how deeply disappointing he found that after having just met Cydya. He knew he was merely enamored of her beauty. But he already considered her impending departure his loss. He asked where she was going.

Her voice was at once throaty and melodic, and she seemed to suppress a smile. "France. My parents are French, so I'm fluent in the language. I studied Spanish in high school, so I'm sort of

73

fluent in that. And I was raised in the States, so English is my mother tongue."

"So why France? Why not Spain?" *Why not Michigan?*

She smiled. "Interpol."

"The international police thing?"

"The International Criminal Police Organization. I've wanted to work there for as long as I can remember. The languages I know are the three languages of Interpol."

"Did you do that on purpose?"

"I didn't have any choice about the French and English, but yes, I studied Spanish so I'd know all three."

"What will you do there?"

"Start at the bottom. After that, who knows? I can hardly wait."

"You've already been hired?"

"I begin next spring."

Jordan sighed. She'd still be around more than six months. "It takes that long to train a replacement?"

"Not really. I involve the children in sports and games, while Mickey and the rest involve the parents in farming and building projects."

Jordan nodded. "The Peace Corps's loss will be Interpol's gain."

He felt silly, and Cydya just turned and stared out the window.

5

JUST BEFORE TOUCHDOWN at Dulles, Felix Granger gently shook Jordan, then produced a business-size NSA envelope. Inside was a cable: *THE SECRETARY HEARD THE KITTY TELL THE PREZ, "NOW I KNOW MY ABC's."*
Jordan shook his head, amazed that anyone, especially among the ranking intelligence community in the free world, thought anyone would be fooled by the simplistic code. Felix interpreted. "*Secretary* is the airport because Dulles was—"

"Secretary of state, I know."

"I'm the kitty, Felix the—"

"Yeah, I know."

"And you're—"

"The prez, JK, John Kennedy. Clever."

"And where does that ABC's line come in the song?"

Jordan sighed. "At the end, so we have to get off the plane last."

"So what was I 'splainin' it for?"

"Why do we have to get off last?"

Felix looked surprised. "You think Lister was workin' alone and now you're safe?"

"Are you telling me I'm going to have NSA guys all over the place?"

"For a while, I suppose. Till they're sure no one followed you over."

Jordan was nearly overcome with longing to see someone who loved him. His knees were weak. His head and back ached. But that cable was clear evidence that anyone who might have planned to meet him had already been told to wait in another room. He would have to deal with NSA red tape first. Just what he needed.

At the entrance to the terminal, Felix took his arm and quickened his pace. They passed families in tearful embrace. Jordan was jealous, wondering what had gotten into him. Already he was turning into some weird combination softy and cynic. And he knew that at least one of his kids would do anything but embrace him.

He wanted someone to rush to him, to hold him, to let him cry. He appreciated Felix and would never forget his kindness. But Felix wasn't family. The big man steered him through the terminal to the Red Carpet room and straight into a tiny alcove.

The place seemed full. The first face he recognized was Blake Bauer's, deputy director for field management and evaluation. Jordan shot Felix a double take. "Didn't expect him."

The stocky, baby-faced exec wore a heavy wool overcoat buttoned all the way up, and his dark, razor-cut hair was sprayed into place. Jordan believed bureaucrats like Bauer always assumed the men on the front line wanted their jobs. Fact was, Jordan had been offered Blake Bauer's job more than once. He'd rather pump gas.

He wished more people in administration had spent time in the trenches the way he and Chuck and Felix and Stan Stuart had. The mere thought of Stu made Jordan wince. If only he could talk to Chuck, tell him what Stu had told him. What were the odds that Chuck or anyone else could find the photos Stu had shown him? And would they mean anything to whoever found them? Jordan knew Chuck would agree there had been no suicide in Germany the night before, but even if they could convince someone of the crisis, NSA brass would be as concerned with protecting the public's confidence in the intelligence and defense communities as with dealing forthrightly with al-Qaeda and their Russian-made MiGs.

Bauer extended a manicured hand, and when Jordan grasped it, the deputy awkwardly tried to embrace him. Jordan stiffened. "Is my family here?"

Bauer was surrounded by clones. He had worked his face into a look of deepest sympathy. "You may have a few moments with them, and then we must talk."

Jordan pursed his lips. "I'll take as much time with them as I want. And we can talk next week, can't we?"

"I'm afraid not. In fact, give Mathews here the

funeral arrangements and he'll see to the, uh, disposition of, uh—"

Jordan scribbled the name of the funeral home and Mathews jogged off. Bauer squeezed Jordan's shoulder. "Just a few details from the director when you get a minute." Jordan was already pulling away. "I'm terribly sorry, Kirkwood."

When he was finally past the cadre of young headquarters types, Jordan saw his in-laws first. Elderly and retired now, the Reverend Holub was bald and bigger than ever, and he looked ashen. Jordan was struck at how Rosemary had always worshiped her father, despite his doting. Was that what Jordan should have done with his own daughter and son?

And there they were. He wanted to drink in the sight. Ken looked good—tanned, robust, older than his eighteen years. His sandy hair and dark eyes set off a handsomeness Jordan had never possessed. He had stood when Jordan appeared, but he made no move to approach or greet his father.

As the others awkwardly welcomed Jordan with only their eyes, Christa broke through and hugged him, sobbing. Her long black hair covered his hands as he embraced her. He wanted to see her olive face with the clear eyes and the high cheekbones she'd inherited from her mother. She felt tiny and frail. Jordan fought to keep his composure, hating himself for it.

His orange-haired mother-in-law approached with a sob in her voice. "Your boss has been so wonderful. He paid for Kenny's flight from California, and he offered us a car, but of course we have one. Christa has your car."

Reverend Holub's voice was a husky whisper. "They have also offered to fly in your mother and someone to accompany her."

Jordan tried to appear grateful, but he was suspicious of every kindness. His employers had to know his work meant nothing to him now, that he would blame his profession for the loss of his wife. "I'll just be a minute."

Bauer was waiting, hands in his pockets. He had apparently learned to speak first when dealing with Jordan. "We'll be at the funeral day after tomorrow, but not in the way. You'll get one more day after that with your family, then plan on three days with us."

"For?"

"Debriefing and testing. We'll be in the medical center first, then the basement of S Building." He must have noticed Jordan's angry look. "It's security, Kirkwood. We have your best interests in mind; you know that."

Jordan wasn't so sure. He'd always been repulsed by the behind-the-scenes guys, especially Bauer and his boss, Kurt Erhard, director of the National Security Agency.

Bauer clapped him on the shoulder. "Spend time

with your family. Granger will pick you up Thursday morning at seven. You may go now."

"Oh, I may? Thank you so much, Blake."

Bauer smiled benignly. "You're welcome, Jordan. Take care."

Less than an hour later, Jordan sat in the living room of his suburban split-level trying to explain what had happened. His daughter sat sniffling. His son still had said nothing. His father-in-law told him what they had been told: ". . . a terrorist attack."

Jordan was hoarse. "There's not much else to say."

His son glared at him. "Did you see it happen?"

Jordan nodded miserably.

His mother-in-law gasped. "We don't want to go through the ordeal again, but not knowing is worse."

Jordan nodded. "I take comfort—and you can too—in the fact that I don't think she ever knew what hit her. You probably read about it."

Mrs. Holub pressed her lips together but couldn't stifle a whimper.

Kenneth still glared. "And you were right there? Were you armed?"

"Armed?"

"C'mon, Dad! You think any of us still believe you're a diplomat? Were you armed?"

"Not really." Jordan winced. He should have

simply said no. Did they *all* know he was more than a diplomat? They looked uncomfortable with Ken's behavior.

His son stood. "'Not really'? Have you ever killed anybody?"

"Ken, if you'd like to talk about this—"

"I want to know! You killed somebody, didn't you? You go overseas and you kill people for the CIA. And because of someone you killed, someone was sent to kill you. He was trying for you and he got Mom!"

Jordan pleaded with his eyes. "That's not true." Ken stormed from the room, and Jordan turned to the remaining three. "It's not true."

Reverend Holub raised a meaty hand. "We know, Jordan. Is there anything more we should know about Rose's death?" His wife covered her face.

Jordan stared at the floor, wishing he could die. "She was among the first hit, so we can be grateful she didn't experience the terror of those who knew they would be next." Jordan's breathing grew shallow. "Mom and Dad Holub, I loved Rosemary with everything in me."

"We know."

Jordan had never been so expressive, especially in front of them. "I don't care about anything else anymore."

"Don't say that."

"I don't. All I'll ever care about is all of you."

Jordan's professional mind argued that he had shown weakness, but he didn't care. He was going to quit the NSA, and then the first thing on his agenda was to reverse all the mind training. It had saved his life more than once. Yet how could he argue with Ken?

If he had indeed been the diplomat the neighbors and relatives thought he was, this wouldn't have happened. He hated his cynicism. His work had made him tough and uncompromising. Realistic. Jaded.

He stood shakily. He hoped he'd be able to sleep. During brief flashes he was able think about something other than his loss, but nothing could blot out that his son was blaming him. And he had no defense.

The funeral was more of an ordeal than Jordan could have imagined. Neighbors, friends from church, coworkers, and family on both sides were kind enough, but their inane attempts to console him did no more than teach him a valuable lesson. Never again would he say anything to anyone who had lost a loved one. Just being there said ten times more.

His mother kept calling him by his brothers' names and asking for Rosemary. "Where is she, anyway? When is she getting here?" Fortunately, her brother had accompanied her.

Jordan's uncle Dexter Lee was a white-haired,

weatherworn, retired furniture magnate who had been Jordan's favorite since he was a child. He looked like a truck driver but dressed like an executive. Jordan wept in his embrace. The big man stood at the casket with his arm around Jordan and cried with him. "Ray Jr. and Walt wanted to come, but they just couldn't swing it. They send their love."

He could have told Jordan how good Rosemary looked and what a wonderful woman she had been and how he had always liked and respected and admired her. He could have promised to do "anything I can." But rather he was just there. A most unlikely angel of support and comfort.

At the airport early Wednesday afternoon, Uncle Dexter finally spoke. "Jordie, you know where I am. Say the word, and I'm on the next plane. Need a day or more with me like we used to do, you've got it. You want to come to Muskegon, just let me know."

Jordan wanted to board with him and be fathered. "Ken hates me."

Dexter put one hand behind Jordan's head and cupped his cheek with the other. "He doesn't hate you. He blames you. Wants to punish you."

"Uncle Dex, he has a right. And I feel like I owe him answers. But there are things I can't tell him."

"I know." Dexter always seemed to know when to quit. "You call me, hear?"

Back at home, Christa dispatched the last of the visitors and said she needed a nap. "You all right, Daddy?"

"Yeah. I need to do something, though. I was going to quit running, but now I feel like I'm going to explode."

"Ken said he was going for a run this afternoon. It's nippy out there."

"Never stopped us before. Where is he?"

She pointed upstairs. Jordan went up to change. Ken was already on his way down with his sweats on. "Mind if I join you, Ken?"

His son shrugged. "Suit yourself."

"Where you running?"

"Morningside."

"Our two-mile course? Perfect."

Ken drove. Jordan gave up trying to chat, hoping their running together for the first time in months would begin a thaw. He suggested a contest Chuck Wallington had taught him years before: run a mile at whatever speed you think you can duplicate for the second mile. Ken shed his sweats. "I think I can do two sixes."

Jordan took a deep breath. "I've been away from running for a few days. But I'll beat that by thirty seconds on both ends."

He hoped for a smile, some hint of the old Kenny. But his son's eyes darkened. "You won't win either one." And he took off, much faster than he should have.

Jordan settled into an easy pace, having run for enough years to know precisely how to turn a five-thirty mile. He wasn't sure he could run two in a row at that speed after a layoff, but if Ken beat him, so much the better.

A half mile out, Jordan caught Ken and could have passed him easily. Instead he slowed and ran with him for several hundred yards. Jordan sensed he was angering his son. Maybe he should just pull away and beat him. He tried. Ken accelerated, panting. At the end of the first mile, Ken surged ahead angrily and collapsed as he finished.

Jordan followed and ran in place. "That's one. You done?" He turned to repeat the course. Ken lay on his back, grimacing, knees raised. Jordan checked his watch. "You ran your six. But I can do it again. Can you?"

Ken rolled onto his stomach, buried his face in the crook of his elbow, and wept. "You're in intelligence, aren't you?"

"I'm not with the CIA."

Ken turned to look up at Jordan. "Don't play games with me, Dad! You're in intelligence."

Jordan nodded. "If I told you I was leaving the profession, would you let me keep all the confidences I've been sworn to keep?"

"Sworn to keep even from your wife?"

"Some, yes."

"Just some?"

"Most."

"More than that, I'll bet."

"Your mother was wonderful, Ken. She didn't pressure me to tell her things I wasn't supposed to."

"So you couldn't even tell her she was walking into one of your cases? You couldn't tell her she would be ambushed while you watched?"

Jordan hung his head. "You can't think I knew, Ken. You can't. I would have sacrificed my own life before I let someone kill her. You have a right to ask questions, but don't you dare accuse me of being responsible for her death. You have to know how much I loved her."

"How? You weren't around much!"

They'd been through this before, had discussed it for hours.

"Failing you by not being around enough is one thing . . ."

Ken stared at his father, snorting in an obvious attempt to keep from crying again. He managed a whisper. "I want to hit you. I want to punch you in the face."

"What's the matter with you?"

Ken got to his feet. "I just want to, that's all! Somebody already killed whoever was after you. Who else can I be angry at?"

How many times as a child had Jordan wanted to punch his own father? But he'd never even raised his hand toward him, never had the guts to even tell him what he thought of his self-righteousness, his rigidity.

So this was the new generation? "You really want to? You want a free shot at me, or would it make you feel better if I put up a fight?"

"What, and beat me up?"

"You tell me, Ken. This is your therapy, not mine."

Jordan hadn't meant to anger him further. Ken moved directly in front of him and punched him hard on the left cheek. Jordan felt tissue give way from bone as his head rocked to the side. He spread both hands on the ground as his knees buckled. He squinted up at Ken and straightened to face him again. The boy slashed at him with a backhand right, catching him beside the right eye, and Jordan knew it would blacken. Now he was on his knees, his hands at his sides.

When Ken took a step back, Jordan saw the boy wasn't through. He saw the rage on his son's face as he fired an uppercut toward Jordan's nose with all the power in his fabled serving arm.

Taking one straight to the face while on his knees before a standing opponent would break Jordan's nose, possibly drive cartilage fragments into his skull, maybe even his brain. At best, he would be knocked unconscious. At worst, his muscled neck would be broken.

His good deed had already been done. He'd taken his punishment, and he expected to feel as good about it later as Ken had felt in administering it. But he couldn't allow this third blow. He snatched Ken's fist out of the air, stepped on Ken's foot, stood, and yanked the arm toward himself. As Ken fell forward, Jordan drew the arm all the way around Ken's back, muscling the boy to the ground. He pressed a knee to the back of Ken's neck and cupped his right hand under Ken's chin.

"Son, you could have killed me. But now you know that I could kill you rather than let you hit me again."

"I hate you!"

"No, you don't." Jordan freed him.

Ken looked small now, struggling to his feet. "You've killed people just like that, haven't you?"

Jordan shook his head. Soon they would have to talk.

"Are you all right, son?"

Ken scowled. "I'm glad I hit you."

So am I.

6

JORDAN, HIS EYE purple and his cheek fiery red, phoned Christa's faculty adviser to find out how she was doing, only to learn that she was one of the most promising students of either gender to come along in years.

"No way are you staying here after the weekend, Christa."

"Daddy, you need me. You just won't admit it."

She was so right. "But I don't need a nanny, and much as I love having you around, I won't keep you here."

Christa seemed to brood. "Maybe I need the break. This isn't any easier for me than it is for you."

"I know."

No one could know the depth of his bonding with Rosemary. His was a faithfulness and a loyalty that had drawn him to her over the years and the miles, that checked him every time he entertained the thought of looking up his old acquaintance "just out of curiosity."

The truth was, he was more than curious about Cydya, and there were weeks, months sometimes, when her memory had plagued him and forced him to try to think of Rosemary instead. The excitement, the passion, the magic had never been as intense in his marriage as it had been with Cydya in Indonesia, yet he couldn't imagine a better wife.

He loved Rosemary deeply and completely and forever. He had chosen her, dedicated himself to her, committed himself, promised himself. And the same loyalty and singleness of mind and purpose that shot his score off the charts on personality and preference profile tests and made him the ideal intelligence operative made him a good husband under nearly impossible circumstances.

Divorce was rampant in his business. Lonely, unhappy wives were the norm. Much of the credit for his and Rosemary's success, he knew, had to go to her. She had been a remarkable, sweet, selfless person, the type people find hard to believe. However, another secret to their success, Jordan was certain, was his resolve to never tell her about Cydya.

Rosemary had told him of her previous boyfriends. One had wanted to marry her, but he cared nothing for God and she had to break his heart. She told Jordan the story carefully and seemed to watch intently for any sign of jealousy or discomfort. How he wished she had a story like his own. Then maybe he would have felt free to share what had happened to him.

But she didn't. And when she teased about his past, he admitted only the usual high school romances. He was amazed now that he could have loved two women for two decades, one he hadn't seen for that entire time. Finally he passed off his infatuation as only that: he decided he was enamored with the memory of Cydya's mere beauty.

Was it lust? It had been at the beginning. But what about his thoughts of her on dark, cold nights in lonely, undercover outposts thousands of miles from home? No, those weren't always pure either. In fact, even his wholesome, otherwise-innocent memories of her as a beautiful, engaging girl from his youth never came without guilt.

How would he feel if he knew his wife was thinking of a long-lost love that way? He would hate it, and he considered himself unfaithful for even allowing Cydya into his consciousness. He had prayed he could forget her, but he wound up doing little other than thinking of her. Worse, in his mind she had never aged. How could she? For twenty years she had been there as she had been in Jakarta—tanned, firm, youthful.

How much easier might it have been had Rosemary become a shrew. But she was a good mother, interesting and articulate because she passed the weeks of their frequent separations with voracious reading. When Jordan's tenuous faith was tested by the lack of anyone who seemed to live a genuine life of servanthood, there stood Rosemary as a beacon.

And she was loyal. Jordan couldn't deny he enjoyed the attention she showed him in public, but it was her consuming interest in him in private that amazed him. Early in their marriage she passionately discussed the dichotomy between her natural curiosity and her contentment with things as they were.

"I've always wanted to know everything, Jordan. It drove me crazy when something was going on at our house and I was the only one left in the dark. That's one of the reasons I read so much. But for some reason, I don't even want to ask you anything you wouldn't volunteer.

"I know you, I trust you, I love you. To my knowledge you've never shared with me a shred of classified information. I hope that's because you're told not to and not because you don't want me to worry. Because I worry anyway. And I pray."

He had told her what he was allowed to. She knew he worked for the National Security Agency, that he was in intelligence, and that he was anonymous even to many in the NSA. She had been made aware how difficult and demanding his job was and also how much he loved it. From the beginning, after she had gone through several sessions with Chuck Wallington, she had to know her life would be abnormal if she married Jordan.

For years he assured her that he had never been forced to use a weapon in the course of duty. On the pistol range, yes. In training, of course. But after a little more than ten years in the agency, he quit saying that. And she had never raised the subject.

Unites States policy prohibits political assassination or murder. However, in Cuba, Jordan had been forced to "eliminate an opponent for the purpose of preservation of one's own viability"—agency language for justifiable homicide. In fact, the incident had been grisly, caused by Jordan's own error.

He had ignored a hunch, the type of thing he should have relied on, based on Chuck's counsel.

"Always follow a hunch that leads to caution; never follow a hunch to take a risk." Something told him to wait. He didn't wait. Then he was jumped, a Luger pressed cold and ugly against his neck.

His assailant disarmed him and should have killed him where he stood. Instead, Jordan was made to lean against a wall while the Cuban agent taunted him and waited for a companion.

Jordan sagged, letting his head drop to his chest so he could see behind himself with peripheral vision. He prepared his body and mind for a technique Chuck had taught him during his years as a student in Washington. Feigning fatigue, fear, and exhaustion, he tripped his adrenal gland into high gear by imagining his own death.

When his body was sufficiently charged, he leaped into the air, driving his feet off the wall and screaming as he turned around in midflight, hurtling toward the Cuban. It was kill or be killed. If you miss the gun hand, go for the neck. He missed the gun hand. It wound up under his arm, pointing toward the wall.

He clamped down on the gunman's arm with his elbow and drove him to the floor. He could release the pressure on the gun hand, provided he could break the man's neck more quickly than the man could turn the barrel and shoot.

The gun was in his ribs at his back when he felt the man's neck give way. And when the Cuban's partner burst in, Jordan had to kill him with the Luger. Wallington and other NSA brass were concerned over how the incident would affect Jordan. They and his uncle Dexter were the only people who knew what he had done.

The killings were legal. Self-defense. Yet they plagued him more than any of the serious injuries he had inflicted before. Those had been a different story. But to kill a man, to feel and see him die, to see the terror in his eyes, then the vacant stare . . .

Though he tried to hide his feelings, Jordan sensed that Rosemary knew. The event changed him, but it didn't make him want to leave the NSA the way the death of his wife did. Telling his bosses was going to be an ordeal. They'd dealt with burnt-out operatives before. He wouldn't say anything they hadn't heard.

Meanwhile, he had to talk Christa into getting back to Salisbury. "You can always come back if I need you. And anyway, I have to be at headquarters for three days."

"But you'll be home for dinner."

"No, I'm staying right there, overnight. There'll be nothing for you to do here. Ken's heading back to California."

"Do you think you should let him go before you . . . you know, get things straight?"

"We almost have. I'll be taking him to the airport, so say your good-byes here."

Christa looked at her father as if she knew him

better than he knew himself. "I hate that your bosses think you're up to being debriefed or whatever they call it. When will they let you mourn?"

"They can't stop me from that, honey."

Her lips quivered and her eyes filled. "But you need time to think, to remember, to cry."

He held her and whispered, fighting his own tears. "You're a special lady. When I get back from headquarters, I'll take the time to rest."

"Promise?"

"I'm quitting, Christa."

"Your job?"

He nodded.

"What will you do?"

"I don't know yet. I just know it's over. I've lost my drive."

"It'll come back."

"No! It won't!"

Christa flinched at his anger. "All right."

"I'm sorry, sweetie. It's just that I know myself. This isn't a phase, something caused by grief. I don't want to get over it."

She pulled away and sat facing him, appearing deep in thought. "Dad, do you feel guilty? Responsible?"

Jordan looked everywhere but at his daughter. "Should I?"

Her tears began again. "Oh, Dad. Kenny was right, wasn't he?"

Jordan's mind was still not right. He fought to

be himself, yet he felt the conflicting patterns of his training rising to his defense. He could be lucid and evasive, even with his own daughter, if he weren't grieving, if he were in shape. But he didn't want to be in shape. He didn't want to mislead her. He didn't want to quit grieving.

"Get your brother."

Then he told his daughter and son he wanted them to know the truth about their mother's death. "But I don't want you to ask me anything. If I don't volunteer it, don't ask." They nodded. "I do feel responsible. I *am* responsible. I don't know why. You make a lot of enemies in my business, but what caused the attack, I don't know. It's clear that I was the target and that the gunman died thinking he had succeeded."

Ken leaned forward. "What reason did he have for wanting to kill you, or is that something I'm not supposed to ask?"

Jordan's mind raced. He rationalized that he didn't know for sure whether the Stuart meeting in Frankfurt had anything to do with it. "If I knew the reason, I might not be able to tell you, Ken. But I really don't know. He was a hired killer, and until I find out who hired him, I won't know the reason."

Christa looked at her brother, then at Jordan. "Until *you* find out who hired him? You didn't mean to say that, did you?"

Jordan forced himself to speak evenly, though

all the rage that had been building, all the grief and guilt and sorrow, threatened to overflow. "Yes, for two reasons." His eyes burned into her. "Revenge and self-preservation."

Christa stood and walked to the window, her back to him. He could hardly hear her. "Mom would want you to leave vengeance to God, you know."

He shrugged, catching Ken's eye. "Sounds good in theory. But if vengeance is God's, I want to be His instrument."

Christa whirled. "Don't mock."

"I'm dead serious."

Ken looked puzzled. "You'll be on the case? Officially, I mean?"

"Of course not. I told you, I'm quitting. But do you think anyone will be as interested in finding whoever hired the assassin? If I don't do it and my people lose interest, I could be the next victim. Or you." He couldn't tell them he trusted only one, maybe two others in the agency. If Stuart's information was good, Jordan's would-be assassin could have been hired by someone within the NSA.

Christa sat back down next to Ken. "That's why you want us both out of here by the time you get back. You think someone might come looking for you and find us, just like Mom?"

Jordan caught the glimmer of realization in their eyes. "I will not have my family living in fear."

97

Ken lowered his head and peeked up at his father. "I'm not scared."

Christa looked first at Ken, then at her father. "Me either."

Jordan had to say it. "I am."

Christa seemed to force a smile. "I thought you weren't afraid of anything."

"Did I ever say that?" She shook her head. "Did I act that way?" They both nodded.

"There *is* something I'm terribly afraid of, besides your safety and my own. I'm afraid you'll never forgive me for costing you your mother."

They embraced him.

Christa lingered when Ken went to pack. "You know he's got some big tournament coming up."

"Tournament?"

"Some tennis thingy. It's intrasquad or whatever they call it, but it's a big deal because if he does well, he could make the varsity."

"Seriously?"

"Yes, Dad. You need to be there. It's in a month or so."

"I should."

Jordan thought he had been tired before. Seven hours' sleep that Wednesday night put a mere dent in the fatigue caused not only by his grief and fear, but also by his anxiety over how to inform his superiors of his plans.

Felix was quiet on the way to the NSA compound. He had not attended the funeral, something Jordan hadn't even noticed until he mentioned it. "Real sorry I couldn't make it. You know how they tie you up when you get back from anywhere."

"How well I know. This is the longest I've ever been back without being debriefed already."

Within an hour, Felix had driven north on the Baltimore-Washington Parkway to a place just about equidistant from both cities. Noting Felix's mood, or at least his evident disinclination to chat so early in the morning, Jordan tried to relax and enjoy the scenery. He found that the Maryland countryside consisted of miles of trees he had never taken time to look at.

"How'd it go with the boy this mornin'?"

"He's coming around, Felix. I promised to attend a tennis thing next month."

"Good for you."

Felix turned onto Savage Road, bringing into view the nine-story NSA headquarters building surrounded by the three-story complex that had preceded it. The very sight of that innocent-looking building threw Jordan back to his early days in Washington when Chuck Wallington had driven this very route to show it to him.

The idea was that the place should not look like what it was: headquarters for the world's largest secret code–deciphering plant. In those days, the NSA had no operatives who worked in the manner that Jordan Kirkwood would—like a misplaced CIA man. Now, twenty years later, he told himself, after this last debriefing there would be none left.

He had visited headquarters at least twice a year since he had joined the NSA. He always hated it. The three fences surrounding the grounds, the electrically charged wires, the barbed wire, the guard dogs, and the television monitors were necessary, but there were days all that security seemed so Mickey Mouse. Today was one such day.

No matter who you were or what your business was, you went through security just like everyone else, including the director. As they mounted the dozen steps to the glassed-in entrance to Gatehouse One, Jordan wondered aloud if he would be seeing Erhard. Felix grunted. "Count on it."

A Federal Protective Service guard matched Felix's face with the photo on the employee security badge around his neck. Then he stopped Jordan.

"You—ain't you an employee too?"

Jordan nodded apologetically. "Forgot my badge."

Felix tried to wave off the guard. "He's with me."

"You know that ain't good enough, sir. If he ain't got his badge, you got to sponsor him just like he was a visitor. Sorry."

Felix swore and dragged Jordan off through

another set of doors to the reception area, where he was processed like anyone else without security clearance. Felix had to sign a promise that Jordan would be accompanied at all times. A striped, one-day badge was pinned on Jordan, and for a moment he really felt like an outsider. *Not soon enough.*

On the way down the long corridor to the lobby, Felix chuckled. "That receptionist woulda had a fit if she'd known y'all was gonna be here three days on a one-day badge." Jordan didn't see the humor. In the mural on the wall, which purported to show the various activities of the NSA, he saw agency employees engaged in listening, writing, and collecting signals. He didn't see anyone killing anyone else or watching his wife die.

At the end of the hall was the gaudy seal he'd passed so many times, its gleaming eagle protecting the NSA. He and Felix took a left and headed toward the elevators in the lobby, past the portraits of former NSA directors and another armed guard.

The bored-looking guard noted their badges and nodded. Felix pushed the Up button while glancing at his watch. "You should see some of the new computers in the basement. But we don't have time." When they stepped into the car, he pushed the button for the top floor.

Jordan had been in room 9A197 before, the office of the director of the National Security

Agency. The secretary ushered them into the empty office and pointed to two leather chairs facing a coffee table and a matching couch. As soon as she left, an edgy Jordan stood and looked out the window, then idly twirled the huge globe.

Felix sat like a gangly junior high basketball player on the bench. "Lots to do today."

Kurt Erhard breezed in, tall and pale with dark wavy hair, brown eyes, thin lips, and hurry-up in his voice. "Good morning, gentlemen." Felix stood and Erhard shook their hands. "Don't sit, Felix. You may be excused."

Erhard unbuttoned his suit coat as he sat on the couch, stretching both legs out to one side. Settled in, he stared long and hard at Jordan. "Tough, tough thing for you, Kirkwood. A lovely service, though. Happy to be there. Beautiful family. Enjoyed getting to meet your mother. Is she well?" Jordan shook his head. "And your father?"

"Dead, sir."

"But the older gentleman—"

"Her brother, my uncle."

"Ah. Nice. Good he could come. You're okay?"

"Hardly."

"Well, of course not. I can imagine. Sorry we have to jump right into things. You could use more time, no doubt."

"No doubt."

"But such is life. Tough, tough thing. Is there anything at all I can do for you, Jordan?"

It was an idle statement, one he had heard many times the past two days. But here was a man with resources. "Two things."

Erhard looked surprised. "Anything."

"I'd like to see Chuck Wallington."

"He's coming! Didn't you know?" Jordan shook his head. Erhard nodded. "Oh yes. We knew he was instrumental in your career. He's coming. Absolutely. Up from Florida. In fact, he'll be involved in some of your debriefing and counseling."

"Counseling?"

"You said there were *two* things I could help you with?"

"But, sir, please, you said counseling?"

Erhard gestured before he spoke, as if coaxing the words from his throat. "In, uh, situations like this, we like to, you know, do a variety of diagnostic and evaluative things, run some tests. There is some counseling involved, mostly interrogative."

Jordan loved the double-talk. "So a shrink is going to ask me if I'm suicidal."

Erhard swung his legs down off the couch and planted his feet in front of him. He put a hand on each knee and leaned forward. "I understand you are one of our top men, Kirkwood, and I can see why. I also know we'll have to fight to keep you around." Jordan was stunned. Had Erhard been tipped off about his decision? "The CIA is always on our case to lend you to them. Same with military intelligence. Anyway, I appreciate your subjecting yourself to this. Tough—"

Jordan nodded. "Tough thing."

"You did say there was something else I could do for you."

"I was going to ask that you get me out of this, but apparently I'm this week's highlight around here."

Erhard studied him and smiled. "I'm impressed you can keep a sense of humor. Listen, I understand how you feel. We'll keep things moving, and the earliest we can get you out of here on Saturday, the happier we'll be. You know this gives us time to be certain of your security and to start working on a suitable new assignment for you. The more you cooperate, the quicker it'll go."

Erhard stood but motioned for Jordan to stay seated. "Two things I want you to know before you head over to Medical. First, you're the boss. Your next assignment is up to you. You want to go to Florida and work with Wallington in administration? Okay. You want to learn a new area? Decoding? Management? You tell us."

So there it was. A plum position. Whatever and wherever he wanted. Resignation was not in their thinking. Neither was bitterness or cynicism or lack of cooperation. Get in line, stay in line, be loyal, and we'll take care of you. The problem was, Jordan wasn't in the mood. It all seemed like such a waste.

But Erhard wasn't finished. "The other thing is this: we're aware you were the target in London. You will be under constant surveillance, and we will be tracking down the perpetrator with every resource available to us."

"Except me."

"We'll use you, Jordan. That's part of what these three days is all about. We must comb through all your activities for any leads."

Jordan sighed. "How far back?"

"All the way back. But first, a physical. Then a psychological. Then a debriefing on the Germany assignment. Then a history search, an inventory of your contacts."

"For twenty years?"

"If necessary."

Jordan had not been easy to talk to. He had not been kind to Erhard. The director would pass that off as bitterness or grief, but in truth Jordan had come to the end of his patience with the work. He wasn't saying what the NSA did wasn't valid or necessary. He just knew the organization was too big, too cumbersome, too corporate, too bureaucratic. And since he'd quit working for Chuck Wallington, it was also too lonely. Besides, he couldn't imagine any possibility of confirming Stan Stuart's secret from the inside.

Erhard extended his hand as if to help him up. Jordan ignored it. He wasn't old and weak, just tired and heartbroken. "I'll walk you over myself." Erhard knew Jordan had to be accompanied, but he could have assigned someone. Apparently it made him feel good to condescend to such a task.

They went back down through the lobby and into the hallway connecting the headquarters tower to the three-story operations building. Getting through the most secure doors required Erhard to reach inside a box and depress the right buttons. At other passageways he slid a magnetic card into a slot. Jordan had been on the second and third floors of the operations building before, where each new wing was color-coded for level of clearance. Some not even the director could enter without permission.

Corridor C at the center of the complex was nearly a thousand feet long, the longest clear hallway in the United States. Jordan felt fortunate he didn't have to walk all the way to the other end. Erhard delivered him to a physician, Dr. Luschel Bradley, a freckle-faced redhead who, except that he was Jordan's age, could have modeled in children's commercials.

He ran Jordan through five hours of the second-most-rigorous physical examination he had ever had. The first had been his initial exam for the NSA before he enrolled at International University. Chuck Wallington had prepared him for that one. "No sense educating you if you're going to fall apart on us."

If anything, Jordan was in better shape now than he had been then. The doctor asked a lot of personal questions Jordan would have expected more from a psychiatrist, and that was coming next. The redhead smiled and thanked him when it was over, extending his hand. "Couple of test results will be back later, but meanwhile, all things considered, you're a thoroughbred."

Did *everybody* know what he was going through? Jordan began to resent his macabre celebrity. The doctor put a hand on his shoulder. "I get to walk you to Dr. Fazio. You know who he is."

Tall and thin, wearing moccasins and his shirt open at the collar, the fiftyish Dr. Fazio was bald with a rim of hair over his ears. He wore glasses he seemed fonder of chewing than using, and rather than employ a couch or even a chair, he preferred walking interviews.

Early in their first conversation, Dr. Fazio stopped at the intersection of two hallways. "Could you briefly tell me your religious background, Jordan?"

"Sure. I'm not too devout now. Having trouble, uh, praying. My wife was—"

The doctor shook his head. "Background. Training. Upbringing. Briefly."

"Uh, Protestant. Fundamentalist. Um—"

The doctor sighed. "Two's enough." He rubbed his forehead. "Oh, boy."

7

BY THE TIME Dr. Fazio and Jordan had walked the length of corridor C, including a brief stop for a snack, Jordan had formed an opinion about the psychiatrist and was certain the doctor had made up his mind about him too. Clearly, Dr. Fazio had concluded that Jordan would hide his true grief in the belief that God knew best, cared personally about him, and was watching over him.

"My fear, young man, is that you will soon turn the blame on God, still assuming that He takes a personal interest in each of His charges, and wonder why He has done this to you."

Jordan shrugged. "Five days ago I saw my wife alive one minute and dead the next. Is it all right if that traumatizes me? I'm not suicidal."

The doctor sniffed. "No need to be testy. I'm just trying to determine how deeply ingrained is your belief in a personal God."

"For what purpose?"

"Unfortunately, some of these childish—excuse me, childhood—myths can be difficult to overcome. When depended upon to assuage grief, well . . ."

"Well?"

"The notion of a personal deity can be comforting. But to a reasonably intelligent person such as yourself, the sudden realization of a lack of substance there could set you back. In other words, if everything is *not* all right and God is *not* in His heaven, what then?"

Jordan shaped his hand in the form of a gun and held it to his head.

The doctor flinched. "That does not amuse me."

"Look, my upbringing resulted in some solid beliefs, but I don't think I have to be a nutcase to be a Christian."

"But you believe God exists as a real person?"

"Yes."

The doctor raised both hands and smiled. "I find you otherwise mentally healthy."

"Is that going in my file?"

"That you're healthy? Yes. I don't worry terribly about you. I *would* like to check on your faith in about six months, however."

"I want to know if you're going to label it some sort of psychological aberration."

The doctor leaned against the wall. "If that would cause you discomfort, I can leave it out. Don't deceive yourself, however. It's not as if they don't know. Why do you think I asked about your religious background?"

"I know they know. Chuck Wallington discovered me on a missionary trip. I've never hidden it."

"Then why the issue with my recording it?"

"The issue is whether you label it a problem."

"Oh, I rarely record my personal opinions. Ready for some dinner? Dr. Bradley will join us."

"Really?"

"He's been assigned to go through the line with you and prescribe your dinner."

"Prescribe?"

The psychiatrist smiled. "You are going to sleep tonight, Mr. Kirkwood. Like you've never slept before."

"I could use that. And he's going to pull it off with food choices?"

The redheaded physician must have overheard because he interjected as he approached. "Partly. Also this." He held out a plastic packet containing two capsules. "Good for hours of solid—and I mean uninterrupted—sleep."

In the cafeteria, Dr. Bradley pointed to high-protein, high-fiber vegetables and a small chicken dish, no dessert, no dairy products. Jordan examined the capsules. "No label. What's in it?"

They sat and Bradley borrowed back the packet and showed the psychiatrist. Fazio nodded and smiled. "Take these when you're finished eating, but find out where you're bedding down first so you can tell whoever scrapes you off the floor."

Jordan fingered the packet again. "I'm not a big chemical man. I even stay away from aspirin as much as I can. You still haven't told me what's in this."

"Ever hear of sodium thiopental?"

"Yeah, for major surgery. Surely you're not—"

Bradley stopped him with a wave. "Of course not. The key ingredient is phenobarbital." He switched into a bad W. C. Fields impersonation. "A white, odorless, crystalline powder."

Dr. Fazio broke in. "Five cc's of which will kill a twelve-hundred-pound racehorse in thirty seconds. You know how much five cc's is?"

Jordan remembered, from somewhere, that thirty cc's made an ounce. "A sixth of an ounce." The doctors looked at each other, obviously impressed. Jordan dug his fork into a stalk of broccoli. "I won't take it."

Dr. Bradley sat back. "No one will force you, but let me encourage you. You've been through an ordeal. Tomorrow and Saturday could be difficult as well. You should be in bed by seven tonight. Within twenty-five minutes of taking those capsules, you will fall asleep and stay asleep for up to twelve hours without dreaming or moving. Be sure to eliminate before you retire."

Doctors were always so delicate.

"Any idea what's on the docket for me tomorrow?"

Dr. Fazio studied his clipboard and raised his eyebrows. "You rate top brass."

"Not the director. He would have told me."

"No, the deputy. Bauer himself and a couple of aides."

"Oh, joy."

"Plus one of the old-timers from out of state—Wallington, the one you mentioned."

Directed to a comfortable but not fancy room, Jordan disrobed to his shorts and sat wearily on the bed. Someone would be by in the morning to escort him to S Building, which was puzzling. Surely they would be in the way in the bronze-colored home of the agency's Communications Security Organization.

Jordan padded around, arranging his room, hanging up things. After brushing his teeth, he stared at the haggard face in the mirror. He felt old and looked older. It wouldn't be long before his natural color would begin peeking out at the roots of his hair. He wouldn't be surprised if it came in gray. Stranger things had happened.

He was exhausted, but he knew he was too wired to sleep. He went to the closet and found the pills in his pants pocket. After a moment's hesitation, he dry-swallowed two of them.

When he slid between the cold sheets, Jordan decided to try to stay awake until the pills took effect, just out of curiosity. Unfortunately, that gave him time to think. He stared at the ceiling, reliving his meeting with Stanley Stuart and the icy feeling in the pit of his stomach at the very thought of more enemies on American soil. He experienced anew the shooting, the trip home,

Felix's compassion, Bauer's prissiness, Christa's sweetness, Ken's anger.

Ken's embrace after their heart-to-heart had seemed genuine, but clearly the two had a long way to go. Hearing the praise of his mother at the funeral had to accentuate all the horror and grief of losing her in the prime of her—and his—life. Jordan realized that after having been less than a father for too many years, now he needed to be both mother and father to his son.

Jordan's own mother had certainly declined. When would she have to be institutionalized? And when would he be jetting back for her funeral? Uncle Dex had been his usual, rare self. Jordan felt fortunate to have had him over the years.

He found himself weeping as he lay there, legs crossed at the ankles, fingers entwined over his chest. The tears rolled over his ears.

He knew when his eyelids grew heavy that he was past the point of no return. A warm glow radiated through his muscles and joints, leaving a floating numbness. He felt giddy, then drowsy. Hallucinations teased him, and he tried to think, to remember. Hadn't that doctor said no dreams? Nonsense. But which doctor? Witch doctor? He saw Bradley with a bone through his nose. In London. On the floor, next to his wife. Or was that Cydya? Whoever it was, she was dead. A train pulled slowly away as he ran leaden-legged along the platform. He ran and ran, waving, but all he could see through the windows were Russian MiG-23s. At the end of the platform he stopped at a huge corrugated steel door, but the train kept moving.

As these thoughts faded, so did all consciousness.

When Jordan's eyes popped open, he reached for his watch and squinted at the luminous hands. Five fifteen. Couldn't be.

He raised the shade. Still dark. Was another clock in the hall? Peeking out, he heard footsteps echoing and moved back in, leaving the door ajar. When the steps came closer, he peeked out again. It was a guard. "Help you, sir?"

Jordan found it difficult to form words. "Jes' wonderin' what time it is."

"Almost five twenty, Mr. Kirkwood. Need anything?"

Jordan shook his head.

The doctor had said he would sleep without moving or dreaming. He didn't say anything about losing even a subconscious awareness of time. He sat on the bed, trying to convince himself he had slept more than ten hours. It was as if he had lain down, thought awhile, drifted off a minute, and then awakened ten hours later.

As life returned to his limbs, Jordan ran in place, did push-ups, sit-ups, and stretching exercises. After he had showered and shaved and followed his escort to breakfast, Jordan met Blake Bauer and two assistants in the basement of S Building. Bauer urged Jordan to make himself comfortable in a room much too large for the few sticks of furniture and the file cabinets dollied in for the occasion.

The chair of honor was a dilapidated green vinyl job with sagging springs and spindly legs. Blake sat facing him in a hardwood, Bank of England chair that caused him to squirm. They shared a small table. The aides sat behind the deputy director in secretary's chairs, on rollers, near the file cabinets.

Jordan thought his case would be considered grunt duty for someone at Bauer's level, but the deputy director smiled as if he relished his assignment. "Mr. Wallington is expected after lunch. Meanwhile, let's get acquainted."

"We know each other, Blake. And please, let's not talk in agencyspeak."

"As you recall, Kirkwood, I joined the NSA from the military some five years after you had already been on board. I had no reason to be aware of you during my climb—or I should say my, uh, progress, as it were, to the level of responsibility which is now mine, or which I now hold."

Jordan felt as if he were in bureaucratic purgatory. "And now you're important enough to know one of the only remaining CIA types within the NSA."

"I wouldn't express it that way, but you have

described yourself well. You know, NSA history shows that when Mr. Wallington received permission for this highly unusual undertaking—developing clandestine operations with anonymous recruits such as yourself—most thought it would fail."

Jordan straightened up. "And it did fail, didn't it? I've heard this pitch before."

Bauer cocked his head and looked hurt. "It's not a pitch, Jordan. We have a job to do."

"And what is that? What *are* we trying to accomplish here while whoever had my wife hit is still looking for me?"

Bauer grew suddenly serious. "Don't be naive. You have to know your protection is one of the primary reasons you're here."

"So what are we doing down here with the files?"

"Your files have never been open to the administration. With your role including investigation of even the agency, so few people inside were aware of your activity and sphere of influence that we hardly know where to begin to look for leads on your pursuer."

"So I'm in the way now that I'm in trouble? You people wish I had been either more visible or less effective."

Bauer shook his head, smiling. "There are those—though I'm not one of them—who are less than comfortable with having had one of our own keeping us under surveillance."

"Most of my time was spent watching other federal agencies."

"For which we are grateful."

"You're grateful someone is watching *them,* as long as no one is watching *us.*"

Bauer stood, his face red. "Enough people are watching us, Jordan. We don't need to watch ourselves!"

Jordan smiled, letting Blake's own statement ring in his ears. "Is that what you meant to say?"

"Well, of course we keep an eye on our people. But we're talking here about a band of a dozen or so young people, some just out of high school—yourself included—who were somehow brought in by Wallington when he was a maverick, and—"

"He's not still a maverick?"

"He's less a maverick. He's a company man, Jordan, and always has been. Anyway, he and some long-since-departed associates got this scheme passed by the former director—heaven knows how—and frankly, for a decade or so it ran amok. Do you not agree?"

"We did our jobs, Blake. We were committed. It was an unusual group. You know, of course, that for a couple of years we weren't even aware of each other. It was an experiment."

"Yes, yes, each big brother—or whatever Wallington and his cohorts called themselves—tried to see how long each could keep his man

117

working without anyone knowing who he was. Didn't work too well, I understand."

"Worked too well. Made the director and your predecessor nervous. They knew we existed but didn't know our names. We were their best people, and they had no idea if they'd ever seen us or ever would. Finally called us in."

"It wasn't quite that clean."

Now it was Jordan's turn to stand, only he wasn't upset. Just cramped. "There were failures, sure. Some were found out; some were lured away by other agencies. Some were bad choices."

"One failed miserably. Stanley Stuart's selection."

"The failure was in the choosing. The man wasn't evaluated the way Chuck studied me. At least Stu still had an interesting job after that fiasco. He wasn't kicked upstairs until fifteen years later when his wife died."

Bauer looked hurt. "A raise and a promotion is your idea of getting kicked upstairs?"

"I didn't get the impression Stu was happy about it."

Bauer pressed his lips together. "You can't blame his suicide on his job."

Didn't anyone question Stu's cause of death?

"What do you think caused it, Blake?"

The deputy stared at the ceiling. "Grief. Depression."

"Four years after he lost his wife? C'mon!"

"Well, who knows, Jordan? Did you see him when you were over there? He requested you, but you worked independently, didn't you?"

"Right. I worked independently."

"So you didn't see him?"

Jordan hesitated.

"A routine check of his calendar to see if anything might have triggered his demise revealed that you spent five minutes with him in the afternoon and that he went home right after your meeting."

"So why'd you ask?"

"To see if you'd deny it."

"That's why we're here? To see if I caused Stanley Stuart's death?"

"Just answer the question."

"I hadn't planned to see him. Five minutes hardly constitutes a meeting. We pretty much just greeted each other. I hadn't even known he was there."

"Get serious. You know where everyone is, especially your old acquaintances."

"I knew he'd been reassigned in Europe, but I didn't know he was at JOSAF. Ask his assistant."

Bauer picked through some documents. "Well, score one for you. She says you expressed surprise Mr. Stuart was there. So what did he want?"

"Five minutes for old times' sake."

"He seem depressed?"

"Tired maybe. Showed his age. Mentioned retirement."

Bauer stared. "That's it?"

Jordan stared back, unmoving as if his life depended on it. The second meeting with Stuart had been private and personal, away from the JOSAF office. "That's it."

Bauer asked one of his lackeys for the Wallington file on Jordan. "It's time to get back on track." He picked through four inches of manila. "Something's missing."

Jordan gazed at him. "I'll bite."

"I'm not being cute. I've been over this and over this. Wallington documents how he met you, baited you, tested you to see if you wanted the position. He's clear on your shortcomings and how you worked to improve. But how did he make that step from seeing an admittedly impressive high school résumé to knowing you were sincere?"

"Sincere?"

"Don't be coy, Jordan. The reason you lasted, the reason you're the only survivor of this crazy twenty-year-old plan, is because you had the ideals for it."

Had Bauer really seen that for himself? "Do you really think so?"

Bauer slammed his fist on the table. "That's just it, Jordan! I don't know! With inside men we can study military records and watch as they climb the corporate ladder. With you, we've got what? You were a Boy Scout and a churchgoer. So what? Most of us were. How did Wallington know you would be a true patriot, loyal, honest, and with the right motives?"

Jordan fought a smile. "He was a good judge of character?"

"Nobody is *that* good! He was taking a risk."

"Isn't a hire always a risk?"

"But someone so young for so sensitive a position? Do you realize how potentially dangerous your appointment was?"

"Not till now, Blake, but you're really bringin' it home. How'd we get on this? I thought we were here to look for a criminal."

Bauer tapped the ends of the folders on the table. "We are. But we can't study your background and activities and contacts without getting into this."

"We were that worrisome for everyone?"

"Oh, you bet."

"Were they that jealous of our freedom?"

Bauer smirked. "You'd like to think that. Maybe some of us *would* rather have been globe-trotting, carrying weapons, playing CIA. But as the number of you renegades dwindled and the dictate came down to quit spying on our own people, folks around here thought the program ought to be deep-sixed. We thought we had you when you snuffed those guys in Cuba. Ho, man, Kirkwood! That just about did it. They could put up with you

121

and yours when nobody but Wallington and a few others knew what you were doing, but when things got noisy, well—this agency was founded to intercept and decode messages, and there you guys were, playing cloak-and-dagger."

"Guilty. Want me to quit? Just show me where to sign."

Bauer looked back at his assistants, who appeared bored. "You know nobody's going to let you resign."

"How can they stop me?"

"You know too much, inside and out."

"So that's it. It's what I know about the agency."

Bauer shrugged. "I'm authorized to offer you a three-step promotion and appropriate raise, which you and I both know you don't need. You make almost as much as I do now, not that I have a problem with that. But first, I feel an obligation to protect you."

"I should think you would!"

"Hey, not many people in this agency get themselves in that kind of trouble."

Jordan stepped in front of Bauer's chair and towered over him in much the same way his own son had looked down upon him two days before. "Who was I working for when I crossed whoever it was I crossed? I may have been one of the only NSA operatives in the world—okay, the only one—doing that kind of work, but it was my assignment!"

Bauer held up his hands. "What do you say we calm down, huh, Kirkwood? Maybe I should have said that in sincere appreciation for your putting your life on the line in the course of duty and in light of your loss, we want to do everything in our power to apprehend the person or persons responsible. Okay? That's going to require careful scrutiny of your entire career. You know the case is otherwise off-limits to you."

Jordan sat. "I figured. But outside Chuck Wallington, whom you've already relegated to some two-bit desk job, you just implied I'm the only man in the NSA with the training and experience to handle the case."

"There's no way you're searching for your own assassin, and that's final. Now, are we ready for our second task here, which, as I recall, was your original question? I have to do the job, with or without Wallington's help, that he should have done when he hired you. He didn't document a thing except your meeting a few challenges and answering a question or two about being gung ho—wherein you waxed eloquent about your father's war wounds. Now don't look at me that way. Your record is good, but we have to retroactively establish the solidity of your character."

The insult was not lost on Jordan. He wanted to dive across the table, but the mind-trigger mechanism so effectively impressed upon him by Chuck Wallington quickly shifted him to calm mode.

"Doesn't my record speak for itself, Blake? Can't we say that even if he hired me on flimsy grounds, I proved myself? Do you need a polygraph? You wanna wire me up and ask me if I'm true blue?"

Bauer dabbed at his forehead with a handkerchief. "Jordan, I have to tell you something, and I hope you'll appreciate that I'm telling you, because it was thought—and I hoped—that I would be more successful if I didn't have to spell this out."

"I can hardly wait."

"The fact is, we don't know nearly enough about your activity for several of the years you've been with us to know how credible you are."

"So I could be subversive? A double agent?"

"I didn't say that! I'm telling you no, we can't just take a look at your record and decide whether any embarrassment might come to this agency over what happened to your wife."

Jordan scratched his head. "Do you see how ridiculous this is? You decide I brought all this on by involving myself in some subversive activity, and what, you leave me to fend for myself? Do I get the promotion and the raise and the protection if I'm deemed okay, or if I'm *not* okay? And will you accept my resignation if I'm *not* okay, but not if I *am* okay?"

"You raise good points."

Jordan let his head fall back and roared. But his

laughter turned on him in an instant and became crying. He lurched forward to cover his mouth and saw pity in the eyes of Bauer and his assistants. He had steeled himself against breaking down, but he couldn't help it. If only the emotion hadn't sneaked up on him . . .

Jordan had wanted to laugh at the horrendous lack of logic. His mind, tuned to the paradox of the opposite frequency, read comedy and spit out tragedy. Now that he had failed and sat there sobbing, he wanted to scream at Bauer, to demand to know how he could impugn a perfect record.

He wanted to rage about his love for his country, his rock-solid belief in democracy and justice and peace and honesty. Yet he would not lower himself to speak while out of control.

Bauer spoke haltingly. "Let's break. Mr. Wallington will be here this afternoon, and we'll take this up again then."

8

THE EASE WITH which NSA brass like Blake Bauer separated business and pleasure had always astounded Jordan. Bauer, his two young aides, and Jordan were picked up in a motorized cart and deposited at a small, institutional, private dining room where they were served sandwiches in a manner all too formal for the fare.

For some reason, Bauer found it necessary to treat Jordan as a guest, like an acquaintance he had invited to join his family for lunch. Jordan refused to engage in small talk with the man who had so recently implied that he might be other than what he had been reputed all these years.

It wasn't enough that they had to make him endure a debriefing for the sake of finding his wife's assailant. No, now they would spring on him the fact that, for years, everyone who hadn't been engaged in his type of work had been jealous, even suspicious of him. The only thing that warmed and encouraged Jordan during lunch was the knowledge that he would be seeing Chuck Wallington before long.

Bauer studied the empty plates before his aides and asked if they would excuse him and Jordan. They left as if shot from their seats.

"Jordan, there is another item, if you don't mind. Did you happen to bring your weapons with you?"

"I never do. You know that."

"But this being a highly unusual visit, I thought maybe—"

"They're at home in the attic, locked in my trunk. Strictly regulation."

"Ah, good. We'd like to examine them for the purposes of this investigation."

"The ones I took on this trip, you mean?"

"All of them. You have what, a couple of hundred pounds' worth?"

"Probably twice that."

Bauer looked disgusted, as if no one anywhere, certainly not in the service of the National Security Agency, needed any weapons, let alone a four-hundred-pound arsenal.

"Some of those are personal weapons, Blake. It's all in my files. I purchased sixteen Colt .45s that had been obsolete since the Army announced it was switching to Berettas. They had over four hundred thousand Colts, not one newer than sixty years old, some as old as ninety years."

"What in the world would you want with a .45, Jordan? What does one weigh? Two pounds?"

"Two and a half."

"And the recoil on that thing is enormous."

"That's what I like about it. That nine-millimeter Beretta is like a BB gun."

Bauer raised his eyebrows as if he knew more about weapons than Jordan Kirkwood. "The Italians know how to make weapons. Our European allies have all gone to Berettas."

"Good reason for us to stay with the Colts. We've helped our allies a lot more than they've helped us, and one of the big reasons was our advanced weaponry. You wouldn't catch me laying out over a thousand bucks apiece for non-American-made toys like Berettas. But then I'm

127

not in purchasing. Got myself a couple of classics, though, and a dozen or so in perfect condition."

"Accurate?"

"That's never been one of the .45's traits. You have to get used to each weapon, learn its idiosyncrasies, and use it, rather than letting it use you."

"You have a license to own those Colts?"

"I was a Boy Scout, remember? Why, I've been in the selfless, patriotic service of my country for more than twenty years."

"No need to be sarcastic."

"Me? Just quit hoping for some local legal technicality. If you want to prove I brought this on myself, that the NSA has no responsibility, base it on my record, not on my guns."

"Your guns *are* part of your record. Anyway, who said I was trying to do what you just said?"

"Just tell me when you need to see my inventory."

"Today or tomorrow."

"Then you're going to have to let me go get my trunk."

"Can't do that. You're quarantined until tomorrow."

"You're not sending one of your flunkies into my home."

Bauer sighed and reached over to clap Jordan on the shoulder. Jordan hated that. "I don't have flunkies, Kirkwood. I'm as proud of my young assistants as Chuck Wallington was of you twenty years ago. They won't disturb your castle, you can be sure."

Jordan stared straight into Bauer's eyes and shook his head. "You're not sending anyone I don't know into my house. Forget it."

"We'd appreciate your permission, but it isn't required."

"So now the NSA owns me *and* my house?"

"This is crucial to our investigation. Those weapons, all but the .45s, belong to the NSA."

"I have a few other pieces."

"Whatever for? Planning something?"

"Only getting out of this organization."

Jordan thought Bauer would jump all over that. But no. "Is there someone who would be acceptable to you, someone you would entrust with your keys?"

Jordan thought a moment. "Wallington."

"Wallington will be working with us today and tomorrow."

"Felix, then."

Bauer flinched. "You expect Granger to run an errand for you?"

"It's not for me, Blake. It's for you."

"I don't know whether Felix is even still in the country."

Jordan stood and moved toward the door. "Wonderful. The man comes over here with me during the toughest time of my life, and no one lets me know when he's leaving? Don't you think I might have wanted to thank him?"

"I assumed you already had. He may still be around. I'll check."

"No one else is allowed in my house—except Chuck—unless you want a noisy suit."

"Would you really do that?"

Jordan smiled. "Sounds horrible, doesn't it? Almost as horrible as breaking into the home of one of your own employees."

Bauer tried his cell phone, then apparently remembered it didn't work inside the thick walls. He used a phone on the wall to learn that Felix Granger was scheduled to be driven to the airport within two hours. He told the driver to have Felix see him for an assignment first. As he walked Jordan back to the basement of S Building, he asked for his keys.

"Can't I give them to him myself, Blake?"

"You'll be busy with Chuck. I'll let you see him before he leaves for the airport."

Chuck Wallington wasn't the type one embraced, not even Jordan, though he hadn't seen his mentor for three years. A few more lines marked the sculptured face, and Chuck had let his hair grow out about half an inch, apparently so he could bend over the result in an attempt at something partable.

He was the same old Chuck, though. Trim, fit,

obviously still running and working out. At fifty-five, he still looked as if he could take care of himself, regardless of the situation. He was guarded around Blake Bauer, which reminded Jordan where he had learned to be that way.

The men shook hands but were given no time to reminisce. Apparently that was calculated. Bauer pointed to a chair for Chuck and began in his formal tone. "You're here for three reasons. First, we're searching for any clues in Mr. Kirkwood's career that might lead us to the identity of whoever might have paid to have him shot. Second, you're here to help us talk Mr. Kirkwood into at least putting off his decision to resign. And third, you are here to be assigned as the head of the field investigation to apprehend whoever is out to eliminate him."

Jordan looked first at Chuck, then at Bauer. "Are you going to be totally frank, Blake?"

"Meaning?"

"Are you going to tell Chuck that you wonder about my competence, my loyalty, his job in selecting and recruiting me, and best of all, that you really want me to delay my resigning until you determine whether I should be dismissed?"

Bauer hesitated and shouldn't have. Wallington was ready. "I can't wait to hear all this. Is that what it's come to?"

For the next forty minutes, Bauer took on Wallington in the same discussion/argument he had endured with Jordan that morning. Chuck pressed his lips together and shook his head. "You might as well know I'm going to be a hostile witness, so now that we've both been so clear on everything, let's get on with it."

It was obvious Blake Bauer was not used to having subordinates argue with him. He may have been in charge, but he was not in command of the situation, and he clearly didn't like that.

Jordan longed for the chance to tell Chuck of Stanley Stuart's terrible secret. If Stu was right, the United States had not been in as much danger since 9/11.

But Jordan never got a minute alone with Chuck. The study of his own file went long into the night. Dinner was brought in, quickly consumed, and cleared. In spite of his inactivity and his good night's sleep, exhaustion still dogged him.

Not even hearing about his own hiring and career kept him alert. His mind stayed on the MiG-23s until Chuck mentioned something that jogged his memory. When his old boss mentioned the days in Washington during his college years, he was reminded of his firearms training. And that brought to mind his weapons arsenal.

"Hey, Blake! You said I could say good-bye to Felix."

"Sorry about that, Kirkwood. They told me during dinner that he had made delivery of your weapons but wasn't able to connect with you. He sends his best."

Jordan slammed his fists on the arms of his chair and glared at Bauer, who had shed his suit coat and was unbuttoning his vest. "What, he didn't know where I was? How could you do that, Blake? It was a small request."

"Breakdown in communications. I tried. What can I say? You'll see him again."

Jordan looked to Chuck. "An example of how I'm to be treated from here on out."

Bauer sighed. "Your cell doesn't reach London? Last I heard we carried unlimited long distance."

Chuck Wallington spoke softly but directly. "Give the man a break, Bauer. He's been through an ordeal you and I can be grateful we'll never have to endure."

Jordan recoiled. "Don't defend me, Chuck! I don't want anybody feeling sorry for me."

Chuck scowled at Jordan, and it was just like the old days when he was the boss.

Bauer, tie loose and sleeves rolled up now, flipped through several more documents. "Kirkwood's training in Washington."

Chuck recited the details of how he put Jordan through his paces of diet, study, sleep, workouts, swimming, running, weight lifting, hand-to-hand combat, firearms training, and mental restraint. All that while Jordan worked in a date or two a week with Rosemary Holub.

Bauer slid his chair back noisily, wood on concrete. "Mental restraint? You mean in case he got put in a concentration camp?"

"Not quite." Wallington briefly explained the basics of his opposite-triggers thought processes.

Bauer sounded impressed. "That your invention, Wallington?"

Chuck shrugged. "I put it together from stuff I'd heard and read. By the time I taught Jordan, I'd been practicing it ten years. There's nothing mystical about it. No trances. No hypnotism. Just concentration, obsession over detail, and the training of your reflexes and reactions."

"How long did it take you to learn that, Kirkwood?"

"I'm still learning."

Wallington chuckled. "False modesty. Best I've ever seen, myself included. I remember the first time I really tested him. Remember, Jordan?"

"How could I forget?"

Indeed, that test had been the most traumatic moment of his life to that point.

He was engaged to Rosemary, earning straight A's at International, and still trying to blend into the crowd in spite of his outstanding natural abilities. He ignored intramural sports, public speaking, and student government, though he would have shone in any of those.

Most of his spare time was devoted to studying

and following Chuck's regimen. Even his visits with Rosemary were regulated, which neither appreciated until much later.

One Saturday morning, Chuck drove Jordan up the ocean shore to a secluded spot. Thirty miles from civilization, they took a long, hard swim, then dried and dressed in military fatigues, carrying full battle gear, guns loaded.

"Follow me." Chuck took off running in the sand with his big combat boots, carrying a heavy rifle, even wearing a helmet. After following him for two miles as fast as he could go, Jordan was about to drop. He was in the best shape of his life, yet this called for all his energy.

If Chuck had shown any sign of fatigue, any sign that he too was human, Jordan might have been able to go on. He knew he would incur Chuck's wrath if he fell too far behind, so he kept pushing himself. But he knew he was in trouble when he quit sweating and felt his body temperature rise.

"Chuck!" His voice was thick and weak. But apparently that had been what the older man had been waiting for. Chuck stopped dead, whirled, and fired his automatic rifle at Jordan.

Jordan froze, expecting the impact to knock him to the ground. There would be pain, blood, trauma, breathing difficulty. Yet there he stood, unscathed.

Chuck circled him like a madman, shooting

again, then again. Each time, Jordan winced, shutting his eyes. Had Chuck gone over the edge? His instincts told him his life was in danger, to return the fire, but from six feet away? He'd have ripped the man's head off. Should he drop his rifle and go for a grenade? His pistol? How quickly could he shoot?

As if reading his mind, Chuck tossed his empty rifle in the sand and drew his pistol. He fired several rounds past Jordan's head. The young man nearly passed out. Chuck's wild look terrified him. Jordan counted the shots. When Chuck was down to his last, he pulled back the hammer and held the barrel to his young student's temple.

Chuck's voice was calm. "If I was just playing with you, would I hold a live, cocked weapon to your head?"

Jordan's instincts were to leap to action, to karate-chop the weapon from his head and attack. He feared his voice would betray his terror, but when he spoke, he surprised both himself and Chuck. "I don't know, sir."

Chuck turned the weapon away from Jordan's head and fired the last round into the distance. It would be three days before Jordan's hearing would return in that ear. Yet he had passed some sort of a test, not breaking down and weeping, pleading for his life, running, or fighting. He'd remained calm, at least outwardly.

Chuck slowly backed away about ten feet and coolly drew a hand grenade from a pouch at his belt. He pulled the pin, released the lever, and lobbed it toward Jordan. It landed squarely between Jordan's feet. Now he wanted to run, to jump, to dive for cover, to pick up the bomb, throw it back, kick it, anything. His entire body prepared for the explosion that would rip him to pieces and fling body parts about the beach.

Chuck shouted, running at him. "Oh, C minus! And you were doing so well!" He deftly kicked the grenade through Jordan's legs, lofting it forty or so feet toward the water. It exploded just before it hit, the force rocking Jordan and sending a water spout high into the air.

Chuck grabbed Jordan and pulled him to a low, sandy shelf, where they sat. Jordan's muscles ached. He was breathless and stiff. Chuck let him catch his wind. "Did you know I wasn't going to kill you?"

"At first I thought you wouldn't. And then I thought you would. And then I knew you would."

"When did you know?"

"With the last shot from the handgun."

"But I didn't. Then what did you think?"

"I didn't know."

"And after the grenade?"

"Then I knew for sure."

"But you were wrong."

"Thankfully."

"When did you know you were wrong?"

"When you didn't dive for cover. I knew you weren't about to kill yourself to kill me."

"Did you think I was really angry with you?"

"At first, but I didn't know why. Then I knew you were testing me."

"What was I testing?"

"I don't know."

"What did I mean by C minus?"

"My grade, I guess."

"You had an A up till then, Jordan. You were beautiful, and you don't even know why, do you?" Jordan shook his head. "You don't know why you didn't run or fight, do you?" He shook his head again. "Your mind training is working. You were dead. I could have killed you if I'd wanted to. Easily. I had the drop on you. You didn't have a chance. Not for an instant. Not even when you thought you did."

"When did I think that?"

"When I held the pistol to your head, didn't you think that I should have killed you when I had the chance, because now, with the gun so near, you had a fifty-fifty chance of subduing me? Didn't you think that?"

"I guess."

"But you failed when you let that grenade lie at your feet. We have to work on that. Your mind was so tuned into opposite triggers that instead of defending yourself—a good thing to avoid when you don't have a chance, but lethal when you do—you were going to stoically take it."

"What should I have done?"

"You knew you had between four and five seconds. It was kill or be killed unless I rescued you. You should have kicked that grenade right back at me."

"And what would you have done?"

"If it came back with an arc, that would have wasted the remaining time and I would have had to dive for cover. If it had come back straight, I'd have kicked it, batted at it, or caught and thrown it."

He pulled another grenade from his pouch. "Fourteen ounces, six of which consist of comp B, which turns serrated steel into fragments when it explodes."

Jordan was still shaken, wondering if Chuck knew what he was doing. Chuck sat there looking pleased with his student, but Jordan had to wonder whether he was a little shaken himself at how long Jordan had let the grenade lie at his feet and what a public relations mess the NSA would have had if he had killed his most promising disciple. Jordan reached for the new grenade and Chuck dropped it into his palm. Jordan turned the device in his hand, idly studying it. He casually pulled the pin and sat staring at Chuck, keeping the spring-loaded lever closed.

Chuck smiled at him. "What're you going to do now, big boy?"

Jordan smiled back and tossed the grenade three feet in the air to Chuck. The lever flew off just before Wallington caught it, chuckled, stood, and threw it about a hundred and fifty feet down the beach. When it exploded, he smiled. "Next time, Jordan, defend yourself. Everything else was perfect."

They walked slowly back to Chuck's vehicle. "Just for the record, Jordan, next time it won't be me. I put you through that test only once."

Blake Bauer shifted his gaze between the two. "You're both nuts."

He stood and paced and soon returned to business. "So by the time Kirkwood was married and out of college, he was ready for this, uh, unusual sort of service within the NSA. Where was he assigned?"

"Everywhere." Wallington began a litany of clandestine operations at home and abroad, within and without the NSA. Jordan noticed he was less than specific about the inside jobs, probably assuming Bauer was aware of those. It seemed, however, that the deputy was most interested in those. Wallington told only the basics, which Jordan appreciated.

But as Chuck got into the bulk of Jordan's work over the last two decades, Bauer held up a hand.

He was digging through several transcripts. "Don't you have supplementary files, Wallington? There are gaps in the record. References to material I don't see."

"Such as?"

"Conversations with Kirkwood that you recorded, but the transcripts of which are not included."

"Some—well, much of that—was classified, sir."

"Nothing is classified in this investigation, Mr. Wallington. I want those files."

"I certainly wouldn't be able to tell you where to start looking. Anyway, I'm sure they're nothing to speak of."

"Then your memory had better be awfully good, because you're going to have to re-create some of them for me."

"Such as?"

"Such as this." Bauer turned several pages slowly, recounting a conversation with Jordan that Chuck Wallington had written of as "pertaining to clandestine activities in Indonesia during several months before Kirkwood's first semester at International University."

Jordan knew immediately the conversation Bauer was referring to. It had centered on his relationship with Cydya and would indeed have called into question Chuck's judgment in selecting him for the NSA. "That's in my file?"

Chuck spoke softly. "Everything went into your file back then, Jordan."

"Everything?"

Chuck nodded.

Bauer looked up, impatient. "But the transcript of the tape of that conversation is not here."

Jordan looked to Chuck. "You *taped* that conversation?"

"Not easily." Jordan saw Chuck trying to signal him with his eyes to shut up.

Bauer was back on the offensive. "This says you engaged in a sensitive conversation recorded in supplementary file JordanKb. What did it entail?"

"That was more than twenty years ago, Blake."

"Then where is the file?"

"Let me save you some time and trouble. If you can trust me and take my word for it, then get this: that transcript and every other document supplemental to these files are no longer in JordanKb. They were typed and maintained for years by Miss Gwendolyn Geoffrey."

"Your old secretary? The one with the highest clerical clearance level in the organization?"

"One and the same."

"And she's no longer with us, is she?"

"Died about two years ago."

"And as for your knowing where this material is?"

"I couldn't say."

"Could be she shredded it years ago?"

"I haven't read it since it was typed, sir."

"Then you'd have a tough time re-creating the file."

"That's right. And you're not going to find it."

9

THREE DAYS LATER, Jordan sat at the kitchen table in his home, desperate to speak privately to Chuck Wallington, knowing the house was being staked out by NSA personnel. He had tidied up, typed out his letter of resignation, and phoned for a flight to Muskegon to visit his uncle, Dexter Lee.

Jordan was embarrassed that he was about to let his old boss and mentor see him unshaven, dressed in grubbies, and without the physical tone he would have had if he'd been eating, sleeping, and running right.

The Friday session with Blake Bauer had lasted until after midnight, and the Saturday ended just before dinner. Jordan had lost his cool Saturday when a ballistics report showed that three of his weapons had been fired within the last several days.

Two of his own Colt .45s and one of the wooden pistols reportedly showed fresh powder burns. Jordan told Bauer that he hadn't fired a weapon anywhere, except on the practice range, in more than six months and that he had never fired the weapons in question.

Jordan knew that if he even implied he was being framed by someone in ballistics, his next step would be to hire a lawyer. He had to wonder, however, if Bauer had purposely kept him from Felix. If those guns had been fired, Felix would have noticed.

Jordan had not hidden his anger from Bauer. "Get me for unreported weapon fire, and you can make me responsible for the Heathrow attack."

"Just stay out of the investigation, Kirkwood."

Jordan was determined to call Felix eventually. And he wanted to know why Chuck covered for him on sensitive conversations from the past, yet seemed to disappear in the weapons dispute. Jordan expected him to vouch for his veracity.

When Chuck finally arrived at the house, Jordan ushered him in and pointed him to the sofa without even offering to take his coat. "I've got so much to tell you. My last night in Frankf—"

Chuck's desperate wave and piercing look stopped him. Wallington pulled a slip of paper from his pocket as he spoke. "Blake's a good man. I think we help ourselves and the agency only if we cooperate fully." Chuck handed him the slip, which read: *House may be bugged.*

"Yeah, I know. Hey, you hungry? Let's go get something to eat. I could use a break."

As Chuck pulled out of the driveway, Jordan unloaded. "Why would they bug my house?"

"Just guessing. They had access to it for three days. Why risk anything?"

"Hey, where were you when they trumped up the weapons charges on me? You sure got quiet."

"It's hard to argue with ballistics reports."

"What, you don't believe me?"

"'Course I do, Jordan. But if they're trying to frame you, don't you think they're going to shoot those weapons so the reports will be credible? Anyway, I couldn't appear to be countering Bauer on every detail if I was going to keep this assignment. You know no one else is qualified and no one else would care. And for sure no one else would get any cooperation out of you."

"Chuck, someone in the agency is behind all this." He told Wallington all he had learned from Stanley Stuart.

Chuck blanched. He kept checking his rearview mirror, then pulled into a forest preserve several hundred yards off the highway. He parked and faced Jordan. "I haven't seen Stu for years, Jordan. Any chance the old man's mind was playing tricks on him?"

Jordan shook his head. "He showed me photographs. They looked real to me, and he was convinced. And let me tell you something else: the man was not suicidal."

"You think he was hit? Because someone saw him with you?"

"What else *can* I think? If it weren't for dumb luck, we both would have been dead within a day of each other."

Chuck clenched his fists and stared out the windshield. "We can't go running to the Pentagon with news of al-Qaeda planes when we don't know where they are and don't know who to trust. We'll need to work fast. I have to get to Frankfurt to see if Stu left the photos or any other documents around. If I can locate his contact, maybe I can get a clue to who the inside man is. Top priority is to find something credible and specific to take to Defense. Wish I could use you somehow."

"Chuck, I feel like I'm leaning over a gas tank with a cigarette in my lips."

"And I have to do all this with the brass on my tail. Who knows how much time we have."

Jordan shook his head. "Talk about first-strike capability . . . I feel like the kid with his finger in the dike."

The older man nodded. "I'd like to expose the creep in the agency, but I don't suppose I can do one without the other. Sure makes what I was gonna show you seem insignificant."

"Which is what?"

"File JordanKb."

"Thought you didn't know where that was."

"I said I couldn't say and that my secretary was

long since dead. The document is not in the file cabinet anymore because I've had it for years. I haven't read it, but I've had it."

"Is it something I should take with me? I leave Wednesday for Muskegon."

"You make your reservation under your own name?"

"K. Johnson."

"But from your home phone?"

"Cell, which means the NSA could know where I'm going. So what?"

Chuck shrugged. "Might just be the best thing for us. You can lie low. I can start work in earnest."

"You think the agency will support what you find?"

"Are you kidding? They let me know that when they put me out to pasture. This assignment is a bone. If they can pin the whole problem on you in time, I'll be back to pencil-pushing."

"Can't let them do that."

"We can hardly stop them unless we find the money behind the assassin. I hate to admit it, but Blake was on the right track. The key has to be something in your history, and unfortunately, it's more than likely hidden in the files I separated from the main body years ago."

"Why did you separate them, Chuck?"

"You won't believe this, but I started feeling guilty about them."

"You're right. I don't believe it."

"I left in everything I had recorded by hand, memories of conversations, that kind of stuff. I took out everything I had recorded and transcribed without your permission."

"Was there a lot?"

"Several thousand pages."

Jordan recoiled. "Why *did* you record me?"

"I needed to. You had insight and remembered details I thought we needed."

"So why not just ask if you could record me?"

"You might have said no, and then where would I have been?"

"You think there's evidence in there of who might want me dead?"

"It's one place to look. Some of the files are right here between the seats. The rest are in the trunk."

Jordan pulled the folders from between the seats. "You're not going to keep me off this case, too, are you?"

"You're going to Michigan, the best place for you. It would take all our energy just to hide you from our own people."

Jordan shook his head. "So officially I tell you whatever you need to know, and then I'm out of it. Unrealistic, wouldn't you say?"

Chuck seemed to study Jordan. "You can't say you wouldn't be emotionally involved."

"It's stupid to think I could stay away from this. Would you if it had been your wife?"

"My former wife, you mean. I'd be a suspect."

Jordan couldn't smile.

Chuck flushed. "Forgive me, JK. That was a dumb thing to say."

Jordan was already thumbing through a file. "I almost quit when you got reassigned. I went from working under the best field man in the business to dealing with a bunch of flabby bureaucrats."

Wallington shook his head. "Look where they put me."

"Yeah. Until now."

"I admit I'm not totally uninvolved emotionally myself. Stu was a friend. He took shortcuts, but I liked the man. And I loved your wife."

"You were special to her, too."

"I want as much as you do to find out who's behind this."

Three quarters of the way through the transcripts of conversations he'd had with Chuck over the years, Jordan found the report of his debriefing on the Cuban assignment.

Kirkwood: Chuck, it, uh, was my own fault. That thing you said, what you taught me . . . you know, about the hunches. About following the ones that protect you and not following the ones that make you take a risk. I blew that. I mean, I didn't follow your advice.

Wallington: Your hunch was to wait; you should've waited. Then you would've had—

Kirkwood: The advantage. And I could have jumped him instead of—

Wallington: Him jumping you.

Chuck interrupted. "I know which one you're most interested in."

"You do?"

" 'Course. And I've got it."

"And Gwen typed it?"

"She never told a soul."

"That was risky."

"So was what you did. When I saw the hand-writing on the wall, when I knew my days as your supervisor were over, I had a feeling it would come to this. For years the agency has been dying for a reason to reopen those files. Rosemary's death was the perfect opportunity."

"So where is it?"

"Sure you want it? Or would you rather I destroy it?"

Jordan thought a moment. "I remember that conversation like it was yesterday. You were kind enough never to bring it up again."

"I kept an eye on you."

"You're not serious."

"You think I wouldn't have known if you'd

checked up on her? That would have been a natural thing."

"You check up on her too?"

Chuck shook his head. "None of my business. You wanna see the file or not?"

"I do."

Chuck got out and opened the trunk. Jordan found himself nervous, about to be brought face-to-face with a past he had tried to suppress for two decades. But when Chuck slammed the trunk, his hands were empty.

An NSA car slid up behind them. By the time Jordan leaped out and joined them, the agent was already briefing Chuck. "So get out of here. Anywhere. Back to headquarters, on a plane, whatever. But not in one of our cars."

The agent on the passenger side leaned over and pointed to a late model, bright yellow sports car. "I can hot-wire that one, if you want to explain it to the owner later."

"Do it. I'll run Jordan to the airport and bring the car back here. Call ahead and get him a ticket under the name of K. Johnson. Route him wherever you want, just make sure he leaves soon and winds up in Muskegon. And get some security assigned to his kids. Make sure they know what's going on before they hear anything on the news."

Jordan hesitated. Again Christa and Ken would hear from the agency before hearing from him. It was past time to retire and be the father he always should have been. But wasn't it also past the time when he could assimilate himself into his kids' lives? What would he do with himself? What would they do with him?

Chuck transferred the stuff from his trunk to the backseat of the sports car as the other agent got it started. The roar brought a young couple running from the trees. As Chuck pulled away with Jordan aboard, the agents flashed their badges and apparently explained what was going on. Which was what Jordan wanted to know.

Chuck streaked from the forest preserve onto the highway. "Your house was obliterated ten minutes ago. Windows blown out of every house on the block, and the houses on either side of yours are burning. Nobody hurt."

"Did the agency do this?"

"Not our style; you know that. We would have gotten the valuables out first."

"You're sure no one was hurt?"

"No one but you, pal. You were killed. Understand? You're dead, as of right now. That's going over the wires and to the papers and broadcast people. Can your kids be trusted with that?"

Christa and Ken would hate this. He was responsible not only for their mother's death, but also for the destruction of the only home they had ever known. For years Jordan had been proud of the fact that all they knew was that he was a government bureaucrat. The charade was over.

Wallington was still talking. "That'll take some heat off you and keep us from spending all our time trying to protect you."

"Yeah, great job so far. How did anyone get past all that security?"

"We had men cruising the area, but they didn't have the place in view all the time. The place was vaporized. Just a black hole now, and what was left of the flooring is burning in the basement."

Jordan held his head in his hands. Any reservations about leaving the NSA disappeared now. He didn't care whether the brass accepted his resignation or not. He was gone.

"Tell me you didn't know about this, Chuck. If you hadn't thought the place was bugged, we'd both be dead."

Chuck nodded. "Even some of our people think you bought it, and they won't know different until they're briefed."

"And what am I supposed to do?"

"Go to your uncle's and lie low until you hear from me. If we can't flush out the perpetrator, we may need to bring you back to life."

"For bait? Not interested."

"You want this guy to keep comin' after you and your family?"

"I've had enough, Chuck. I'm through."

"Don't make any hasty decisions. And take any of these files you want."

"Well, maybe that one we were talking about."

During a two-hour layover in Cleveland, Jordan used his K. Johnson credit card for toiletries, a suitcase, and a couple of changes of clothes. He did not call his uncle, lest he give anyone a clue where he was going.

He finally arrived in Muskegon on a puddle jumper at nine that evening and took a taxi to a block and a half from his uncle's home. He went down an alley and through a gate to the back door of the rambling, two-story white frame that had hosted many a family gathering when he was a boy. Now most of the rooms were sealed off. His uncle lived alone, occupying only a portion of the basement for his workshop, the living room and kitchen above that, and a bedroom and bath one more floor up. A light burned in the old man's bedroom.

Jordan set the suitcase down and tried to freshen up in the reflection of the back door. His normal color had started to peek through his greasy and matted hair. He had gone two days without shaving, so his every-other-day five-o'clock shadow showed.

He rang the bell and glanced up to see his uncle peek out. Jordan waved apologetically, but Dexter Lee was already bounding down the stairs. He burst through the storm door wearing a plaid, floor-length, flannel robe over pajamas. His reading glasses were low on his nose, his eyes red and swollen. The old man embraced him. "Oh, Jordan! You survived!"

His uncle carried his suitcase and led him up the concrete steps and into the kitchen, where they sat at the table. Dex's feathery white hair pointed several directions, and he couldn't quit talking. "I don't believe it. Does anyone else know you're alive?"

"Not many."

"It was a setup, then? Something your people staged?"

"Where did you hear about it?"

"It was all over the news. I've been trying to call your kids all night. Jordan, I cried and cried. I couldn't imagine having to break it to your mother. I prayed it wasn't true, but now I can't believe you're here."

"You couldn't reach Christa or Ken? I'm not happy about that."

"Tell me they know you're all right."

"They know, and the agency likely has quarantined their phones so they're not getting calls from the press . . . or the culprits. I just hate this, Dex. I'm being forced to face the ugliest side of me. There's no making up for lost time, is there? I've just royally screwed up my relationship with my kids."

"Are you worried about what it's cost them? Or you?"

155

Jordan winced. "Well, that sure makes me feel better."

"You know you'll always get the truth from me, Jordie. I've told you and told you over the years that as much as they were missing out on, you were costing yourself even more. I know you better than you know those kids."

Jordan just sat, shaking his head.

Dex leaned forward. "Hopefully we'll have time to talk about that, but you've got to tell me what's been going on."

Jordan told his uncle the whole story. Dexter had always been the only one other than Chuck Wallington who knew everything. He even knew about Cydya, though Jordan had never admitted his lingering curiosity.

His uncle sat studying him, as was his custom. "You need a shower and a bed."

By the time he was out of the shower, his uncle had opened a heating duct to a spare bedroom. "So you're in hiding. Anything I can get for you?"

"I'll give you a list in the morning. I'm going to need to make myself look like an old friend of yours. Emphasis on the *old*. Gray hair, the whole bit. And don't worry if you hear me digging around in the basement in the morning. I'll just be checking your phone. I hate to put you through this, Dex. If you don't want to be involved, I'll understand."

His uncle waved him off. "I wouldn't have it any other way."

Jordan collapsed into bed on his stomach, one arm hanging over the side and a hand atop the file he would read as soon as he felt up to it. All he wanted was enough sleep so he could think clearly, check his uncle's phone, get in touch with Christa and Ken, and get back into the hunt.

That wouldn't please anybody at the NSA, including Chuck. But he didn't have a choice. Avenging Rosemary's death, protecting his children, and solving this case—the only one in his life that had ever really mattered—were the only reasons he could think of to keep getting up in the morning. Would his kids miss him any less if he didn't?

10

JORDAN WAS UP long before dawn and felt refreshed, surprising himself.

He sat on the edge of the saggy-springed bed he'd shared with a brother many times as a child and retrieved the JordanKb manila folder from the floor. The transcription of his conversation with Chuck Wallington seemed to begin in the middle. Chuck had scribbled in the margin, "Gwen, I wrote on the permanent file that when Kirkwood reacted to my checking out Rosemary by saying

157

he might have to think about the job some more, he was kidding; that I checked her out carefully, found her solid, etc. Let's hold the rest here for file JordanKb."

Wallington: Have I misjudged you, or do we call it quits right here?

Kirkwood: Just call me Tuesday as early as you can.

Wallington: (Unintelligible.) While we're talking about women, I've got to ask you about Cydya LeMonde.

Kirkwood: Who?

Wallington: Don't give me that. Who do you think you're talking to?

Kirkwood: There's not much to tell. I met her in Indonesia.

Wallington: You worked with her.

Kirkwood: You asking or telling?

Wallington: (Expletive.) You were supposed to replace her, and you wound up working with her for months. You like her?

Kirkwood: You already did my debriefing for Jakarta. You saw that diary you had me keep. Nobody else saw it.

Wallington: I'm asking you about Cydya LeMonde.

Kirkwood: You mean was she CIA?

Wallington: Do I have to spell it out for you? Don't you think I know most of what happened, what you did there? We were watching you.

Kirkwood: I figured. Did you infiltrate the corps?

Wallington: Yes! With you! You were our only person on the inside, but there were visitors. They were with us. You didn't suspect anyone?

Kirkwood: Huh-uh. Should I have?

Wallington: No demerits for not noticing, but don't change the subject. Tell me about her. Everything. She's a puzzle to us. You know where she's working now?

Kirkwood: Yeah.

Wallington: She could be a friend in the future.

Kirkwood: Not mine.

Wallington: Don't be silly. We work closely with international agencies.

Kirkwood: Interpol?

Wallington: 'Course. But listen, if there was anything there between you two, a relationship, then I should know about it.

Kirkwood: What did your people tell you, if they know so much?

Wallington: I didn't say they told me anything.

Kirkwood: Then how did you even know her name?

Wallington: You spent more time with her than with anybody else there. Tell me how the relationship progressed.

Kirkwood: Who said there was a relationship?

Wallington: (Expletive.) You're making me angry.

Kirkwood: Do I have to tell you every time I go to the bathroom? Don't I get a private life?

Wallington: 'Fraid not. I don't need to know every detail, but I do have to know if there's anything, uh . . . LeMonde was a real looker, huh? Did you find her distracting? I mean, you worked together, and you got to see this gorgeous girl playing with the kids.

Kirkwood: It wasn't like I stood around watching her all the time. I had things to do too, you know.

Wallington: What're you, a homosexual, Kirkwood?

Kirkwood: What're you talking about?

Wallington: My people tell me this girl would make any guy freeze in his tracks, and you're tellin' me you worked with her all day every day, yet you weren't the least bit distracted?

Kirkwood: Okay, she was fun to work with. Smart. A good talker. Said what she meant.

Wallington: And she wasn't making it with every guy there?

Kirkwood: Who told you that? She never was that way!

Wallington: Some girls are like that, you know.

Kirkwood: Not this one.

Wallington: You know that for sure?

Kirkwood: You bet I do.

Wallington: Yet you had no relationship with her?

Kirkwood: You mean—

Wallington: Can't you answer a simple question? Admit it, you followed her around for weeks with your tongue hangin' out.

Kirkwood: So you didn't send me there to check on CIA involvement. You were just watching me.

Wallington: We did want to know about the CIA thing, but yeah, you were under surveillance. And you did well. You kept your mouth shut. You'd be surprised how many guys shoot their mouths off first chance they get, telling everybody they're undercover.

Kirkwood: I didn't do that.

Wallington: I hope not. Not even to Cydya?

Kirkwood: (Pause) Never.

Wallington: You had the chance, though, didn't you? You somehow won her over, didn't you? And then your work even suffered. You two started talking more than working and just got the kids involved in something so you could talk while you watched them. Right?

Kirkwood: (No response.)

Wallington: Once a kid got away from you and was across the road before you both went running after him, leaving all the other kids unprotected.

Kirkwood: Nothing happened. We got the kid back and the others were all right.

Wallington: Lucky for you. That would've been something, wouldn't it? Peace Corps volunteers letting a kid get hurt when they're supposed to be watching him.

Kirkwood: So that's what I'm in trouble for?

Wallington: You're not in trouble, Jordan. But you have to learn to tell me the important stuff.

Kirkwood: Cydya wasn't related to what I was doing there for you.

Wallington: But she was important.

Kirkwood: Why?

Wallington: Because you were in love with her.

Kirkwood: How can you say that?

Wallington: You were pretty quick to defend her honor.

Kirkwood: Well, I . . . How should I know if I was actually—

Wallington: (Laughs.) You're still in love with her!

Kirkwood: I'm not, Chuck! When I had to come back, you know, for my, uh—

Wallington: Your father's funeral.

Kirkwood: Yeah, afterward she was gone.

Wallington: But you knew she would be because she was supposed to leave around that time.

Kirkwood: Anyway, that was the end of it.

Wallington: Of your affair?

Kirkwood: We didn't have an affair!

Wallington: You were in love with her.

Kirkwood: (Pause.) I might have thought I was.

Wallington: You gave everyone else that impression. Holding hands, gazing into each other's eyes, long walks, going off to Jakarta together, talking about each other all the time.

Kirkwood: So it was a summer romance.

Wallington: You're not still writing to her?

Kirkwood: Just once. I'm sorry—twice. I told her we were through. But when she kept writing, I finally wrote and told her I wasn't going to open any more of her letters.

Wallington: Why not? What was so important about breaking up with her?

Kirkwood: (Long pause.) There was no future in it. She was too far away.

Wallington: Did she keep writing?

Kirkwood: Yeah.

Wallington: How many letters?

Kirkwood: Two.

Wallington: And you never opened them?

Kirkwood: I opened them, but I never responded.

Wallington: Jordan, either get back in touch with the girl or forget her. Toss the letters and be done with it.

Kirkwood: Someday. When I find someone else.

Wallington: You think this Rosemary is it?

Kirkwood: That'd be a little hasty.

Wallington: That's your style.

Kirkwood: It's not!

Wallington: You didn't waste any time with Cydya. Jordan, I have to know: was your relationship with her appropriate?

Kirkwood: You mean, did we—?

Wallington: Yeah.

Kirkwood: We couldn't have if we'd wanted to.

Wallington: Why not?

Kirkwood: For one thing, I had the fear of God in me. I told her all about my faith, church, God, everything.

Wallington: So she would have been disappointed in you if you'd tried anything inappropriate?

Kirkwood: I guess so. I would have been disappointed in myself.

Wallington: Was she, um, experienced?

Kirkwood: I don't think so. She hadn't even dated that much.

Wallington: What happened that night the two of you spent in Jakarta?

Kirkwood: Why do you need to know that?

Wallington: Jordan, if your morals were compromised, it's significant to us, to me.

Kirkwood: (No response.)

Wallington: The night before she was supposed to fly back to the States and then on to France, you went to Jakarta with her.

Kirkwood: We had the day off. We went shopping.

Wallington: But you didn't go back to corps headquarters that night.

Kirkwood: We missed the bus. I called Mickey and she checked with her supervisor. We stayed in separate rooms.

Wallington: So you weren't in her room?

Kirkwood: Well, just to kiss her good night. But we didn't sleep together.

Wallington: Bet you wanted to. Bet you were excited to be alone with her, miles from anyone who knew you and nearly ten thousand miles from home.

Kirkwood: (No response.)

Wallington: Jordan, I have no way of knowing whether you slept together, but I do know you were in her room until two in the morning. Are you telling me you didn't actually fall asleep with her, or are you saying you weren't intimate with her?

Kirkwood: (No response.)

Wallington: I know something happened that night because the next morning, when you got the news that your father had died and that you had to get back to the States, you left without telling her. Why?

Kirkwood: It was over. That's all.

Wallington: No, it wasn't. Maybe it is now, or maybe it will be when you can forget her, but I think you slept with her that night. And when the news about your father came, you couldn't separate what you'd done from what had happened to him. Maybe you even felt you had been judged.

Kirkwood: (No response.)

Wallington: Jordan, let me tell you something: I believe that you were in love with this girl and that she was in love with you. If she'd had a bad reputation and could drag you down with her, I would lose all interest in you for the NSA. But I believe your failure was honest. Don't be so hard on yourself. It was a passionate mistake.

Kirkwood: It was still wrong. But it's over now.

Wallington: I'm no psychologist, Jordan. And I'd be the last person to argue with anybody over his religion, but if nothing else ever comes of this conversation, I've got to get you to separate your mistake—if that's what you want to call it—from your father's death. Can you do that?

Kirkwood: Not easy.

Wallington: Will you think about it?

Kirkwood: I guess.

Twenty years later Jordan still regretted his lack of willpower, for going against his convictions, for taking advantage of the girl he loved. But worse, he had always felt more remorse about his failure with Cydya than about the loss of his father. And never having told Rosemary about such a deep, intense love, one he had never been able to shake, a curiosity he had never been able to satisfy, made him feel unfaithful. Something told him that Rosemary would have been her typically wonderful and understanding self.

But now it was too late.

11

THE SMELL OF eggs and sausage made Jordan ravenous. He buried the file in his suitcase and padded to the shower. A few minutes later he discovered his bed had been made, a signal that breakfast was ready. He threw on new clothes—cuffed trousers and a pullover shirt.

His uncle had never been one for small talk. The old man straddled his chair, sat heavily, and prayed aloud. Jordan had always enjoyed hearing his uncle pray. He was personal, informal, and somehow specific. He never just rattled off the blessings of life, but rather prayed humbly and thanked God. ". . . For loving us in spite of ourselves, for never changing or even casting a shadow of turning. We don't understand what's happening and confess that, in our finite wisdom, we wouldn't have allowed what You have allowed. But we love You and we trust You."

Jordan wished he himself could pray that way again. He loved God and trusted Him, but how long had it been since he had really prayed? Things were so different now, so removed from his childhood, when everything was black-and-white and made sense. He wasn't doubting, wasn't challenging. As a boy, he'd had an experience with God. A transaction had taken place that nothing could take away. He had prayed to receive Christ under the guidance of his mother. But he had drifted so dreadfully far. What did his faith mean now, today, with his wife in the ground, his country in peril, and his heart full of vengeance and anger? Could it be, he wondered, that God had brought him back to this place, this person?

Rosemary and Uncle Dex had been the only people outside the NSA who even knew the name of the agency for which Jordan worked. And not even Rosemary knew precisely what he did, except that he used disguises. She had never known about Cydya either. Dex Lee had.

It had been Jordan's uncle who pointed out to him the irony of his continuing, schoolboylike guilt and curiosity over a long-lost love, in contrast with a sort of utilitarian angst over having to kill two men in Cuba.

Jordan had thought about that one a long time, trying to reconcile his feelings with his faith, his morals, his upbringing, his training. Over the years he had quit talking to his uncle about Cydya, hoping Dexter would suppose he had forgotten her. Well-placed questions from the old man exposed him, however. Their visits had grown less frequent, but they were always poignant. Whenever Jordan got an R & R pass from Wallington, he considered himself assigned to Muskegon before flying home to Rosemary.

Therapeutic. Being with Dexter always was. Strange, he thought, to read that old transcript in this very house and then to eat in front of his life-long confidant without letting on.

His uncle sighed. "How long can you stay? Nothing to rush off for, is there?"

Jordan shrugged. "Depends on what Chuck finds. See, Dex, I don't know that anyone con-nected with the London thing followed me to the States. The fact that I'm without a house should be a clue, but so far, none of our people have seen anything or anybody who could be linked with the attack."

Dexter pressed a thick palm over his mouth, then pulled it away. "And even if someone did follow you from London—assuming whoever had the shooting done also had the house bombed—I s'pose there's little chance he followed you here."

"Unless he was fortunate enough to see me leave with Chuck, talk with the other agents, and switch cars. Then I'd be fairly easy to track. But I doubt it."

"Did you check my phones?"

Jordan shook his head, trying not to give away his own surprise at the lapse. He had said he would, but then he started reading that file. "You still don't have a cell phone, right? Those are a nightmare, so easy to bug remotely."

"Never have, never will."

While his uncle washed the dishes, Jordan crawled around in the basement with a flashlight. It was clear no one had messed with the phone lines in that house for years. He fished in his uncle's tools till he found a voltage tester. He used a tiny alligator clip to dig through the extension phone wire and picked up the receiver.

He listened for the telltale click that would have exposed an old-fashioned bugging device hooked to the line from outside the house. Nothing. He dialed for local information and asked for the number of time and temperature. Was it just his imagination, or was there a fluctuation of voltage when the call was placed?

He watched the meter carefully as he dialed the time and temperature number. There had been a minute change when he picked up the receiver, of course, and when the dialed phone began ringing. But when the call was answered, there was a noticeable diminution of power. He slammed his fist against the wall.

He grabbed pliers, two screwdrivers, and a hammer and headed upstairs and out the back door. He followed the poles to the third one, which had a series of drab green boxes at its base. Jordan determined he was out of the line of sight of any nosy neighbors. Only one of the boxes appeared to have been tampered with. Paint covered the screws and bolts on the other two.

Jordan quickly opened the box and there, attached to several thin wires, sat a platinum-colored strip no bigger than a child's watchband. Only one intelligence organization in the world was even aware of such a device. It served as a self-contained transmitter that put tapped conversations on a special frequency, which could then be monitored by cellular technology from miles away.

Jordan left the bug in place and secured the box again. He ran back to the house. His uncle sat at the kitchen table, reading the paper. "Everything all right?"

" 'Fraid not. The only outfit bugging this place is the NSA. I've had it."

His uncle put down the paper. "What are you talking about?"

"Your phone is being tapped from the area signal box by NSA equipment!"

"When would they have had time to do that?"

"Somebody knew I was coming, so they would have just assigned local people. If I don't talk to Chuck soon, there's no guarantee where I'll go or what I'll do. I just hope he's not already out of the country."

Jordan marched into the living room, where he flopped onto the couch, hands behind his head.

Dexter Lee joined him, sitting in an easy chair with his feet on an ottoman. He mirrored Jordan's pose.

"Do me a favor, would you, Dex? Call my kids from a pay phone. Give 'em my love. Tell 'em I'm all right and that I'll be getting back with them as soon as I can."

"You sure you want *me* to make that call? They don't want to hear from me."

"Tell me about it. But I can't go out, Dex. Wallington's the only guy I trust right now. Well, him and the guy who flew over here with me, but he's back in London. Chuck thinks I'm safe and sound for a while. He's doing what he's supposed to be doing, and I'm getting bugged by my own people."

"Maybe they're just bugging me, seeing if you'll show up. They don't know you're here yet."

"Enough of 'em do. And that puts *you* in danger. You know what happened to the last place I was living."

While Jordan fumed, his uncle sat calmly. "I've never seen you this way."

"Well, forgive me, but I've never lost my wife and home before. Or been pursued in this country. Do you realize that nobody in the international community, until now, even knew where I lived? That was the beauty of working with the NSA."

"You're usually so calm and rational, much more than I would be. You seem paranoid now, not that you don't have a right."

The phone rang and Jordan bolted upright. He stooped to put his ear next to Dex's.

"Mr. Lee? This is Western Union with a telegram for you."

"A telegram? How quaint!"

"The message isn't long, sir, but you might want to jot it down." He read it aloud.

HAVE YOUR MONKEY TRAVEL FIVE
CENTURIES ON THE HOOSIER EGG AND
HE'LL BE RIGHT WHERE THE BEEF
WANTS HIM, WELL-DONE. WORTH HIS
WHILE. TWO HUNDRED AND FORTY POUNDS
OF YOURS, MINE, AND YOU-KNOW-WHOSE.
YOUR COCCINELLIDAE.

"And this was sent from where?"

"The origination point is in code, sir, and I'm not aware of it myself. The message came through our New York facility."

When Dexter Lee hung up, Jordan was a different man. "I *love* Chuck! *Love* him!"

"You understand this?"

"All I know is, it's from Chuck. He's never sent me one I've figured out in less than four hours. I need paper and a place to work."

"Sure, but—"

"And could you run some errands for me? I hate to put you out, Uncle Dex . . ."

"You know I'd do anything."

"Call the kids. Anything you can say that will help me somehow start fixing things with them, I'd appreciate it. And call my guy in London for me? Here's his number—Felix Granger. And be sure to talk only to him. Just tell him I know he knows what's going on and that I appreciate him more than I can say. Someday I'll try to make it all up to him." Jordan also made a list of items he needed from the store: makeup, dumbbells, running shoes and sweats, hair dye.

By the time his uncle returned midafternoon with a late lunch, Jordan had cracked the telegram. His uncle seemed fascinated by Jordan's explanation.

"The first thing you have to decide with a piece like this is whether the sender is playing word games. That's not Chuck's style, but he's good at it."

"Is that what this is?"

"No, this is deductive. The telegram is to you, right?" His uncle nodded. "And so who would he be referring to by sending you a wire in code?"

Dexter shrugged.

"C'mon, Dex. He'd have to be talking about me, right?"

"You're my monkey?"

"If we can make that make sense."

"And can we?"

"Well, if I'm your monkey, what are you?"

"What am I? Hmm. I'm a monkey's uncle!"

"See how easy it is?"

"No. I'm lost."

"Stay with me. What does he want you to have me do?"

"Travel five centuries on the Hoosier egg."

"Good!"

"Good nothin'! I'm readin' it verbatim!"

"Don't take it at face value. The word *travel* is the tip-off that *centuries* doesn't mean years, get it?"

"No."

"You don't really travel in time. You travel in distance. So traveling five centuries would, or could, mean five hundred miles."

"Yeah?"

"Does that make anything else make sense?"

"Well, Hoosiers are from Indiana."

"Good, Dex! Ever hear of anything in Indiana connected with traveling five hundred miles?"

"The Indy 500!"

"Right!"

"He wants you to go to Indianapolis?"

"I don't think so. Look how he words it. What's the Hoosier egg?"

"How should I know?"

"What shape is an egg?"

"Oval."

"So?"

"The egg is the track?"

"I think so."

"Then he *does* want you to go to Indy."

"Look at it this way: if you did get to Indy and you did travel five hundred miles, start to finish, where would you be?"

"In the winner's circle?"

"Not unless you won. All the guys who make the whole five hundred miles wind up somewhere. Where?"

"Right back where they started from."

"Exactly."

"Exactly what, Jordan? I'm glad to be just an old lumberjack turned furniture man!"

Jordan laughed. "He may want someone who intercepts this message to think I'm going to Indianapolis to meet him at the track, but to me it means, stay right where you are. Move and run and travel five hundred miles if you want, but—just like at Indy—you'll end up right where you started. So I stay here."

Dexter Lee looked dubious. "So how do you know it's from Wallington?"

"That was the easy part."

"I was afraid of that."

"No, look. He says that's where the beef wants me. Almost too simple. *Beef* is another word for *chuck,* isn't it? Chuck steak? A *beef* is a chuck and Chuck Wallington is the beef. And the next phrases, 'well-done' and 'worth his while,' mean just what they say. They fit the parlance, but he wants me in shape for a good assignment. Which can only mean he's got a place for me on the case."

"I thought you weren't allowed."

"What else could he mean? I think he wants to see me in ten days. Don't know if I can wait that long."

"Where in the world do you get ten days out of that crazy message?"

"'Two hundred and forty' relates to the missing word implied by 'yours, mine, and you-know-whose'—which is . . . ?"

"Ours?"

"Right, but phonetically. *Hours.* Two hundred forty hours is ten days."

"Why not pounds?"

"Because things are never as they seem."

"They sure aren't. Could you be totally off on this, Jordan? Could you have missed the whole point?"

"Doubt it. One of my specialties."

"You seem almost high on this."

"Beats sitting around. Never thought I'd say that again."

"Staying with the NSA?"

"No. But I'd go anywhere, do anything for Chuck Wallington."

"The beef."

"Right."

"And what's the strange sign-off?"

"Didn't know myself until I looked it up. The term was obviously biological, so I started there. It means ladybug, Dex. He's 'Your Coccinellidae' or 'our bug.' That tells me that *he* had the phone tapped, so I can quit worrying about it."

"You made all this up."

"Chuck and I used to communicate like this all the time. Actually, it's amateurish. We were decoded many times."

"You won't be this time."

"I hope not."

12

DURING THE NEXT week, Jordan worked out hard every day, mostly indoors. He ran in place and did multiple series of push-ups, chin-ups, and isometrics. He alternated periods of exercise—when he tried to keep his pulse at around 140 for twenty minutes—with ten-minute breaks, when he sat perspiring in his new hooded sweats.

Dexter Lee busied himself with errands, always sure to be home when Jordan was out running. Jordan told him precisely when he planned to return. "If I'm forty seconds late, come looking for me." But he was usually early, to set his uncle's mind at ease.

From dinner until bedtime, night after night the men chatted, going over old ground, dredging memories. Dex Lee raised subjects Jordan had long forgotten; he seemed to be working into the conversations areas he thought it necessary for Jordan to deal with.

Jordan felt his uncle urging him to talk about Rosemary, about his grief, his guilt, even his short-circuited spiritual life since her death. "I gotta tell ya, Jordie, I wish you'd act more consistently with what you believe."

"Uncle Dex, I'm not sure I know what to believe anymore."

The old man was curled up on the end of the couch near the fireplace. "Ah, who am I to prescribe how a person should respond to a trauma like yours. I lost your aunt in what was supposed to be the most natural, humane, easiest way. She fell ill, she got worse, and the doctor prepared me. Still I cried for weeks. Being prepared, and knowing she was, didn't cushion the shock. I felt punched in the gut. I can't imagine how it must have been for you. Eventually, though, even in a dark spot of grief, comes that 'peace that passes understanding.' "

"I could sure use some of that."

Dexter sat up and planted both feet on the floor, elbows on his knees. With the dancing fire illuminating one side of his face, he looked like a wizened prophet. "Oh, but you have. Did you fire your weapon when you knew your wife was dead? Did you go crazy, kill yourself?"

"Only because of Chuck Wallington's mind training."

"No, Jordan. That worked *because* you have that bedrock peace, the knowledge that God is sovereign."

Jordan wasn't convinced, but as the hours passed, he found himself quicker on the emotional trigger, weeping when they spoke of Rosemary. His uncle advised him over and over to express himself when he felt angry, ignored, cheated. "When you feel the whole situation is God's fault, say that, too. When you disagree with me, say so."

As Jordan opened up, especially about Christa and Ken, he began to feel healthier. He couldn't deceive himself, however. The climb to reconnect with them looked as steep as the international crisis he found himself in.

The conversations with his uncle covered more than Jordan and his troubles. Dexter Lee was well-read and a thoughtful historian. He loved to gas about politics and economics.

Jordan grew more eager to see Wallington, but he was still careful to check the area around the house every night. Sunday, in his old-man disguise, he ventured out to church with his uncle. It was awkward because the people in the tiny congregation were friendly and curious, but he had to maintain the false identity.

Late Sunday night, after another meaningful talk with Dexter, Jordan found himself anxious, pensive. It was still a few days before he expected Chuck, yet he was energized. He paced his room, his body lean and hard, his mind sharper than it had been since Frankfurt.

Jordan turned off his light and sat on the bed, listening to a light rain. He heard splashing footsteps in the street. A jogger at this time of night? Jordan peered out, worried about the man who bounced along past the house.

Could the jogger have studied the house as he ran? Jordan chastised himself for being paranoid, but didn't the man take longer to pass than he should have? He appeared young and stocky, an orange-clad, plodding type whose thighs looked like they could handle more speed. Jordan wondered whether the man would double back.

Was he oversensitized, too excited about Wallington's promise of an assignment? He began to breathe deeply to counteract his pulse, and just as he felt his body relaxing, the jogger reappeared. The man slowed and carefully regarded the house.

Adrenaline flooded Jordan and his mind shifted into opposite-trigger mode. He crept downstairs in the darkness. Not knowing whether his adversary—if that's what he was—had a weapon called for the coolest head. If the jogger was more than a jogger, Jordan would have to surprise him.

He peeked between the drapes in the living

room. The man should have run under the light at the corner by now, but he had not appeared. Was he on his way back, or had he cut between houses to head through the alley toward the Lee home? Either way, Jordan would feel safer outside.

He grabbed his sweats from a pile near the front door and pulled on his shoes. While his uncle snored upstairs, Jordan slipped out the front door and knelt in the cold, damp earth behind the bushes. The jogger was no longer on the street.

Jordan crept around back, where the outside light was on. He stopped to listen, but his pounding pulse and shallow breathing made that difficult. He willed his system to relax, and as his body began to respond, he heard footsteps in the alley. He squinted in the mist and was startled when the orange figure emerged from the bushes and casually strode up the back walk. The man pulled a small slip of paper from his sweatshirt and peered at it under the light.

He studied the house, sighed, and sat on the bench at the side of the steps, his back to Jordan. He breathed heavily as if he had run a long way.

Jordan stepped lightly in the grass to within a few feet of the jogger, then leaped at him, throwing his left forearm around his neck, pressing hard but not lethally on his Adam's apple. With his right hand, he pressed on the back of the head.

Jordan was shocked at the hardness of the man,

wondering if he had been wise in attacking. Rocklike fists reached up and back in an attempt to pull Jordan over, but he had prepared himself for that. All his weight was on his heels, and he lifted them from the ground, making himself a dead weight, a choking, suffocating albatross.

He knew both windpipe and voice box had been incapacitated and that to breathe, the man would have to relax or move with Jordan's pressure. Jordan spoke near the man's ear, through the hood. "Talk to me."

A straining, gurgling sound came from the jogger's throat, but when Jordan loosened his grip, he felt the man tense for action. He reapplied the pressure, soft tissue constricting around the larynx. The message had been sent, and Jordan loosened his grip again.

The voice was husky. "Wallington."

Jordan flinched. "What about him?"

"He's here. Wants to see you."

Jordan slid his hand from the man's throat and felt his pockets for a weapon. The man tensed again, and Jordan would have gone for his throat once more if the man had not raised his hands. Jordan stepped back and wheeled around in front of him. "I'm not expecting Chuck for three days."

The man shrugged, swallowing. "I know nothin' about that. I've got a van around the corner, and I can take you to him. He's at the beach."

"Lake Michigan?"

The man nodded and extended his hand. "Roscoe. Wow, I thought you were younger. Wait. Disguise, right?"

"You could be anybody, Roscoe. How do I know you're with Wallington?"

Roscoe loosened the string at his neck and pulled his hood down. His face was wide with pale blue eyes and close-cropped blond hair. He looked to be in his late twenties, over six feet and at least 240 pounds. "Ask me somethin'."

"What's my wife's name?"

"Rosemary, sir. Maiden name Holub."

"Am I happily married?"

"You were, sir. I'm sorry."

"Lots of people know that."

"I'm answerin' *your* questions, sir."

"You military?"

"Was."

"Now?"

"I work for Chuck, same as you used to."

"Can't be."

Roscoe shrugged.

"Did I surprise you, Roscoe?"

"No, sir. Chuck said to make myself obvious and you'd come to me. You were a little earlier than I expected, but Wallington's seldom wrong."

Jordan studied him. "He give you any passwords?"

"J.K.B., sir, whatever that means."

"And what did Chuck say to try if I said a lot of people knew about J.K.B.?"

"He said you might say Bauer's people knew about that and that I might be workin' for them. But he said they wouldn't know about C.L. from France."

Jordan fought for composure. "And you do?"

"No, sir. He just said that would convince you."

Jordan nodded. "Meet you at the corner."

He poked his head in the front door to be sure his uncle was still asleep and left a note on the mat inside. Ten minutes and a silent drive later, he found himself sitting under a bluff, his back to the wind, with Chuck Wallington. Roscoe stayed in the van.

Jordan eyed Chuck. "I wasn't expecting you yet."

"What do you mean 'yet'?"

"I figured three days."

Chuck studied him in the faint light from cottages on the shore. "Why?"

"Your message said 240 'yours, mine, and you-know-whose,' which I took to mean 240 hours. That would have been ten days from when I got it."

"What are you talking about?"

Jordan was embarrassed. "Okay, apparently I misunderstood part of it. At least I didn't head off to Indy."

"I don't follow."

Jordan shuddered, and not from the rain and wind. "Your telegram—the one telling me to stay put for ten days and stay in shape and you'd make it worth my while. You signed it, in essence, 'My bug,' which told me you were the one who put the NSA tap on the phone."

Chuck looked out across the lake and rubbed a hand over his mouth. "What else did it say?"

"You didn't send it?"

"What else did it say, Jordan? You'd better be sure about the timing or we're going to have to get your uncle out of there."

Jordan recited the telegram from memory. "You've got to admit, it sounds like you."

Wallington rose and headed toward the van. "Your uncle have a garage?"

"Uh-huh."

"And you're sure the bug is ours?"

"Pretty sure."

They drove back to Dexter Lee's place, where Roscoe waited in the van at the end of the alley while Wallington took some tools and followed Jordan to the phone box. He removed the tap and put it in his pocket, swearing under his breath. "Can we put the van in the garage without waking your uncle?"

"Think so."

In the kitchen Jordan showed Wallington the telegram while Roscoe sat silently. "I thought it had you written all over it."

"It does. And that scares me. I do have an assignment for you, but I wouldn't have thought I needed to encourage you to stay in shape. I would have assumed that."

"Who else knew you had an assignment for me?"

"Not many. Of course, we're always under surveillance. You're sure there's no bug in here, other than on the phone?"

Jordan nodded.

Wallington sighed. "Looks like we've got three days, then, before company arrives."

Roscoe stirred. "You want us out of the country before that, don't you, sir?"

"Uh, I haven't mentioned that to Kirkwood yet."

"Sorry."

"The question is what do we do about whoever is coming here. Leave an empty house? Or if he's looking for action, do we not disappoint him?"

Jordan shook his head. "I think about Rosemary, Stu, my house . . . I'd just as soon stay and fight."

"And risk your uncle's life, not to mention your own and my career."

"When has that ever bothered you?"

"All I need is the brass knowing I let you onto the case. I'd rather get your uncle out of here, stake out the place, and see if we can surprise someone. Meanwhile, I've got work for you and Roscoe. And if you don't succeed, it'll cost me my job."

"Chuck, who sent the telegram?"

The older man looked tired. "I hate to admit I don't know."

"Any doubt in your mind that Stanley Stuart was right about this being an inside job? It's someone who knows I'm here, has access to agency devices, knows your style, and even knew you had plans for me."

"I know."

"So why are you here, Chuck?"

"To report on my trip to London and Frankfurt."

"I'm dying to hear."

"Spent a day with Felix. He appreciated your call—or your uncle's call, anyway."

"Good guy."

"Then I went straight to Germany. Jackpot. I was there three days and scored; that's all I can tell you."

"What do you mean? You're gonna tell me everything."

"I got a peek at Stu's personal effects. Sorry to tell you, but it *was* a suicide."

"I don't believe it. It doesn't sound like him."

Wallington spread a photocopied sheet before Jordan. It was Stu's handwriting, and it read: *The news from the northwest is true, and it's my fault.*

Jordan covered his mouth. "Reference to Heathrow?"

"Has to be. Assumed you had been killed. When his contact confirmed it, he took the blame for

192

dragging you into this. Among the items in his apartment were bills he'd paid and receipts from the post office. The man settled his affairs first. The place was tidy, even his work was up-to-date. He had to go back to the office that evening to do that."

Jordan shook his head. "That sounds more like the Stu I knew."

"But I believe he saved your life and tried to preserve the security of the United States before he died. One of the receipts was for an overnight package to the States. He listed the contents as 'Returned catalog items' and addressed the package to CW Ltd. at my post office box in Florida. You and Stu are the only people in the agency who know that address."

"So what'd he send?"

Chuck suppressed a smile. "I slipped the receipt out of his effects so no one else would see it and come nosing around. Picked up the package yesterday. I was lucky enough to locate Roscoe last night and find him hungry for work."

"You *stole* evidence from an NSA suicide scene?"

"Hey, JK, they put me on this case. I'm in charge of stuff like that."

"They didn't assign you to Stu's case."

"Tracing your whereabouts up to the attack led to Stu, okay? You wanna see the package or not?"

Jordan sat back. "I've seen the pictures."

"There's more." Chuck pulled the envelope from his bag. "I'm going to visit Western Union tomorrow and find out where that telegram came from. We're safe tonight. Anywhere we can sleep?"

"The living room."

"And scare your uncle when he stumbles over us? Why don't *you* sleep there and we'll sleep in your room."

"Deal. Now show me."

Roscoe sighed. "I've seen all this. Where do you want me to sleep at?"

Jordan led him upstairs. When he returned, Wallington was just opening his eyes. "One hundred twenty seconds."

"What's that?"

"You were gone 120 seconds. I prescribed myself an intense, two-minute nap. The subconscious—"

"I know, keeps perfect time."

Jordan recognized the three photographs. Chuck said he detected no clue as to precisely where the hangar was. "Foliage sure looks southern U.S., though, doesn't it? I saved the best for last."

Chuck slid a sheet across the table. In neat, hand-printed, block letters, Stanley Stuart had written:

DESPONDENT OVER YOUR LOSS. THEY'RE MOVING THE BALTIMORE CLUB TO

ALABAMA, AND PREPARATIONS FOR SAM'S RITES WILL BE HELD AT THE MALDONADO FUNERAL CHAPEL NEAR 78TH AND 1ST, THE 20TH OF THIS MONTH. THE ENTIRE FAMILY WILL BE THERE. IF OUR MUTUAL FRIEND DID NOT GET TO YOU BEFORE HIS DEMISE, THIS WILL BE MEANINGLESS TO YOU AND ALL IS LOST. FOR MY CONTRIBUTION TO THAT CATASTROPHE, I PRAY FOR ABSOLUTION. SEE ATTACHED.

Attached was a copy of Stu's hand-scrawled note to a Michala Diego at an apartment in downtown Frankfurt:

The London activity convinces me I'm in over my head. I'm out. Count Florida contact in, the one I told you about. He'll see you the 20th.

Jordan looked to Chuck. "I'm lost."

"Don't feel bad. This one took me six hours and several faxes to Interpol. If this Diego trusted Stu, we're making progress. If the suicide spooks him or he finds out that the Florida contact—that's me—goes back a long way with you, he'll smell a rat."

"What was Stu saying? And who's Diego?"

"Okay, my 'loss' that he's despondent over is

you. He thinks you were wiped out in the London attack. The 'Baltimore club' would be the Orioles, right? The birds. The jets. 'Alabama' is obviously a clue to the location of al-Qaeda's MiG-23s. 'Sam's rites' took me a while, but he's referring to the death of Uncle Sam if we don't do something about Alabama. The next part took the longest. I looked up funeral homes in a hundred cities and didn't find anything remotely close to Maldonado's or anything at an address like that. I discovered what he was talking about by accident.

"Frustrated, I took a walk through the library, noticed a globe, and found myself staring at the latitude and longitude lines. Guess what's near 78th and 1st?"

Jordan spoke in a monotone. "Maldonado, Ecuador."

"Been there?"

"Not right there, but I had those two assignments in Ecuador, one in the late eighties and one in the early nineties that took me south of Quito into that sweep of four fairly big cities—Ambato, Riobamba, Guaranda, and, um, that northernmost one."

"Latacunga."

"Hated it. Reminded me of Indonesia."

"But you got north, near Maldonado?"

"Seems we flew in or out of Ibarra. Probably out, because I remember being happy."

"That would have been in '93, right?"

"Probably. They were celebrating some anniversary, I want to say of when the government was overthrown and they went away from the 1967 constitution and back to the 1945 one."

Chuck nodded. "Good memory."

"A curse as well as a blessing. So what's happening there on the twentieth?"

Chuck scratched his head. "Best I can figure, a strategic meeting about the MiGs. If the entire family is there, I expect al-Qaeda and people from Mexico, Cuba, and South America. No Russians, though. I'm still convinced they thought their planes would be used in the Middle East."

"But where in Maldonado are these people supposed to meet? And what do we do if we find them? You remember how hard it is to get weapons into South America?"

"That's your job. As to where, that's mine. I'll track down this Diego in Frankfurt. Got a lead on him from Interpol. If everything works, I'll win him over and come to Maldonado with him. You and Roscoe can bring weapons in from the other direction, and we'll rendezvous."

"What's Interpol got on Diego? And how did you know to start there?"

"I didn't. I tried him with everybody else first. FBI, CIA, NSA. They all had something on him, but of course he uses many aliases. Interpol provided the most information. He's from the Galápagos Islands."

"What's he doing so far from home? The islands are, what, five or six hundred miles into the Pacific from Ecuador, and he's in Germany?"

Chuck nodded. "Only he and al-Qaeda know. Like Lister, he's a hired man."

"Like Roscoe."

Chuck flinched. "Don't put criminals in Roscoe's category. He's a mercenary, but he's always on the right side."

"Tell me about Diego."

"Well, the only time he was even spotted on the Ecuador mainland was about four years ago when Interpol was on his tail for narcotics traffic as far north as Texas and as far south as Chile."

"So he's aware of the radar gap."

"That's probably how he got connected with others who wanted to do the same. He was into weapons, too."

"Like MiGs?"

"Not before this. I think this is his first time in the big leagues. I mean, he's a bad guy, but he's never played at this level before. He's got to be the junior man in this operation, just a message carrier. Most likely, he told Stu he was going to have you killed because Stu talked to you without his permission. When the London attack was broadcast, Stu apparently told him I was a better bet anyway and then blamed himself for your death."

Jordan stretched and shut his eyes. "I want this

guy. I know how important the big picture is, but I want him for myself."

"Don't get carried away. Until we learn Diego's contact in the agency, all we can do is try to get next to the guy. That won't be easy because Diego's not going to immediately trust the new recommendation from a guy who tried to go behind his back and then killed himself when the thing blew up."

"How you gonna get around that?"

Chuck shook his head. "I'll have to turn on the charm, I guess. Convince him I've been stiffed by the NSA and the United States for so many years that now I want to do something for myself. I could sure use the money."

"And you want Roscoe and me to get to Ecuador from the other direction?"

"I've made almost all the contacts already. The rest will be arranged by the time you get there and need them."

"When do we leave? I have to do something before I go crazy."

"First off, you realize this is a wholly clandestine operation."

"They always are."

"You didn't hear me. I said *wholly*. That means *no one* knows about it. No one but Felix and me, you and Roscoe."

"I need to know all about Roscoe if I'm going to be depending on him for my next breath."

Chuck told Jordan he'd met Roscoe when the young man was a Marine recruit. "Different kind of a kid. Doesn't have the double dose you've got with the body and the brain, but he's not stupid. Just quiet. Could beat you in a sprint and a mile."

"I still break five minutes in the mile."

Wallington smiled. "Not bad for a middle-aged man. Would you believe four-thirty-six for this monster? Never seen anybody that big do that. Plus top proficiency in self-defense, kill skills, hand-to-hand combat, especially strength tests."

"*You're* still ahead of me in those, Chuck. Does he beat you?"

"By a third, all the way around."

"Firearms?"

"Skilled, but he doesn't know what makes 'em tick the way you do."

"So what's he doing here? Trying to become NSA?"

"Strictly freelance. Didn't like military pay, so he hires himself out. Anything legal for a flat fee. Only none of the fees I've ever paid him have been flat."

13

THE NEXT MORNING, while Wallington was visiting the local Western Union office, Jordan sat at breakfast enjoying Dexter Lee's giving Roscoe the third degree. The husky man dragged a napkin across his mouth, pale eyes darting everywhere except at Dexter.

"What made you leave the military?"

"Besides that Wallington's a legend? Bucks."

Dexter was smiling. "I don't mean to offend, but you're apparently a multitalented man. Yet you're motivated only by money?"

Roscoe shrugged and rested his elbows on the table. " 'Course. Aren't you? Looks like you've done all right for yourself."

The smile remained, but the twinkle had left Dexter's eyes. "I'm not motivated by great amounts of money. No."

"Well, then what motivates you?"

"It might sound a little pious to you, Mr. Roscoe."

Roscoe shot a glance at Jordan. "Wallington told me Kirkwood was a Holy Roller. So it runs in the family?"

Jordan perked up. "Holy Roller? Chuck said that?"

"Not in so many words. Religious though, you know."

Jordan rolled his eyes.

Dex cleared his throat. "Let me speak to this, Jordan. You're not in any condition—"

"To do what?" But that he had snapped at his uncle in front of a stranger only proved Dex was right.

"Mr. Roscoe, our faith is not in religion. It's a way of life, yes, but we believe in a Person, not in a creed."

Roscoe shook his head. "I've heard that Person business before. But the Person is Jesus, right? If you don't think believing in *that* person makes you religious, you're kiddin' yourselves."

"So we have a semantics problem. Faith, religion, Christianity, Christ, whatever—the fact is, He is my life, and that's a better investment than any I could ever have made in the stock market."

Roscoe looked around. "A few shekels have come your way. C'mon! I've never been taken in by a preacher with his hand out."

Dex winked at him. "Neither have I."

Roscoe stood. "I can see where this is goin'. You're going to wind up workin' on me. Let me tell you something. I was raised in Indiana on a dirt farm. Picked vegetables from the time I got up in the morning till it was time to go to school. My daddy figured that if his kids picked until eleven minutes before school started, we could wash up, jump on the back of the truck, and be drove to school—he'd get more bushels out of us than if we took the school bus that came by twenty minutes earlier."

"Seems to have made quite a man of you."

"I wouldn't say that's what did it. I did it. I had to pick when I got home, too, ya know."

"No playtime?"

"I didn't mind that. Wasn't much to play with. I played in my head." He looked away as if he wished he hadn't said that. Jordan got the feeling Roscoe rarely talked about himself. But Dexter Lee could get anyone to talk.

"So you're not afraid of hard work, but you want to be rewarded. That's fair."

Roscoe pursed his lips. "When I was fifteen, workin' barefoot in the cabbage patch, dust making me gag, Willie Floyd come drivin' past, honking and waving from his red and black convertible. Sucker was just sixteen years old, and he had a brand-new Merc. A beauty."

Lee nodded.

"When he come back by, I knew he wanted me to come runnin' and see it and all. He skidded up to the fence, and I could see him from maybe fifty feet away, only I pretended I didn't. He honked and hollered and waved, and I just kept pickin'. He never dared pull that thing onto our property. Might get it dirty."

Dexter smiled. "Surely you didn't want to be like him."

Roscoe shrugged. "I figured if I could ever get a

car like that, that would be enough. People would know I had to have *some* money, and they might guess I was free, too. I wouldn't have to be a rotten guy like Willie."

"And did you get it?"

"Soon's I got out of the service. Big monthly payments. Lived in a cheap apartment. Hated living there, but I loved drivin' that car. Got a nice place now too. Lots of stuff. Want more."

"So you—"

"Do whatever anybody wants me to that's legal and that they'll pay for."

"And who hires you?"

"First the military, but now Wallington for about three years."

Jordan looked up. "He never told me about you."

"Told me enough about you, man. Made me look forward to workin' with you, but I never thought I'd get the chance."

Jordan raised his eyebrows. "This case has to mean more than money to you. Can you get worked up about al-Qaeda jets in Alabama?"

Roscoe shrugged. "I'll do the right thing, if that's what you mean. I know the good guys from the bad guys, but for me it's also business. If I get dead, I don't get the bread. Follow?"

Dexter Lee broke in, gently. "And if you get dead, as you say, before you deal with God's claim on your life, then where are you?"

"I believe in me, and I've taken care of myself all right up till now."

"But sometime during this mission, you might want to discuss this more with my nephew."

Jordan supposed he cared as much about Roscoe's eternal soul as Uncle Dexter did, but he sure didn't feel up to that kind of responsibility just then. He needn't have worried. Roscoe pointed at each of them. "Tell you what. That'll be my business, okay? I'll thank you to stay off my case. Deal?"

Jordan nodded, but his uncle wasn't finished. "Just don't wait until it's too late."

Roscoe waved him off. "Gotta admire your persistence."

Jordan still worried about the case. "If this is just business to you when we may be on the verge of war, maybe you're not right for this."

"Don't worry. I work for whoever's payin'. Just don't expect me to get into it the way you do."

Jordan trusted Wallington to have handpicked the right person. "If I decide to do this, Roscoe, I'll need to count on you."

Roscoe tugged at his belt. "You've already decided, and you know it." So he wasn't as slow as he sounded. The young man smiled. "If you'll both excuse me, I'm takin' a walk."

With Roscoe gone, Dexter leaned forward. "Look after that young man, Jordie. He may find he needs something more to believe in than himself."

Jordan didn't feel comfortable pushing his faith on anyone, but he wasn't up to arguing with his uncle about it either. "Hey, can I still get an ear around here myself?"

Jordan reminisced about his early days training under Wallington, developing his mind and body. Chuck would argue with him, berate him about his Pollyanna beliefs about America and patriotism and his faith. He would argue about capitalism, world hunger, peace, social issues.

Wallington would play devil's advocate, arguing against the establishment, against the United States, against the traditional system of justice. He pressed Jordan to articulate his ideals.

"Chuck couldn't shake me. He told me no one else had ever been able to stand under his barrage. One day he came to me acting very cold and somber and sad. He drove me to a country road where we just walked for miles. He told me he was leaving the NSA, had lost his zeal. I laughed, told him I didn't believe him, told him it was too late to fool me. But he convinced me. He told me who my new supervisor would be and that there were no guarantees about my assignments. By the end of that hike I was pleading with him, arguing with him, nearly crying. For the last half hour he quit talking. I asked him over and over if he would reconsider, what was he thinking, wouldn't he sleep on it?

"All the way back to my apartment I begged him to consider his worth to the United States, to the agency, to the world. When he wouldn't answer, I just trudged up to my apartment. I didn't sleep."

"Obviously, he didn't carry out his threat."

Jordan laughed. "The next morning he showed up early and dragged me out of bed for our usual workout. When I asked where his head was now about leaving, he asked what in the world I was talking about. It was almost as unfair as the grenade test. I was mad and let him know it. I told him I wouldn't have done that to someone. He said he was glad he had because it gave me the chance to finally convince him I was genuine. He said, 'None of us can tell what makes us or anyone else genuine in his passions, but once we become convinced, there's no wavering.' "

When Wallington returned, he pulled Jordan off to the side. "Some things I can tell you; some things I can't. I'm working on a few leads from the scene of the shooting and some interesting ones from Felix and Huck Williamsby, but this telegram still has me baffled. Western Union gave me zip. I gave the code at the top to our ciphering guys in Washington, but all they would tell me was that the message came through New York from Europe and that the text originated in Spanish."

207

"Spanish?"

"I don't know what to make of that either, Jordan. Regardless, it's no joke. I'm going to get your uncle out of here by tomorrow and stake out the place myself."

"Not with my help?"

"This Ecuador thing won't wait."

"But what about all the—"

"Arrangements? You remember what it was like working for me, don't you? The first thing I did was get your weapons from headquarters. Told them I needed to examine them myself, all but the ones that had been fired. They wouldn't let me touch those anyway. And we're going to have to talk about those someday."

"Let's talk about them now, Chuck. I never fired those."

"Frankly, I was kinda hoping you had and that there was some creative reason for it. Would have made my job much easier. Anyway, I've stored the extra weapons, the wood pistols, and so forth, and I've shipped a half-dozen .45s to Ecuador. They'll be waiting for you. You'll fly from here to Chicago, then to Mexico City, take a puddle jumper to Panama, and two boats to San Lorenzo. Roscoe has all the contacts. You know one of 'em. Paul Paveli."

"Really? Good."

"He'll be your man for the second leg, will take you right into the harbor on his fishing boat.

You'll still be about fifty miles from your destination, and you're on your own after that."

"How will I keep in touch with you?"

"I'll find you."

"You're pretty confident."

"Shouldn't I be? I've got the best in the business and three others who know how to follow orders."

"And the weapons?"

"Roscoe has that contact too."

"And the other two men?"

"Cubans."

"Ouch."

"Should be good for you."

"They have a vested interest?"

"'Fraid not. They're just like Roscoe."

"They know about me?"

"About your eliminating two of their countrymen? No, and if they did, they couldn't care less. They wouldn't be any more sympathetic to their government's agents than to ours. I've worked with these boys before. They know the jungle and the languages. They may have the best idea where Diego and his people are meeting. They'll also have motorbikes. They'll get you only so far. Then you'll be in a canoe or on foot. You leave tonight."

"I need gear."

"You still the same size you were three years ago?"

Jordan nodded.

"Check the van in the driveway."

The crisp morning air felt good. Jordan climbed in the back and dug through several bags from an Army surplus store. He couldn't have chosen better himself. Some of the stuff was obviously for Roscoe, but they both would be fully outfitted, and the gear was exactly right. Even the sleeping bags and tents were super-lightweight. Jordan's juices were flowing again.

He spent the afternoon and early evening on the phone with his son and daughter and in intense planning sessions with Roscoe and Wallington. By that night, he felt better about Roscoe. The young man was full of bluster and make-believe earthiness, but he was a brilliant strategist, able to distinguish between the wise and the foolish. And Jordan had no doubt he was fearless.

At the airport, Roscoe got everything checked and loaded while Wallington stood outside with Jordan and put a hand on each of his shoulders. "I want to tell you something important, but only if you promise to not act upon it. Swear to me you won't do anything until I get there."

Jordan nodded, wondering if he could keep his promise, not knowing what he might do if he learned who had tried to kill him.

"Felix tells me that about six months ago he began getting inquiries about you from Interpol."

"As a criminal, a suspect in some case?"

"No."

"Cydya?" The name sounded strange in the night air. "But why?"

"I don't know. The first came as a formal request on official letterhead. Felix told no one in Washington and ignored it."

"Why would she write to Felix?"

"Maybe she didn't want to get too close to where you were. I don't know. She even visited him, finally dropping the official charade and admitting it was personal."

Jordan tried to make it all make sense. "Why didn't Felix tell me?"

"He never put the pieces together until I was over there investigating."

Jordan was incredulous. "You told him about her?"

"I told him the types of things I was looking for in your tenure with the agency. Then he recalled the inquiries."

"What'd he tell her?"

"He stalled her. Hasn't heard from her for a while." Wallington seemed to study him. "You all right? Can you sit on this?"

Jordan felt a compulsion to fly to France and ask what Cydya wanted. What he really wanted was to eliminate her from suspicion. "Do I have a choice?"

14

BY THE TIME Jordan and Roscoe boarded a Spanish freighter bound for Malpelo Island, over two hundred miles due west of Buenaventura, Colombia, they had endured delays in both Mexico City and Panama.

Wallington had told Jordan they were to speak as little as possible, and only to the captain. Their fare was to be $1,000 each, and they were to provide their own food. They didn't know whether the captain was a friend of Wallington's, a mercenary, a criminal, or neutral. Jordan's clandestine aides could be anything from Chuck's old service buddies—like Paul Paveli—to mysterious, closemouthed types like this one.

The captain, haggard and bloodshot, spoke with a voice gravelly and weak. "Roscoe?" Jordan nodded toward his young companion. The captain spoke again with a thick Spanish accent. "Two thousand American dollars each."

Roscoe dug deep in his clothes for a roll of bills and peeled off $2,000 in hundreds. "Not each. Total."

The captain pocketed the cash, pointed down into the hold, and held up three fingers. They lugged their stuff down but could find no light in the narrow hallway. Roscoe lit a match and found a battered door with 3 hand-painted near the handle. Inside, a single bulb hung from the ceiling on a long cord that swayed with the ship. There were nine crew members, Jordan and Roscoe were the only passengers, and all shared a toilet not convenient to cabin 3.

Jordan opted for the top bunk. Imagining Roscoe falling on him in the middle of the night made his decision easy. A small round table was bolted to the middle of the floor, but there were no chairs. With their gear, the two had barely enough room to get from the bunks to the door. With the door shut and the light off, the cabin was tomb black even at noon.

Roscoe sat on the bottom bunk. Jordan leaned against a trunk and studied him. "Prone to claustrophobia or seasickness?"

Roscoe shook his head. In the dim light he looked weary. He lay back and put his hands behind his head, one shoulder against the wall, the other hanging over the side of the bunk. "Not sure about that tostada in Panama is all."

Fortunately, the weather was uneventful and the sea calm. The captain didn't appear in any hurry, and occasionally Jordan had to ascend to the bridge to assure himself the craft was moving at all. His only clue was the deafening clack of the engine not twenty feet from his bunk.

Thankfully, he was able to sleep anyway.

He and Roscoe occupied their days talking and working out in the corridor. It was clear the crew had been instructed not to speak to or even look at them. They were avoided as if contagious, though Jordan wasn't sure the crew avoided their cabin when they weren't there. He and Roscoe subsisted on sausage, cheese, fruit, crackers, bread, and bottled water.

Jordan was amazed at Roscoe's strength. He would wrap his hands around an overhead pipe and do slow-motion pull-ups, forcing himself to spend fifteen seconds on the way up and ten on the way down, resting no more than three seconds between each. Roscoe's massive arms shook with the effort, and he repeated these until he could do no more.

Jordan had seen the exercise before, but never so many repetitions. The last took everything Roscoe had. His biceps, triceps, deltoids, and trapezii contracted into grotesque knots. Eyes clenched, cheeks puffed, face purple, body quivering, still he kept his ankles together and legs straight.

When Roscoe reached the zenith, he exhaled slowly but still forced himself to lower his weight gradually. He dropped to the floor and staggered dizzily toward his bunk.

Jordan shook his head.

Roscoe spoke between gasps, massive chest heaving. "Won a hundred . . . bucks . . . from

Chuck . . . doin' those. Said I could do five . . . times as many as . . . him. Ha!"

Jordan whipped through a daily routine of speed and high-rep strength exercises, but after watching Roscoe, his seemed more like just limbering up. Roscoe did his push-ups the same way he did his pull-ups. On toes and fingertips, back perfectly straight, in slow motion.

Late into the night the new partners talked, mostly of Wallington. Roscoe had endured many of the same training regimens as Jordan, yet Wallington had apparently almost exclusively emphasized physical discipline with Roscoe. Jordan's training, nearly twenty years before, had blended in the mental. Roscoe had been conditioned as a machine.

"Wallington ever wax eloquent with you after an assignment, Roscoe?"

"Nah. You?"

"Oh yeah. I think he thought I always came back depressed, so he would pep-talk me, hard-sell me. Once I was in the agency full-time, his patriotism came out. He could go on for hours about how democracy was the only sensible, humane political system on earth.

"He would remind me of injustices all over the globe, the real stories behind the wars and the egos that affected the lives of millions. By the time he finished, I was ready to head back out and do anything for him and for the country."

• • •

When the ship finally docked on Malpelo Island, Roscoe seemed logy. Still he lugged ashore more than his share. He turned a trunk on its side and sat atop it. He sounded weary. "Wallington said you'd know Paveli's boat."

Jordan snorted. "Paul will have the rattiest-looking tub in the drink." He scanned the horizon. "Two more hours of daylight. He'll be along."

Roscoe appeared to be daydreaming. Jordan lifted half the gear and trudged closer to the pier, where they might more easily blend into the crowd. Roscoe was slow on the uptake but eventually followed.

"You all right, Roscoe?"

"Not ready for a jog, but I could take you in arm wrestling."

"Not unless I can use two hands."

As daylight faded during the next hour, Roscoe sat in the sand, his back to the trunk. Fifteen minutes later he stretched out, feet crossed at the ankles, hands clasped over his chest. His cap was pulled down over his eyes, and he was soon snoring.

When the sun was gone and the temperature dropped, Roscoe turned on his side and drew his knees up. Jordan draped a khaki fatigue over the wide shoulders and worried.

Jordan strolled the beach, keeping an eye on his companion and their gear. He heard Paul Paveli's forty-foot junker before he saw its lights on the horizon. He even imagined he could hear Paul singing.

Jordan waited until Paul had docked and taken on fuel and supplies, knowing the tiny, wiry Italian could see him. Jordan headed back to Roscoe and thought about waking him, but the young man was sleeping so soundly that he decided against it.

Finally Paul approached. His black beard and stringy hair were grayer than Jordan remembered, but he had the same pointed nose, big ears, and telltale, sea-weathered forehead and cheekbones. His black eyes were nearly invisible in the low light.

They embraced, the seaman giving Jordan a viselike hug around the waist. "Bad news about your wife, Jordan. You doin' all right?"

Jordan nodded and thanked him.

"And this must be Rip van Roscoe?" Paul helped carry things to the boat.

Jordan fell in step behind. "I'm trying to remember what he ate that I didn't. He's been out of sorts the last few days."

Paul turned to look back. "You had your own foodstuffs, right?"

" 'Course."

"Maybe just tired. You'll both sleep well on my rig. You got the cash? This is gonna be a risky one, ya know."

"Roscoe has it. Need it now?"

The Italian shook his head. "It's gonna take both of us to load Sleepin' Beauty if you don't wake him."

Jordan laughed. "I will." He looked around. Although Paveli's boat was a fraction the size of the freighter, there was living, walking, breathing, eating, and sleeping space.

Paul stood with his hands on his hips. "We're gonna be a little heavy with the extra fuel, but I'm gonna stoke 'er up and push hard tonight. Once she's up to speed, you can hold 'er awhile and I'll fix you boys hot beans and cornmeal. Even see if I can scrounge up some canned meat chunks. Good stuff—U.S. government surplus."

To Jordan it sounded like heaven.

He went ashore and knelt near Roscoe, putting a hand on his shoulder. "Time to get aboard, big guy." Jordan patted him. "Let's go, Roscoe." Finally he shook him and spoke in his ear. "Get up! We've got to move!"

The man staggered to his feet and walked stiff-legged toward the boat. On board, Jordan guided him to a cot, where Roscoe collapsed and immediately slept again.

Paul leaned close to look at him. "Young one, ain't he? Bet he won't remember the walk to the boat. Should I fix him anything?"

"You'd better. Otherwise *you* can deal with him if he wakes up while we're eating."

But by midnight, when Paul and Jordan had finished bringing each other up to date, Roscoe had not stirred. Jordan threw a wool blanket over him. "Paul, he's still shivering."

"Give 'im another blanket. I got plenty. Somebody poison that boy?"

Jordan didn't want to consider that. It would mean the freighter had been compromised. He spread another blanket on Roscoe and heard his teeth chattering. "Wonder if he's got a fever."

"If he does, it'll wake him up and we can fill him full of aspirin, huh? You're not worrying about malaria, are you?"

"Crossed my mind. If he's got it, he'll be no good to me. Could be out of commission for weeks. And what would I do with him?"

Paveli shook his head. "If it's malaria and we can't treat it with chloroquine or primaquine, you're gonna wind up leaving him in Tumaco or Valdez. There isn't much you or I could do for him."

"You've got medication?"

"Just those two. If it's your basic treatable type, we might be in luck. Can't guarantee how fresh it is."

"Worth a try, but let's not assume the worst. I'll sleep near him and try to get some medication down him at the first sign he's awake."

Paveli let Jordan pilot the craft while he dug in his supplies for the medicine. "What's he sup-

219

posed to be doing for you anyway? I mean, without tellin' me any specifics."

"I really can't say, Pauly. I'm sorry. The most I can tell you is that he could wind up as my bodyguard or fellow soldier. Clear enough?"

Paul nodded. "Good man?"

Jordan shrugged. "I'd rather be on his side than not. Strictly mercenary."

"Like me."

"I don't believe that for a second, Pauly. You care."

"I care for friends, not ideas."

"Sure. You care for Wallington because of his ideas."

Paveli shrugged. "What do I know? I'd work for Chuck for nothing. And I wouldn't work for the other side for any price." He smiled wide. "But a deal is a deal, and I'm not doin' this job free."

Jordan laughed and clapped him on the shoulder. "Well, sick boy's got the money. You want to wake a giant, he's all yours."

Paul waved him off and they switched places. Jordan approached Roscoe, whose body was now shaking and heaving. Jordan put the chilly back of his hand against the big man's forehead. "I don't like this. Hot."

Paul cut the engine and let the boat drift. Jordan stepped aside as he approached. "Let's get 'im sat up and you can pour somethin' down him. Wanna start with a handful of aspirin?"

"I'd rather go straight to the strong stuff."

Paveli nodded slowly. "I don't know doses for that stuff. Pretty potent, though. I oughta know."

"What do you use?"

"Prima, but that's only after I was tested and experimented on and everything. Maybe neither of them will work, so one's just as good or bad as the other. Thing is, if it's food poisoning or worse, this is the wrong stuff for him."

Jordan studied the tiny bottle in the scant light and pried the cap off. He didn't know if the medicine should smell strong or weak, but he assumed it was fresh when he heard air rush in. He replaced the cap, buried the bottle in his palm, and slapped Roscoe's face. "Let's get some medicine down you, big guy."

Roscoe stirred and squinted at Jordan. "When's your friend getting' here?"

"We're aboard his boat."

"Tired of lyin' on this beach. Hot."

"Take a drink."

"Watcha got?"

"Something cold."

Roscoe held out a hand. Jordan ignored it.

"Here, I'll give you a drink. Open up."

Like a child, Roscoe opened his mouth and tilted his head back. Jordan assumed he would gag if the medicine tasted anything like it smelled, so he decided to pour in as much as he could, hoping Roscoe would swallow enough to make a difference.

He put the bottle to Roscoe's lips and upended it. A huge swallow was followed by a gurgle and a roar. The big man swore. "What was that?"

"You need it. You're sick."

"Gotta take my coat off. Hot!"

There would be little arguing with Roscoe. Paul shook his head. "He's your patient."

Jordan helped him get the coat off. Then Roscoe wanted his shirt off. Soon he lay there bare-chested, barefoot, in only khaki camouflage pants. He was sweating and breathing heavily. Finally he labored to his feet, leaned over the side, and vomited.

Jordan knelt next to Roscoe and tried to calm him.

"Too hot. I didn't trust that crew. Trying to kill me."

"I know, but you've got to lie still and cover up."

"No covers!"

Jordan worried whether he too had been poisoned, but so far he hadn't felt even queasy. He found it hard to believe Roscoe wasn't freezing in the breeze with the boat at full power. Roscoe took a labored breath and hissed.

When the big man's breathing evened out, Jordan hoped he was asleep, but still the man squirmed. Eventually he curled up and tucked his hands under his chin. Jordan piled blankets on him, then fished through Roscoe's pockets until he found the roll of large bills.

Jordan paid Paul and settled into his own cot. He was more than a continent from home, with mystery behind and ahead of him, and still his dreams raced immediately to Rosemary.

But he awoke with Cydya on his mind. Something gnawed at him. That same something bothered him for hours in the sun, while he helped Paul guide the boat through the ocean, played nursemaid to Roscoe, and planned his mission.

Roscoe seemed to be coming around, but he didn't look any stronger. What would he do if Roscoe couldn't help him in this strange and unforgiving climate with an agenda of unknowns?

15

JUST BEFORE MIDNIGHT Monday, Paul Paveli shut down the engine and raised a tattered sail. The balmy tropical air made Jordan feel good, but it was clear Roscoe was no better. Worse, Jordan kept imagining that he too would soon come down with whatever ailed the big man. The two largely ate the same food, so if someone had poisoned any of it, only dumb luck would keep him from ailing too.

Roscoe wasn't talking much and seemed reluctant to say anything in front of Paveli. Jordan couldn't blame him for not trusting anyone. With Paul busy at the other end of the craft, Roscoe motioned Jordan close and recounted more of their instructions from Chuck Wallington.

Paveli maneuvered the craft between rocky bluffs north of the harbor town of San Lorenzo. Jordan kept focused on the shore but detected no signal from their contacts.

"Feeling any stronger, Roscoe?"

The young man shook his head. "I'll carry my share, though."

"Let me do the lugging tonight. Save your strength for the interior."

"There's nothing to riding a bike. I'll be all right."

Paveli kept his craft as close to the rocks as he dared. "Want me to hang around until you've made contact?"

Jordan looked to Roscoe, who furrowed his brow. "Nah. You're probably scarin' 'em off as it is."

Paul shrugged and shook Roscoe's hand, clapping him on the back. "Get well."

Jordan embraced Paul. "Be careful."

The Italian looked away. "Greet Chuck for me when you get back."

More than half an hour later, after Jordan and Roscoe had slogged ashore with Jordan carrying most of the gear, they heard Paul start the engine and knew he was dropping the sail. Jordan was amazed at the seaman's ability to elude detection.

He'd gotten them into Ecuador easily; now all they had to do was make contact with the Cubans.

Roscoe sat with his head in his hands. "Hungry. But afraid to eat."

"I don't blame you."

"You sick too?"

Jordan shook his head. "Just figure my turn's next."

"You don't want what I've got."

"What'd you eat that I didn't?"

"Don't know. I think I had more sausage than you."

"I stayed away from that."

"It's what I'm hungry for, but I don't dare."

"It's probably bad by now anyway, even if someone didn't get to it."

Roscoe stretched. "Why would anyone on that ship want to do us in?"

"Money. Somebody got to them."

Roscoe fell silent a moment. Finally he sighed. "Whoever that somebody is sure has a long reach."

"Tell me about it. Question now is, what do we do if the Cubans don't show with the weapons and bikes?"

"They'll show."

Jordan hoped that was true. Except for a little morphine, there was no more medicine, and he didn't relish carrying the behemoth through the jungle. "We're pretty vulnerable, unarmed."

Roscoe was rubbing his eyes. "The only people who would be out here already know we're here. If they want to take us out, they'll take us out, armed or not."

Jordan froze at the sound of fingers snapping Morse code in a staccato rhythm.

Roscoe turned toward Jordan. "Hope they repeat it. I missed a lot."

"I got most of it. S-H-U-C-K."

"You'd think even a couple of Cubans could spell *Chuck*."

Jordan whistled back W-A-L-L-I-N-G-T-O-N in code, and the response was H-E-L-L-O.

He and Roscoe left their gear and scrambled in the sand toward the sound. Silhouetted against the sky was a short, stocky figure beside a motorcycle he had apparently pushed for miles. Jordan was amazed at the immense load the bike carried. Stacks of boxes and cans towered high over the Cuban's head.

Roscoe extended his hand. "Chuck."

The Cuban secured the bike by gingerly setting the kickstand on a rock, then responded in a thick accent. "Wallington."

"I'm Roscoe. This is Kirkwood."

The Cuban slumped to the ground. Jordan helped Roscoe lay him on his back. "You're alone?"

"*Sí.* Bad news for you. Message from States. Uncle safe. Mentor dead. Machala Diego staying in Germany. I no go with you. My partner no come. You get no guide."

Jordan could hardly breathe. He wanted to scream, to beat his fists on the ground. Could Chuck have sacrificed himself for Uncle Dex, or was the message a sham? His mind wouldn't let him dwell on it.

"Where's the other bike?"

"In box." The Cuban nodded toward the pile. "Instructions and tools inside. Easy. Both bikes hold extra petrol. Long range."

Jordan could see from the unusual construction of the assembled cycle that several areas had been expanded to hold fuel. "And the weapons?"

The Cuban nodded toward the pile again. "Five American .45s."

"Should be six."

"Five."

"You received them?"

"My partner."

"Why would he steal one of our guns?"

"No need. He got plenty of guns."

Jordan kicked at the ground. The Cuban sat up. "I leave now."

"Why?"

"You're on your own."

He ran off across the sand. Roscoe looked to Jordan. "Want me to run him down?"

"No. He's spooked. So's his partner, I guess. Surprised they're afraid of Diego, though.

Thought they knew what they were getting into."

Roscoe surveyed the pile of gear. "Must be a thousand pounds."

"Can't believe he didn't hang around for the money."

"Where'd you put my dough after you paid Paul?"

"Same pocket of your jacket."

"Both empty."

"C'mon, Roscoe."

"Really." Roscoe pulled the pockets inside out.

Jordan closed his eyes. "All hundreds?"

"Right. He had to pickpocket me when we laid him down."

Jordan toyed with dumping the supplies off the bike and heading after the Cuban. But the noise would have drawn more attention than the money was worth. "Got any more?"

"Eight hundred in my shoe and about two thousand in the trunk. I know he didn't get in there."

"How do you know?"

Roscoe headed back down toward their gear, moving more quickly than he had in days. Jordan heard him swear.

"What'd they get?"

"Just the money—no, the morphine, too!" Roscoe swore again. So the Cuban's partner *had* been there, doubling back behind them while they were helping the other.

Jordan helped Roscoe—now panting—carry

their stuff toward the cycle. "Not like Chuck to put us with a couple of losers."

Finally Jordan sank onto the sand, exhausted and feeling hopeless. Could Wallington really be gone? He'd been sure Chuck wrote the first telegram, and he'd been wrong about that. Was it possible this message was true, even coming from a cowardly mercenary who had ripped him off?

"Better find the .45s first."

Roscoe was already searching. "Guns here, but no ammo."

"Got to be there somewhere."

"I don't know, Jordan. The rest of the stuff is just canned food, fuel, and cycle parts."

"You mechanical?"

"If it's got wheels, I can put it together."

"Good. Let's get out of the open and find a place to sleep."

By the time they had carted everything into the underbrush and set up a small tent, Roscoe was faint and feverish again.

"Roscoe, we're out of medicine, so don't do this to me. I need you."

"I won't let you down. You know that."

Jordan spread out his sleeping bag and climbed in. "All I know is that you're not as dense as you'd like people to believe. You could make off with the guns and the cycle, and I'd be in this thing alone."

Roscoe studied him and managed a smile.

"Maybe that'll keep you on your toes. You'll sleep lighter."

Jordan ached at the thought of losing Chuck. No man in his life had ever meant as much to him. Not even Dexter Lee. He wanted to bury his head and sob, but he knew his physical and mental training had been complete when he felt his mind shift gears. He was fully into opposite-trigger mode, his mind occupied with the next morning's schedule. He wanted to sleep deep and sound and rise at dawn to assemble the other bike.

Roscoe lay on his back and sighed. "Think our Cuban friends'll be back for more?"

Jordan turned on his side. "Only if they think I'm totally unprepared." From deep inside his bedroll he produced two full clips of .45-caliber ammunition. "It may be all we have, but it'll be more than enough."

Roscoe loaded the automatics. "For tonight, maybe. But is this all we have for when we run into Diego, too?"

"Hey, we're only after him and a few companions, right?"

Jordan awoke well before sunup, mourning. Much as he tried to tell himself it was a lie, he couldn't shake the dread. Who knew Chuck and his itinerary well enough to pull off such an assassination? Cydya? It couldn't be. It mustn't be. With

230

his wife and his oldest friend gone, he needed more than ever the elusive dream she embodied.

Jordan was tempted to check Roscoe for fever, but he didn't want to wake him. He thought of trying to doze another half hour himself, but something caught his eye from far down along the waterfront. He pulled the flap of the tent wider. A light. Dancing. Moving, as if coming up the beach.

It was a flashlight, he was sure. No one looking for him would give himself away like that. Jordan slowly raised himself to his elbows and knees and buried the handle of the .45 deep in his palm. The figure paused where he and Roscoe had first set their gear, then moved to where they'd met the Cuban. The flashlight shone around and followed their trail in the sand toward the underbrush.

Should he wake Roscoe and risk a noisy response? Jordan didn't want to be caught on his hands and knees in a small tent. He slipped out and circled to kneel behind foliage where the tracker would come if he followed the trail to the tent.

He gingerly released the safety and cocked the gun. The figure passed within inches of him. He was about to leap out and press the barrel against the back of the man's head when he recognized him. "Pauly?"

"Ah!" The little man jumped and fell to his knees. "Oh! Jordan! Oh!"

"Pauly, what're you doing here?"

"Am I glad I found you! I was afraid you'd be on the trail by now."

"Shh!" He led the Italian out of the underbrush away from the tent.

"Whoever's tryin' to get hold of you thought it was worth breakin' radio silence. At first I almost didn't notice they were transmitting through all the static and everything, but I finally made out the message. They even used your names."

"You're not serious."

"Roscoe and Kirkwood. Repeated several times. Anybody who wanted that message must have heard it. I think it was sent from a U.S. military ship somewhere down here."

"They give any indication of where we are?"

"No, they tried to make it sound like an international call. I wrote it down. It's in code." He swore. "I never thought I'd find you. Hope this is important enough for me to be riskin' my boat." He handed Jordan the slip. "If they get my boat, I'm with you."

"What do you mean?"

"If I spot anybody nosin' around it, I can't go back. I'm in restricted waters. Forget it. I'd be joinin' your expedition."

"Not unless you've got a cycle, you're not."

Paveli held the flashlight so Jordan could read. The man's handwriting was atrocious, but the message was clear.

Delay vacation. Travel agent closed for good. New info on tour host in closest capital. Ignore cigar smokers. They got a better deal up the road. Signed, adviser.

"Pauly, you got any medicine left?"

"Just morphine and aspirin."

"I also need that money we gave you. I'll wire it back to you as soon as I can."

"Sure, but we've got to go get it now. As soon as the sun is up, I'm nothin' but a target."

Jordan followed Paul through the darkness to the water, debating what to tell him. The horizon was growing pink when he filled his pockets with cash and medicine. "I'm going to leave Roscoe to recuperate awhile. What's the closest capital?"

Paveli pulled a roll of maps from a drawer. "Looks like Ibarra and Tulcán are about the same distance."

Jordan looked over his shoulder. "Yeah, but if I go southwest, Esmeraldas is closer than both, right?"

Paul nodded. "And the message came over the water, so they must've figured they'd catch you before you started inland. If the message got to you in the jungle, you'd have to figure Tulcán."

"I'll try Esmeraldas."

"Anything else in that message you can tell a curious ol' captain?"

Jordan swallowed. "Pauly, our contact told me

he got a message that my mentor was dead, and Wallington was the one who arranged this trip. He's the travel agent."

Paveli looked stunned. "What does the rest of it mean?"

"Nothing I can talk about, except we've already been hoodwinked by the cigar smokers—our Cuban contacts. Apparently they've been paid more by the other side. Anyway, I thought you'd want to know about Chuck."

Jordan had never seen Paul Paveli weep. Now the old man cursed the rising sun and turned his back on Jordan to get his boat ready to move. No more talk, no good-byes, just a stiff, formal wave as he pushed off. Chuck had been their only link, and Jordan doubted they would ever see each other again.

In Esmeraldas he would try the International Telephone and Telegraph office for anything addressed to any of his aliases. He would leave Roscoe to assemble the other cycle, use the medicine as necessary, and get himself in shape for whatever might be left of their mission.

While Roscoe dozed, Jordan packed necessities and his only change of civilian clothes. Then he fired up the cycle. It brayed harsh and annoying but evidenced enough jumpy power to help him elude any curious authorities.

Roscoe rolled onto one side and squinted at Jordan. Jordan gave him the news. Roscoe sat up in his sleeping bag, Indian style, like a toddler. He was quiet, shaking his head. "So who do you think you're supposed to see in Esmeraldas?"

"One of our guys stationed there, maybe. Might even be CIA, but I doubt it. Wish it was somebody from Washington." Jordan told himself he wouldn't even mind seeing Blake Bauer right then if he could get some definitive word on Chuck.

He left food and water for Roscoe and was about to walk the cycle back up over the rolling sand hills when an explosion from the water rocked the beachhead. He left the motorcycle, grabbed his .45, and hollered to Roscoe. "Stay with the stuff!"

He scrambled down the rocky shore, tumbling, scraping elbows and knees, and reached the water in time to recognize fragments of Paveli's boat in the distance. Someone had to have planted a charge in that boat while Paul had been talking with him on the beach.

He scanned the horizon and thought he saw bubbles a hundred yards from the explosion. *A diver.* He sprinted up the beach, determined to not let the man reach the shore alive. A head appeared from the water, and the diver pulled off his mask, surveying his handiwork.

Paul couldn't have survived, but why bomb the boat? Did someone think Jordan had been with him? They had to know better.

No way would his .45 be effective from that distance, so Jordan slipped behind a rock to wait for the diver to swim closer. When he drew nearly within range, Jordan dropped to a crouch, both hands on the weapon. He edged out onto the shore and drew a bead. The diver was still a minuscule target, but incentive and adrenaline were on Jordan's side. Ten feet closer and he knew he could kill the man.

But the diver stopped and bobbed. Jordan heard a motorboat fire up, though he couldn't see it. The diver would wait for the boat and wouldn't get any closer! Jordan had to close the gap himself. He charged into the shallow water and fired, screaming for his partner. "Roscoe, the boat! The boat!"

Jordan's shot splashed within two feet of the diver and sent him underwater again. The only possibility now was to sink the getaway motorboat. It sped wildly into view from behind a bluff, and Jordan fired again. It was no bigger than a rowboat. The occupants dove into the hull for cover as the bullet splashed in front of them. Jordan only hoped his shot had not skipped too high off the water. He wanted to put a hole in the craft under the waterline. *Where's Roscoe?*

As he aimed again, he heard shots ring out from up near the tent. Roscoe knew better than to think he could come close from up there! But as Jordan listened in horror, nine shots were fired, all with the same deliberate second between them.

By now the boat had picked up the diver and

sped beyond Jordan's range up the coast. Jordan had seven bullets left, but—he feared—no allies. He stayed close to the rocks as he crept up the shore to directly beneath the tent site. When he came within sight of the tent, he pressed against a rock and waited, calming his heart and listening. He slithered to the back, where a light breeze made the tent flap smack against the side. He wanted to call out for Roscoe, but he had no idea what or whom he might encounter.

He crawled along the side, weapon in front of him. Satisfied no one was around, he peered into the tent. The young mercenary lay on his back, feet and legs spread, eyes and mouth open. His weapon lay on his sternum, just beneath his heart, through which nine .45-caliber slugs had passed. Someone had wasted Roscoe with his own gun.

Jordan trembled, near collapse as he backed out of the tent and stood. "I'm here, you cowards! Try me! Come on!" He waved his automatic. "There'd better be more than seven of you! Come on! Come on!"

The response was nothing but the maddening billowing of the tent flap. Jordan fell to his knees, more alone that he had ever been, shuddering at his crazed reaction. He could have easily been cut down by snipers. Either they didn't want him or they were gone.

Why had he reacted so impulsively, so unlike himself and his training? It was the carnage.

Roscoe was just another in a line of five—*five*—that led back to his wife. While there were still exasperating puzzles, one thing was clear: this was more than espionage, more than politics. Millions, maybe tens of millions, of lives were at stake.

Jordan had been willing to take on all the Cubans or al-Qaeda or whoever had killed Paul and Roscoe, because it seemed that nearly everyone he cared about was gone now. But as he forced his pulse and nervous system to calm, he realized there were still Uncle Dex, Christa, Ken, and Felix.

Most important, Islamo-fascists had soon-to-be-nuclear-equipped planes on United States soil. For the future of the country, he vowed to never react irrationally again, no matter who else was slaughtered in an attempt to get at him. Jordan Kirkwood would tune his mind to a sharpness that would make Chuck Wallington proud, and he would complete this mission, even if it was his last.

16

THE TWENTIETH OF the month was two days away, and the beach had not proven safe, but still Jordan took the risk of burying Roscoe. As he shoveled the last grains of sand over the hole, he remembered his uncle warning Roscoe not to wait too long to consider God. And Dex had urged Jordan not to wait for Roscoe to raise the subject. Now Jordan couldn't even bring himself to say anything or pray over the grave. He carefully noted the area so someone could eventually exhume the body for return to the States, in case Roscoe's family would want that.

Jordan hid the still-crated cycle and other equipment he couldn't carry and pushed the assembled motorbike half a mile up the sandy beach to a back road, wondering how the turncoat Cuban had managed such a load. As soon as he hit asphalt, he jumped aboard and slowly got the feel of the machine.

Within minutes he had the bike up to seventy miles an hour, and when no other vehicles were in sight, he opened the throttle all the way. The wind felt good in his hair, but he felt exposed without a helmet and wondered if the Cubans had made off with those as well. The day was heating up.

By midmorning he grew nervous about the stares from people in pickup trucks and buses. With only a compass, Jordan kept to the back roads as he tried to stay on course to Esmeraldas, coastal capital of the province of the same name.

He crossed two rivers via bridges before the longest part of the trip, knowing he would likely have to ferry across the Río Esmeraldas. The back roads were tortuous and slow, but he felt safer there. When he came within sight of the big river just before noon, his shirt was soaked through and he guessed the temperature at more than ninety.

Jordan steered off road along the bank until he thought his kidneys would burst from the constant jostling. He kept looking for narrow, shallow crossings and was even prepared to wade across with the bike on his shoulders.

Eventually he realized he was going to have to head north to Tachina and take the ferry directly across to the capital. At midday, the crossing was busy. Jordan knew he looked conspicuously foreign, but he refused to return stares.

The man at the gate held up both hands to signify that the ferry was full, spurring an outburst from the half dozen or so hopefuls in front of Jordan. They jabbered and shouted at the man while Jordan calmly held up an American $100 bill so only the gatekeeper could see it. The gatekeeper's eyes grew wide and he bellowed in broken English. "Yankee emergency! Medical!" The crowd parted.

By midafternoon, Jordan was a spectacle in the capital city. He didn't intend to disturb anyone's siesta, but he couldn't wait to get to the telegraph office. He found it, naturally, closed until late afternoon, so he chose a spot on a side street to park the bike and sit in the shadows until the town slowly came back to life. Still ignoring curious looks, he made his way back to the telegraph office and entered a swinging screen door that slapped shut behind him.

Jordan pretended to be more interested in the messages on the walls than in talking to the woman behind the desk. He didn't know which name to use in asking for a message, so he just browsed until he could steal a glance behind her where large envelopes bore the names of recipients. There were just five, and only one appeared printed in other than Spanish.

When she reached for the phone, he leaned forward and was rocked to see the name he had used the night his wife was killed. Whoever knew that had to be intimately acquainted with the attack. But Jordan carried no identification bearing the name P. Gaston Blanc. Could he get a phony ID on the black market? And how long might that take?

The woman hung up and smiled at him. In his best French accent he tried to speak rudimentary Spanish, telling her he didn't understand her language. He sputtered in French, pointing to his message. She asked for identification and pantomimed reaching in her pocket. Jordan pleaded with her in French and flashed another big American bill. He had worked himself up to near fake tears by the time she smiled at him, took the bill, gave him a few centavos in return, and handed him the envelope. He hurried outside, tearing it open.

WELCOME. YOU ARE BOOKED AT THE
ESMERALDAS GRANDE. DINNER AT NINE
IN THE LOUNGE. SIGNED, ADVISER.

Jordan wheeled his bike onto a major street and stopped in front of a taxi, drawing an angry honk and shouts from the passengers. He leaned in the driver's window. "Esmeraldas Grande?"

The driver cursed him but pointed north and held up two fingers, then pointed east and held up one. Jordan found the place quickly. Had he been in a normal state of mind, the breathtaking marble lobby would have made him feel like a pilgrim at the portals of heaven. Under present circumstances, however, the reception area had an antiseptic, funereal feel. Jordan was sticky and miserable, in desperate need of a shave and a shower.

Nothing was more representative of the contrasts in the busy capital than the palatial hotel. Within its shadow lay squalor, yet inside its revolving doors an air-conditioned world of opulence glistened. Apart from his grief and the grim task at hand, such would have been just what Jordan needed.

He approached the desk. "Blanc."

The clerk asked in three languages which he preferred—Spanish, French, or English. Remaining in character, he chose French. He couldn't relax until he had changed one of his hundreds, tipped the bellman, checked his room for bugging devices, and double-locked his door. Finally alone and safe, he shaved and showered, letting the questions roll around in his head.

Something was working on him, but it wasn't coming together. He dug deep into his pack and laid out slip-on shoes, socks, knit pants, a cotton pullover shirt, and a light sports coat. They were a mass of wrinkles. He hung them over the shower rod, turned on the hot water, and closed the door to let the steam smooth them out.

He lay on the bed, .45 in his hand. Was his "adviser" CIA, NSA, or military? Someone in Ecuadorean intelligence? Whoever it was must have had contact with Wallington, Granger, or Williamsby. Others in the agency knew of his Blanc alias, but they wouldn't have known where to find him if Chuck was dead, unless Felix had briefed them. Whoever it was should be able to confirm the news about Chuck.

In his anxiety, Jordan needed every ounce of mind training he'd ever had to allow himself to sleep for a few hours before dinner. He accomplished it as a tribute to Chuck. As he dropped off, Jordan tried to focus on one set of questions, hoping his subconscious could make the answers somehow come together as he slept. Why had the NSA thought he had fired weapons he hadn't fired? How did someone get past NSA security to level his house? How was he tracked to

Muskegon? How had they gotten to Chuck? And why had Cydya LeMonde been talking to Felix?

When Jordan awoke, one thing was clear: he needed to know who his adviser was before he dined with him at nine. He also needed to be armed. He checked his watch. It was only seven, but he was anxious. He paced, sifting the details, trying to force them to make sense. He dressed, then wished he hadn't because he felt too warm. He went to the lounge to casually scout which table would give him the best view of the rest of the place, particularly the entrance. He reserved the table for eight thirty, pressing more money into yet another palm.

By eight o'clock Jordan was back in his room, wondering whether he was going to be briefed by someone who would add to his knowledge of his prey, or whether he himself was about to become the prey. Half an hour later, he left for the lounge again with the .45 in his waistband at the back. Calming himself was more of a chore than he expected. He hated the unknown. Finding out, knowing in advance, setting up his own scenarios had been Jordan's specialty for twenty years. And now, inside a few weeks, his wife had been slaughtered; an old friend driven to suicide; his home demolished; his oldest, dearest friend killed; a valued contact man and sailor eliminated; and Chuck's handpicked compatriot for him assassinated while Jordan was within earshot.

He felt dread with every step. Was it foolish to subject himself to this surprise? He would be armed and in public and able to get a good look at his adviser as he approached. Still Jordan felt vulnerable.

Maybe he should stand up his host, stake out his own room, and see who came knocking. No sense sitting there with his back to the wall if he was hopelessly outnumbered. Jordan couldn't remember being this squirrelly and indecisive this late in a scenario.

As he passed a bank of telephones, he spotted a tall, black-haired man on the phone with his back to him. Felix! The image was so comforting that Jordan felt weak-kneed. What a relief! Felix would know what happened to Chuck. He would know everything. And he would care.

He approached the big man and gently put a hand on his shoulder. The man turned, and Jordan was stunned. "Sorry, sir. Mistook you for someone."

The headwaiter waved at him from the lounge. "Your table is ready, Señor Blanc." He led Jordan to a table in the back that was set for two, and Jordan took the seat that faced the entrance. "My guest will be another half hour."

Jordan pressed his fingers to his temples and shut his eyes. Mistaking that man for Felix tied things together in his mind, and a shudder raced from his tailbone to the top of his head. He would have known Jordan was meeting his wife in London after his meeting with Stanley Stuart in Frankfurt. Lister blew the assignment, missing that Jordan and his wife would not be on the same plane, but the hit directive had to have come from Felix Granger!

Granger had to be the high-level NSA man Stu had warned him about—though Stu never suspected. Felix had removed any suspicion of himself by accompanying Jordan back to the States. He had access to the house, to the weapons, to Chuck's confidences in England while Jordan was in Muskegon. He could have planted the house bomb, fired Jordan's weapons, and then had the NSA-style bug planted outside Dexter Lee's home. He could have sent the telegram in an attempt to keep Jordan at his uncle's home until it was bombed or ambushed.

He must have killed Chuck trying to get at Jordan. And once Chuck was out of the picture, Granger tried to jump back in as Jordan's protector by sending the message Paul Paveli received. But that had to just be an attempt to keep Jordan from his assignment. If Chuck was dead, who else would know where to reach Jordan?

Jordan couldn't imagine a motive besides greed. Felix was one of his oldest and most-favored acquaintances in the agency. True, he had been passed over as a mentor for one of the new recruits when Chuck had Jordan and Stu was also assigned a protégé. And before Felix was named deputy director of UKUSA six years before, he had been an expert on radar as the U.S.'s last line of defense. He was the perfect inside man for al-Qaeda.

The question was how much Wallington had told Granger about what he learned in Frankfurt. Felix had to know why Jordan was in Ecuador, and he also had to know that Jordan didn't know where in Maldonado Diego and the others would meet regarding the MiG-23s.

Adrenaline pumped through Jordan's body. All Felix had to do was make sure Jordan didn't find out where the meeting was or learn any more about the location of the MiGs. No one alive but Jordan could slow the process.

How long had Felix been involved with al-Qaeda? His whole life? It was hard to imagine. Many Islamic cells had been traced to England. Maybe they got to him after he was assigned to UKUSA. Yet even if he was a recent flip, clearly he was well connected. He had already proved able to dispatch hit men, bombers, and guerrillas.

And all the while, he remained in the good graces of the NSA director and Deputy Bauer, not to mention Wallington and Jordan and virtually every other influential person in the agency. Felix's connection to Cydya and Interpol jarred Jordan. Had she really come to Felix, or had he gone to her? Could Felix have known about

Jordan and Cydya? Surely Chuck had never mentioned that. If Cydya was involved in Felix's scheme, why would Granger have told Chuck Wallington about her?

Jordan suddenly felt exposed again. Would Granger send another hired gun? If Felix himself came, would he eliminate Jordan at the first opportunity or still pretend to be an ally? It was ten to nine when Jordan casually stood and told the headwaiter, "I'll be back shortly. Would you direct my party to my table? He'll ask for me."

He trotted up one flight of carpeted stairs to a mezzanine portico that overlooked the lounge. Anyone at his table would have to crane awkwardly to even notice him. Moments later, a beautiful woman appeared in the lounge. From Jordan's perch, she looked to be in her late thirties or early forties, long, lithe, and tanned in a cream-colored chiffon dress. She followed the waiter to Jordan's table and sneaked a peek at herself in a mirror from her tiny handbag. Her hands shook as she put the bag next to her on the seat and crossed her legs. As she turned to survey the room, Jordan saw her huge, green eyes.

He couldn't turn his eyes from her, marveling at how the years had done nothing but enhance her beauty. Jordan feared that if he dared even to blink, she would disappear.

So she was involved. But what was her motive? His legs felt rubbery as he headed back to the stairs. He moved his weapon to the hip pocket of his coat. Might the lost love of his life try to cut him down in public, perhaps with a weapon from her handbag?

Jordan knew he should check the area for accomplices, but he was so curious, so drawn to her. He strode the length of the lounge and approached her from behind. The long neck, the majestic carriage, the velvety hair. He would touch her shoulder and greet her by name as he had done to the man at the phone. Only this time, he would not be mistaken. Would his voice fail him? At the periphery of his consciousness, his mind tried to shift into opposite-trigger mode, pushing him to be calm. It was no use.

His hand brushed her shoulder as he came around the table and sat across from her. "Cydya."

His anxiety must have been obvious. She looked at him pleasantly, but without a smile, as if she knew everything, knew what he was going through, and understood. He was looking into the eyes of the woman he had dreamed of for two decades—the expression, the direct, knowing gaze. She delicately put her elbows on the table, cupping her face in her hands. And when she spoke, he was transported to Indonesia. Why had he only ever seen her thousands of miles from home?

"Jordan Kirkwood. We meet in the strangest places."

There was a mature timbre, but he would have recognized the voice anywhere. He had questions, but neither the breath nor the nerve to ask. He had instinctively slipped his hand into his jacket pocket and now sat with his fingers wrapped around the .45. He could no more shoot this woman than a member of his own family. If she played a part in any of this, including a plot to attack her own homeland from within, he'd just as soon she dropped him on the spot.

He felt himself flush as he stared. She was radiant, but what was she doing here? Jordan noticed a waiter approaching. "Are you hungry, Cydya?"

She smiled and shook her head. He pressed a bill into the waiter's hand. "We'd like to be left alone for a couple of hours."

"Sí. Bueno."

How like her younger self she was! "Cydya, forgive me, but I wasn't expecting you."

She was still smiling. "Really? Whom were you expecting? Mr. Wallington?"

She had to know about Chuck if Felix had sent her. "Not funny. I was expecting Granger."

Her smile faded. She reached and covered the back of his hand with her palm. "Jordan, Felix Granger thinks you're dead. He thinks Wallington's dead, too."

"Chuck's alive?"

"Yes. In case Felix's people intercepted the message to the boat, we wanted them to think you were being informed of Mr. Wallington's death. That couldn't be better for us right now, but I'm sorry you were misled. I know how close you are to Mr. Wallington."

Jordan felt as if he could breathe for the first time in hours. "If what you're saying is true, that message also told them Roscoe and I were still alive, if not exactly where we were. I'm so confused now, you'll have to straighten me out."

"I will; I'll tell you everything. I've been involved in this only since the night you left Michigan with the mercenary Chuck hired. Is he with you?"

"No, I, uh, left him back where Paveli dropped us. You'd better start from the beginning." This was still making no sense. He watched for any sign of deceit.

"Right. Well, one morning last week, I got a call at Interpol from Mr. Wallington. He said it was three a.m. in Michigan, but he'd been thinking about me and wanted to come talk to me right away."

"You didn't know him, did you?"

"Well, I had met him in Indonesia, but back then I thought he was CIA."

Jordan shook his head. "He was in Jakarta without my knowing? What was he up to there?"

"He said he was checking on whether any branches of the U.S. government were trying to infiltrate the Peace Corps and wanted to know if I had any knowledge of that. I told him I didn't, and he asked that I not mention our meeting to anyone."

"You didn't even tell me."

"I was going to be working for Interpol, and I didn't want a reputation as one who couldn't keep a confidence. Anyway, I certainly didn't suspect you were NSA. Shortly after I arrived in France and started at Interpol, Mr. Wallington visited me again and admitted he was with the NSA and that actually he had been evaluating your performance. I was proud of you that you had said nothing about your real mission, but I'm afraid I wasn't very good at covering my feelings about our, you know, our—"

"Relationship."

"Well, that's what I had thought it was, Jordan. When I learned you were actually an NSA trainee, I wondered if we'd had a real relationship at all. Mr. Wallington said I didn't have to answer his personal questions, but he did want to know if I thought we would eventually marry. Since you had made that clear in your letter, I told him no."

Chuck had met and talked with Cydya twice? Jordan wanted to assure her their relationship had been real and that his NSA involvement had nothing to do with its end. But that would have to wait. Somehow he had to assure himself she was to be trusted.

"Cydya, I need to ask you something."

"Anything."

"Did Chuck ask you about the night we spent in Jakarta?"

Cydya looked away and shook her head, her eyes suddenly moist. "Did he ask you?"

Jordan nodded. "I just wondered if he had heard about it from you."

"You're saying he knew about that before he came to see me?"

"He knew about it before he talked to *me*." Jordan entwined his fingers and rested his chin on them. "Did you keep in touch with him?"

"Never heard from him again until last week. I did keep tabs on you, though. I suppose you figured that. You know Interpol has files on almost everyone, from international criminals to everybody in the intelligence world."

"So what have I been up to?"

"You've been everything I knew you would be, but I confess I wondered if you'd have staying power when things got tight. You're a globe-trotting specialist in political and criminal undercover work, the best disguise man in the business. Devoted family man. I was so sorry to hear about your wife."

Cydya's eyes filled again. She opened her small bag and searched for a tissue. Not finding one, she closed the bag and stood. "Sorry. I'll be right back."

As she hurried away, Jordan impulsively ran his hand over the bag she had left on the table. Nothing hard or heavy. He quickly returned his handgun to his waistband. Jordan reminded himself to not be careless. Cydya could have dreamed up this whole story by piecing together information from Felix. Had she left the bag on purpose to put his mind at ease, all the while planning to come back with a weapon? She may have felt she deserved an answer to her letters, an apology for running perhaps, but revenge? On the other hand, that she could be the same straightforward woman he had met so long ago would be too good to be true.

Jordan signaled the waiter. "Is your lobster good?"

"Oh, *sí*! Fresh from the Pacific!"

Jordan ordered Cydya's favorite meal, everything from the lobster tail to the salad dressing.

He stood when she returned, and as she sat, she appeared to be looking for someone. "You know, I am a little hungry now."

"Me too, but let's wait a bit. There's so much more I want to hear."

17

JORDAN WOULD NOT be played for a fool simply because he had bailed out of an adolescent romance. It had been more than that, but he didn't know what Cydya thought. Could she have held a grudge all these years? He had trusted Felix Granger like family. Yet now it was clear that Felix, whom Jordan had watched torture a fly just to pass the time, was slowly pulling off Jordan's wings and would crush him between his thumb and forefinger at the first opportunity.

Could Cydya be Granger's pawn? What else had Chuck done or said that Jordan never knew about? Rosemary was dead, and Chuck could be too, for all Jordan knew. This was no time to let his emotions take over.

"Felix told Wallington that you wrote to his office, officially requesting information on me for Interpol, and that you later visited him on your own and admitted your interest was personal."

Her gaze was steady, and there was no dilation of the pupils. "No, as I told Mr. Wallington, I was at UKUSA in London on Interpol business and asked an agent if he was aware of an American-based operative named Jordan Kirkwood. He said of course, but that he had never met you. He said his boss was an old friend of yours, and he introduced me to Mr. Granger. Frankly, I was impressed with him, the down-home charm, the wit, the personal interest."

"What did you tell him about us?"

"I told him I had met you in the Peace Corps and that we had been friends. He offered to remember me to you, and I asked him if he would please not. He agreed and didn't ask why."

"What *was* your reason, Cydya? I would have been pleased to hear that you had asked about me."

She hesitated, looking shaky. "If you wanted any reminder of me, you knew where I was. Not only did you not read my letters, but neither did I hear one word from you over the next twenty-plus years. Once you were married, I didn't expect to. I knew your principles. I shared them."

"Felix never contacted you again, nor you him?" She shook her head. "Then why did he imply to Wallington that you were trying to find me, even to the point where you could have had something to do with the attempts on my life?"

Cydya narrowed her eyes. "I haven't even finished my story about Mr. Wallington contacting me last week, and you're letting Felix Granger color your view of me? It's been a long time, Jordan, but you should know me better than that. Is Mr. Granger a credible judge of character?"

"Please finish."

Cydya tilted her head back and shook out her

hair. "When I told Mr. Wallington about my brief encounter with Mr. Granger, he asked about my life since he'd seen me last, then quickly got to the point. He wanted to know if I had been aware of the attempt on your life and the death of your wife. I was shocked, but for him to call me from the States in the middle of the night and then come immediately to France, it had to be something big."

Cydya said Chuck gave her a rundown on everything that had happened to Jordan from the time he met with Stanley Stuart until he left for Ecuador.

Jordan stared. "You're not serious. Wallington told you all that?"

Cydya looked hurt. "You don't believe me?"

"It doesn't sound like Chuck to tell anything, let alone everything."

"Maybe he sensed he could trust me, even if you don't."

"There's nothing I would rather do. But the stakes have never been higher."

Her voice was quavery. "Mr. Wallington said he couldn't sleep the night you left. He rolled the thing over and over in his mind and concluded that Felix Granger was the only common denominator, the only one who knew everything and everyone and had access to you and your house and your weapons."

As usual, Jordan thought, Chuck had beat him to

the solution by a week. But did it make any sense that he would tell all this to Cydya?

"He was certain someone would try to kill you before you left for South America."

Now *that* sounded like Chuck. "So he hustled back to Michigan to get my uncle out of the house and make it look like both he and I were still there when, what? The place blew?"

She nodded.

Jordan told himself not to jump to conclusions. This could still all be the work of a very crafty Southerner. *Southerner.* Felix was from Mississippi, but his family owned acreage throughout the South! If the al-Qaeda MiGs landed on property Felix owned, no one within a hundred miles would have noticed or cared. If Jordan could be certain about Alabama, then land owned there by a Granger would be a good place for U.S. Air Force reconnaissance pilots to start looking.

When their meals were delivered, Cydya glowed. "Jordan!"

"Cydya, I have to be frank. Everything you've told me up to now is known by many within the NSA. A few nuances sound like Chuck. But isn't there something that will assure me you're working with Chuck and are not someone who just knows him well?"

She shook her head and her face contorted to fight tears. He felt a fool. She couldn't know he had never begged anyone to convince him before. Wariness was an occupational hazard, and his had allowed him a longer-than-average career in a dangerous business.

She picked at her salad. "Remember what you used to do? You prayed before every meal, whether or not we were alone. It didn't bother you. You were a good, devout boy. Are you still?"

He shrugged. "I still believe, if that's what you mean. The devout part—not so much just now."

A smile played at the corners of her mouth. "Would the fearless international operative have the guts to ask the blessing right here in the middle of nowhere, just for old times' sake?"

Jordan bowed his head, thoroughly embarrassed. The only prayer that came to him had become meaningless through repetition as a child. "Lord, for what we are about to receive, may we be truly thankful."

He lifted his head wondering if he would find himself staring down the barrel of a gun. All he saw were Cydya's tears. Somehow he and she had been transported back more than twenty years and across thousands of miles. For that instant, he was no longer a middle-aged widower whose world was crashing in on him, not a spy whose old colleague was trying to kill him. For a few seconds Jordan had again been the devout eighteen-year-old who had won Cydya's heart. And they had come to love each other so deeply that they had promised each other that nothing would ever come between them.

When they slept together that last night in Jakarta before he was suddenly called home to his father's funeral, he knew it violated every standard she had ever set for herself. As awkward and fumbling and passionate as they had been, it had also been obvious from her countenance that she—like he—considered that night a mistake, a failure, wrong.

She could not, however, have expected it to come between them. She had to assume that when he got back to Jakarta, he would write to her in France, and they would pick up where they left off, except that they would resolve never to be intimate with each other again until after they were married. That was what they both wanted, what they both believed to be right.

But he had written only twice—once to tell her it was over and once to tell her he would not open any more of her letters. And that's when she had to know she was on her own, her dreams shattered like his. It had to hurt her that her love and commitment were deeper than his. But if he wouldn't read her letters, all she could do was get over him. From her expression now, it appeared she never had.

If he could trust her.

Cydya seemed to work at composing herself.

"Mr. Wallington told me to tell you about the receipt he stole from the evidence in Mr. Stuart's apartment."

Now they were getting somewhere. Or were they? Could Felix have known that? Could JOSAF have recorded that receipt before Chuck got there and then reported it missing?

"What was it for, Cydya?"

"For sending a package to Mr. Wallington at his private post office box in the States."

This was too neat, too pat. Jordan's head ached from the possibilities. *Your own mother couldn't convince you she was trustworthy.* If JOSAF had recorded the receipt, the address would have been on it.

"What was in the package?"

Cydya swallowed and dabbed her lips. "Photos of Russian planes and a message to Mr. Wallington about the Maldonado meeting."

Jordan held his breath. "Anything else?"

"Such as?"

His heart sank. Anyone could guess that Stu would have sent the photos and a message. But who would know what else he sent? Only Wallington. And Cydya, if he told her.

"Anything else at all?"

"A copy of Mr. Stuart's note to Machala Diego, opting out and recommending Mr. Wallington."

Chuck might have told Felix all that before he began to suspect him. JOSAF or the local

261

authorities could have discovered the copy in the apartment.

Jordan was still troubled and couldn't hide it.

Cydya's shoulders sagged, and she held up empty hands before him. Her hard look frightened him. "What are you afraid of? What do you want? What do you need? Jordan, face it. You don't have a choice. You have to trust me. If I'm lying, then Wallington is dead and Granger knows where you are. But if I'm here because Wallington sent me, because he was pretending to be dead while actually doubling back to follow Diego to Maldonado, then you have to stick with me."

Jordan had a bite of steak in his cheek. "That's his plan? Stay out of Felix's sight and follow Diego? Very risky. Very difficult."

She cocked her head. "He said you'd say that."

That sounds like him too. "Cydya, what would you say if I told you that I saw Paul Paveli blown to bits this morning and Roscoe shot dead?"

She squinted and shoved her meal aside. "Don't play games with me. I'm too tired."

"It's true."

She scowled. "That would mean Granger knows you're in South America."

"You see why I would be wary of anybody? I have to think Chuck wouldn't know who he could trust, and so he wouldn't trust anyone but me."

Cydya looked cold and stony. "And you trust only him, is that it?"

"Do you blame me? I need something rock solid that will convince me everything you have told me has come straight from Chuck."

"Of course you do, if you really saw two men die today. But do you see the position Wallington is in? What if Granger finds out he escaped the bombing of your uncle's house and *then* something happens to Wallington? He needed to tell the whole story to someone he could trust, but his options were limited. He trusted his intuition and took a chance on me."

He stared at her long and hard. "Until I hear something Granger couldn't have gotten through NSA channels, frankly, I fear for my life. But it's not just my own hide I'm worried about. If Chuck *is* dead and I fail, nobody else anywhere can do anything about those MiGs in Alabama."

Cydya dabbed her face. "Could we go for a walk?"

Jordan paid in cash and followed Cydya out. Had she given up trying to convince him? He wasn't being unreasonable, what with the very security of the United States at stake. Was she taking him somewhere to be eliminated?

While her back was to him, he moved his weapon again, this time to his right trouser pocket. He didn't want to offend her by suggesting they stay on the main boulevard and avoid dimly lit side streets, yet he wasn't willing to die for his manners either.

Cydya pointed to a pier with a concrete bench surrounding a miniature lighthouse, and they started toward the ocean. He found her silence ominous. Nearly ten minutes later, they reached the sand. She held his arm as she removed her shoes, and he was hit with a wave of anxiety he couldn't shake. As she held out her hand to return the favor while he slipped off his shoes, he remembered that that same polite gesture had been offered his wife just before she was killed. A man showing courtesy had innocently confirmed to a mistaken assassin that he had found his target.

They worked their way a hundred yards across the sand to the pier, which jutted another fifty yards into the ocean. The farther they got from the road, the darker it became. Finally they reached the pier and stepped up out of the sand. Steadying each other again while they put their shoes back on, they headed out toward the little lighthouse. The pier was just ten feet wide, yet Jordan didn't feel comfortable more than touching her arm occasionally when she appeared too near the edge.

As they came within the radius of the lighthouse, Jordan couldn't help but notice that Cydya had virtually not changed in twenty years. He recalled how naturally and easily they had once walked with their arms around each other's waists. Under other circumstances he might have reached for her now. But the woman carried an aura the girl had not. Resentment? Bitterness? Vengeance?

When they reached the circular bench surrounding the light, Jordan sat facing the ocean, his back to the beach, listening to the lazy slap of the waves against the pier. She sat a couple of feet away. Jordan had always found the ocean therapeutic. Cydya's light perfume was other than therapeutic. For years he had not been able to think of her without being reminded of the terrible news about his father.

There had been so much guilt—still was—regarding his relationship with his father. They had never been close, and he had often felt oppressed under the man. It wasn't that his father had died young, just unexpectedly. And for a teenager who had just broken one of the commandments, the news came at the worst possible time.

Jordan had eventually outgrown the belief that his father's death was a direct result of his own sin. Even though Rosemary never knew of Cydya, it was she who had introduced him to a view of God based in love and understanding and forgiveness. His faith had matured over the years, and while he still believed in a righteous, holy, just God, he quit believing that God killed his father to punish him for his sin. Rather, he came to believe that God gave His Son to forgive him for his sin.

Jordan's voice sounded eerie over the water. "This walk was your idea. Did you have an agenda?"

Her face, lit from above, looked just as she had looked twenty years before. "Yes. I need to tell you something. Jordan, I never married."

"I wondered."

"I was mad at you but never fell out of love with you. Friends and family knew I'd had my heart broken. They worried about me. They still do. They wanted me to forget. To forgive. To get on with my life." Cydya stood and moved closer to the water. "I did get on with my life. I gave myself to my work. I don't know if you care, but you might be proud to know that the kid you used to hang around with is the only Interpol employee of either gender to win two personnel citations in the same year."

"I *am* impressed."

She shrugged. "What can I say? They love me. So, you see, I didn't just sit pining for you."

Was she fishing for an apology? Regardless of the reason, he had dumped her, rejected her, then ignored her, in effect making it appear their mistake was her fault. But he wasn't ready to deal with their past, not until he was certain about her role in the present.

Cydya pulled her wallet out of her purse and popped it open to the pictures. She held one up to the light and he rose to step close for a better look.

"That's Mother and Dad. Their hair's white now, but you'd recognize them."

"I remember the pictures you showed me in Indonesia. And I can see the resemblance."

"Here's my sister and her husband and their kids. She teaches at Vassar. He's coaching."

"Uh-huh."

She flipped to another photo. "Recognize her?"

" 'Course. It's you."

"Look again."

He took the wallet from her and held the picture up to the light. "It's you twenty years ago."

She shook her head. "We didn't wear dresses like that in the eighties, Jordan."

"Another niece?"

"No."

Jordan was uncomfortable with small talk, given the reason for their being in Ecuador. He grew impatient. "I'm out of guesses. If it's not you, it's a relative."

"It's a relative all right. Katrina."

"Pretty name until the hurricane, hm?"

"Pretty girl, don't you think?"

"Beautiful. She looks just like you. Who is she?"

"My daughter."

Jordan grimaced. He couldn't help himself. He handed the wallet back. "So you didn't marry, but you didn't waste any time before bedding down with someone."

What was the matter with him? It was all right for him to sleep with her in a moment of passion and then run, but not all right for that to happen with anyone else?

Cydya accepted the wallet back, then sat with it facing Jordan, open to the beautiful young girl. Her voice was barely audible. "For a brilliant operative, you can be pretty dense. You kept track of the years, Jordan. But you didn't keep track of the months. She goes by Katrina LeMonde, but she might have been named Kirkwood."

Jordan sat and buried his face in his hands. He wanted to see the photo again, but he couldn't bring himself to look. "Are you sure?"

She stood and looked down on him, pushing the wallet into his hands. "How dare you? There was no one after you! I didn't so much as date anyone else! I loved you and you loved me, but you ran. Look what you missed."

"Why didn't you tell me?"

"I wrote you about missing two months, but you weren't opening my letters."

"But I *did* open them! And I read them. I only said I wouldn't. Which letter?"

"The third, but who's counting? You didn't answer any of them."

"Cydya, I never got a third letter!"

He had silenced her, but only momentarily. "And what if you had?"

"I'd have done the right thing."

"The right thing? What would have been the right thing?"

"I would have married you."

She nodded knowingly. "Because I was in trouble."

Jordan blinked back his tears and looked again at his daughter's face. "No!" He was shouting and didn't care if the sound carried to the islands. "Because I loved you! God, forgive me, I never stopped loving you!"

Cydya LeMonde gently took the wallet and laid it on the bench next to her bag. Then she embraced the sobbing father of her child and laid her head on his shoulder.

"I'm sorry, Cydya! I was young and scared, but that was no excuse. And I didn't know. Forgive me, I didn't know."

18

JORDAN AND CYDYA sat by the little lighthouse until midnight, interrupting each other with questions. Jordan was compelled to explain himself, to tell her every emotion he had felt about her from the moment he awoke in Jakarta with remorse over their intimacy until the week before, when Chuck Wallington raised the possibility of her involvement in the terrorism.

Naturally he wanted to know everything about

the daughter he had never known—her tastes, her interests, what she knew of him, what she thought about him. "I can't wait to meet her. Does she want to meet me?"

Cydya shifted. "That's our biggest conflict. We've always gotten on well together, but she's angry with me beyond reason because I will not tell her who you are. I told her that we once loved each other very much and that she was a product of that love, but I also told her that you were now married and that I had no idea whether you had ever told your wife about us. It's been a very, very difficult thing for her, Jordan; yet I just felt I could not do that to you."

"To *me?*"

"When you get to know her, you'll realize that if I'd given her one solid lead, she would have immediately tracked you down and introduced herself."

"One look and I would have known who she was." A low whistle escaped him. "What would I have done?" *And how in the world will I break this to Christa and Ken?*

Cydya told Jordan that she had surprised even herself with her reaction to his rejection. "I had dated before; you knew that. I'd even had disappointments. But somehow, even before that night, I believed we were meant for each other."

"I never knew you felt that way."

"That wasn't something a young woman said

270

back then. I felt it so deeply, was so certain, that learning I was pregnant only confirmed it. I never even considered having anyone but you help raise Katrina."

"You have reason to hate me."

She smiled. "I did for a while. It was a strange, mixed emotion. I loved you so deeply I could hardly face living without you, yet I hated you so much I wanted to punish you. I made Mr. Wallington swear he would never say a word about Katrina."

"*He* knew?"

"It moves me to know that he's a man of his word."

"If he had told me, I'd, I'd—"

"You'd what?"

"What could I have done? I'd have had to tell Rosemary. I would have wanted to see Katrina, to help support her. I can't wait till this is all behind us and I can meet her. I owe you so much. But I need you to believe I didn't know."

"At first I thought you knew and that's why you had dropped me. But Mr. Wallington assured me that if you knew, he would have known, because he could read you like a book."

Jordan nodded, staring into the distance. "And because I never kept anything from him. I can't explain it. I was so sure God was judging me for what we had done, I really believed we should try to forget each other."

"I tried that, too. It never worked."

"It was my fault, Cydya. I see that now. Even if it hadn't been for the fact that you were, you know, that you had Katrina, I can see I was wrong. I've known that for a long time, but I didn't trust myself to admit it to you. What if I had made just one contact to apologize, to see how you were doing, to make sure you were all right? My love for you had been so overwhelming, I was afraid it would rush in on me again. Worse, what if I found you didn't even remember me?"

Cydya laughed. "You, through that gorgeous daughter of ours, have dominated my life, probably more than you would have if we'd been married and you'd been gone all the time."

"Can you find it within yourself to forgive me, Cydya? Nothing can repay what you have endured, but I want to help you with Katrina's education or whatever else she needs."

"Oh, Jordan! This had nothing to do with money or support."

"I know, but I *want* to. I really do."

"There were trade-offs. You suffered too. You had a daughter all these years you never knew."

"You'll never know how close I came to looking you up." He touched her shoulder as if she were a fragile porcelain doll. "We're parents. I can hardly believe that."

She put her hand over his. "You'll love her."

"I do already. Let me see the picture again."

He lifted the photo to the light. Cydya chuckled. "You'll be proud of me. She's devout."

"What do you mean?"

"Just what I said. What do *you* mean when *you* say someone is devout?"

"Tell me."

"You made an impact on me; what can I tell you? I started taking her to church from the beginning. She grew up just like you, Jordan. A believer."

"And you, Cydya?"

"Me too. I told you all about it in the third letter and promised to raise our child as a Christian."

He shook his head. "She's in school? Graduated? Working? What?"

"You won't believe it, Jordan. Graduated early from the American University of Paris, majored in global communications and minored in European and Mediterranean cultures. Somehow she found the time to be involved in the Christian Union and some volunteering club. Fluent in several languages. I don't know where she gets it."

"What's she planning to do with all that?"

"Already doing it. She's the youngest licensed tour guide serving both Greece and Turkey."

"I wish I could leave for Europe tonight."

"We've got a little work to do first, wouldn't you say?"

He nodded. "And I'm tired. Man, am I tired. We'd better get back."

When they reached the sand, he stopped her. "Forgive me. I was wrong."

She avoided his eyes. "You owe me one first."

"What? Anything."

"Tell me you trust me. Would the mother of your own daughter come to kill you?"

"I trust you."

He interpreted her embrace as forgiveness.

When they picked up their keys, the night clerk told Jordan his brother-in-law was there. His eyes met Cydya's and he froze. "I beg your pardon, sir?"

"He said you were expecting him, señor."

"Did you—?"

"*Sí*, I gave him an extra key."

"What did he look like?"

"I'm sorry, señor. Average. Dark hair maybe. Middle age."

"American?"

"*Sí*, I believe so."

"Alone?"

"*Sí.*"

"Upstairs?"

"*Sí.*"

"Ring my room, please."

The clerk dialed and handed Jordan the receiver. No answer.

"I am sorry, señor."

Jordan hurried to the elevator with Cydya right behind him.

"Jordan! What are you going to do?"

"Who else knows I'm here?"

"Only Mr. Wallington. He made the arrangements before he left France. He even wrote the cable for me."

"And no one else saw it?"

"No one but the telegraph office."

They reached Jordan's floor. "Does Interpol know you're here?"

She hesitated. "Yes, but Wallington cleared that, so they know none of the details."

"Then you're here with diplomatic privileges?"

"After a fashion, but—"

"All I want to know is whether you have a weapon."

She hesitated again and Jordan didn't hide his impatience. "Well, yes, I do, Jordan, but don't you? You didn't come through customs. I didn't bring mine to dinner because I thought it would make you suspicious."

"Good thinking." He pulled his from his pocket so she could see it, then hid it inside his jacket. "We need to get yours."

She pushed another button. "I'm on seven, but you know Interpol can't be involved in anything political."

"This isn't Interpol *or* political. This is someone in my room or waiting somewhere with a key until I'm in bed. Now unless you'd like me to go in there alone, I'd appreciate it if you were with me, and armed. When this whole case blows sky-high, you're not going to get in trouble for acting a little outside the bounds of your own agency."

It didn't seem she was gone long enough to change, but within minutes she returned to the elevators wearing a top and slacks with a bulge in the right front pocket. "Sorry, it's just a .22."

"Better than nothing." They stepped out at his floor again. "Stay back and let me know if anybody else comes along. I'm going to knock. If I get no answer, I'll use the key. If the door isn't bolted or chained, I'll move in quickly, weapon up. You want to follow or wait and listen?"

"Follow."

"I'll pass the bathroom, immediately on the left, and cover the main room. You've got the bathroom."

Ten feet from his door, she dropped back. He knocked, his ear to the door. Cydya moved closer. He moved away from the door and reached to unlock it. It opened half an inch. No bolt, no chain.

Jordan crouched before the door, and Cydya stepped directly behind him. He kicked the door open and it smacked the wall and flew back, forcing Cydya to fend it off. Jordan bounced past the bathroom in a crouch, his .45 in front of him.

"Chuck, you dog! I could have killed you!"

Wallington sat on the bed with his back against the headboard, hands behind his head. He wore street clothes and was barefoot. "You wouldn't shoot an unarmed man, would you?" He smiled at Cydya. "Hello, dear."

She collapsed in a chair.

"Why didn't you answer the phone or the door, Chuck? Like to scare me to death."

"Gotta keep my troops in shape. Not many of you left."

"So you know about Roscoe and Pauly?"

Wallington nodded, looking weary. "Al-Qaeda has Diego and his multinational task in their back pocket, and Michala ordered those hits personally."

"I want Diego, Chuck."

"You know if we can get by without any shooting—"

"But if he does us the favor of resisting—"

"Shut the door, Jordan. We've got work to do. I'm bunkin' with you, and we've got an early wake-up call tomorrow."

Jordan gestured at Cydya. "We're beat, Chuck. She traveled most of the day, and I've been up since before dawn. I caught a siesta early this evening, but that's it."

"This won't take long. Let me spread some stuff on the table." Jordan and Cydya joined him. "I know you didn't expect to see me, but we were wrong about Stu's message. Or maybe he was wrong. Anyway, the twentieth is no meeting date. That's the day Diego and his people truck nuclear warheads from a ship to an airport to fly them into the States and equip those MiGs. The Maldonado meeting was today. Everything's set for . . . well, we're after midnight now, so everything's set for tomorrow. Twenty-eight, twenty-nine hours from now."

"How do you know all this?"

Chuck sat back, looking self-satisfied. "Wasn't easy. I staked out Diego's place in Frankfurt a few days ago and recognized one of his security men. He's been loyal to Diego for two years and apparently has won his trust. His name is Jamsheed Majeed. That should ring a bell with you, Cydya."

"Al-Qaeda and one of the FBI's ten most wanted. Interpol thought he was in the Far East."

"So did I, but it was him all right. I followed him home, knowing he would notice me. He's one of the best, very elusive. I employed a couple of local contacts, and we paid him a visit, threatening to bring him back to the States. We made a deal."

"You and Majeed?"

"Yep. He's got a twenty-year sentence hanging over his head for international flight to avoid prosecution. It's automatic. He sets foot in the U.S., twenty years minimum, no parole."

"He couldn't have acquiesced without a fight."

Chuck nodded. "Probably would have killed me if I hadn't had help. This is one strong boy. The three of us wrestled him to the ground and dragged him to his room, and there we came to an amicable settlement. I told him I'd see to it that he served no more than seven years if he told Diego he had to get home to his father's funeral and that he recommended his oldest and most trusted bodyguard as his replacement. Yours truly. It was risky because there are a lot of ways for him to warn Diego now. But he'll be incommunicado for a few weeks anyway."

"You used an alias with Diego?"

"Sure. Good thing, too. I wasn't with him a day and a half before he spat out his contempt for the NSA and Stanley Stuart, who tried to pawn Chuck Wallington off on him. 'Do you know who that is?' he asks me. 'Who?' I say. He says, 'Only the best friend of the guy who met with Stuart, the one we tried to kill in London.' He blamed that screwup on Felix. A couple of days later, he informed the group happily that 'Felix got Wallington.' I had wondered how long it would take that news to get to him."

Cydya leaned forward. "So he's convinced you're dead."

"While I'm actually one of his three body-guards. Don't you love it? We rotate, forty-eight hours on, forty-eight hours off. Since I'm off, he sent me on ahead to the port city in the Yucatán Peninsula to make sure everything is in place. I have to be there when he arrives at midnight tomorrow to assure him everything is on schedule."

Chuck smoothed out a hand-drawn map and turned it right-side up for Jordan and Cydya. "What looks like a Mexican government ship is expected before dawn on the twentieth. It's actually an al-Qaeda vessel bringing more warheads and MiG-23s from Las Martinas, Cuba. It will dock at the harbor in Progreso on the Campeche Bank of the Yucatán Peninsula. Then, just before sunrise, a truck will leave the ship—"

"Wait a second; the truck is coming with the ship?"

"Right. From there it's about thirty miles to Mérida, where there's an airport with a runway long enough to get a jet off the ground toward Alabama. Look at this, Jordan." Chuck pulled another map from his pile. "See how short that flight will be, straight into the United States from the peninsula? We're farther than that from Yucatán right now."

"How are we supposed to get there, and what are we supposed to do?"

"Our job is to stall them. I'd like to see that cargo stay right in the harbor, but if they get to the airport, the plane must not take off. I'm in touch with the only man from the Pentagon who trusts me implicitly, and he has the power to dispatch military aid at a moment's notice. I want to wait to give him all the details until we're certain that ship is on its way to Progreso. By the time we get there, Felix could have found out that I'm with

Diego. Or Diego could find out who I really am and kill me in a second. Felix would too, but as long as I'm inaccessible, he'll just try to stifle me by spreading stories all over Washington that I've gone crazy and used you without permission and whatever else he can think of. All he needs is to keep us from interfering until they can get that plane in the air. If for any reason I have trouble getting military help in time, we have to ensure that plane stays on the ground. Once airborne, it's as good as in the U.S. We can have the Air Force combing Alabama, but my guess is Felix will hurry things along by telling al-Qaeda I've infiltrated. Then they just green-light an attack from within our own borders."

Jordan straightened and stretched. "You don't want the truck off the ship before the Air Force gets there, assuming the Navy doesn't have a battleship close enough to help."

"You got it."

"If they do get the truck off the boat, how are they going to get nuclear warheads on board a plane in a major airport?"

"You forget, the Mexican government is in on this."

"What's in it for them?"

"I'd hate to guess. Oil, probably. Whatever the reason, they're in this one up to their elbows."

"So what's your plan? How do we keep the truck from getting off the ship?"

"Well, it's a surprisingly small operation, because obviously al-Qaeda and the Mexican government want no attention drawn to it. It's supposed to look like a routine dock, unload, and transport, from the ship to the road to the airport to the jet and into the air. But the route is right through the radar gap—our soft underbelly, as Felix himself has called it. So plans? I've got a few, none of them pleasant. Because even though Diego and his buddies total only a half dozen, including me, Mexican military and governmental support and al-Qaeda backup people exist all along the route. We have to strike quickly to stall the process.

"There are only three of us bodyguards, but it'll be my turn to stick close to Diego. He likes me. I have suggested to him that I be alone with him in the cab of the truck. My thought is that I would wait until he's maneuvering the vehicle into position to leave the ship, then disarm him and, in effect, hold him hostage."

Cydya squinted. "Of course he carries a piece."

"An Uzi and sometimes an automatic. But I'm counting on his being nervous about driving a rig loaded with that many warheads. At first no one will understand the delay, but as they approach, I'll threaten to kill him or detonate the warheads."

Jordan walked to the window and looked down on the quiet city. "I don't like it."

"That's what we're here for, JK. Poke holes. Tell me where it's faulty."

"You don't know how long you'll have to hold him hostage. What if it turns out to be hours?"

"I can handle hours."

"What if it's twelve hours?"

"That's where you come in. I'll be in command if I have his weapons and control of the truck. I can make demands. You two will constitute my demands. We can spell each other."

Cydya leaned back in her chair and stared at the ceiling. "I don't know either, Mr. Wallington. It goes against conventional wisdom to try to control a situation from the middle rather than from the outside. You know you'll be immediately surrounded by military and al-Qaeda and their multinational force."

"I'll have enough firepower to wipe the Yucatán Peninsula off the map. Besides, how would we control this situation from the periphery when there are only three of us and they have the nuclear power?"

Jordan thrust his hands deep into his pockets. "You're going to show us where to station ourselves?"

Chuck nodded. "I don't know how carefully the area will be sealed off. It's so hush-hush, I assume the military is counting on Diego and his people to not be too visible. That's the irony of it. This begins and ends with al-Qaeda, and you won't see a turban within a hundred miles."

"That could work to our advantage. But I have a bigger question for you, Chuck—one you've asked me for years. Are you prepared to die?"

"Well, it's not on my to-do list."

"What if someone calls your bluff?"

"I wouldn't be bluffing."

"So someone who knows they can't shoot at you without risking a nuclear explosion approaches the truck. What do you do? Kill Diego?"

"If necessary."

"And suppose they keep coming?"

"With Diego eliminated, I would shoot to kill them."

"And if there are more than you have ammunition for?"

"I would expect help from you and Cydya."

"Dozens rush the truck, and you have threatened to detonate the warheads. How would you do that?"

"With a grenade into the truck bed."

"Finally, Chuck, would you really do it? Sacrifice your own life?"

"For the future of the free world? In a heartbeat."

Cydya spoke. "Even if it means having to sacrifice who knows how many innocent lives in the Yucatán?"

"Justice sometimes carries an awful price. You think Bush wouldn't have shot down United 93 on 9/11 if it had breached Washington airspace? The

Mexican government is responsible for its citizens. They put their heads on the block when they agreed to help al-Qaeda invade the United States. The Islamo-fascists would not hesitate to sacrifice innocent civilians for their cause. Otherwise, why MiGs in Alabama in the first place?

"Any one of us could wind up with the blood of innocents on our hands. If we're not ready, we'd better back out right now."

Jordan saw anxiety in Cydya's eyes. "I'd better walk her to her room, Chuck."

He nodded. "Before you go, I want to know: could *you* detonate?"

Jordan's mind was flooded. Yes, he would give his life and even sacrifice civilian lives in defense of his country. But in his mind's eye were friends and acquaintances with whom he had never pursued the great mysteries of life and God and the hereafter. He bore real fears about their welfare.

And there was the daughter he had never met. Yet what kind of world would she live in if al-Qaeda brought America to its knees?

"I could detonate."

Wallington turned to Cydya. "And you?"

Her voice was monotone. "I could. But don't ask me to sleep well tonight."

19

AT BREAKFAST, CHUCK sketched Progreso harbor for Jordan and Cydya and recommended they split up but stay within sight of each other. "It will be impossible for me to communicate with either of you, even through signals. So be close when Diego brings the truck into position for off-loading."

Cydya was studying the map. "And you say that'll be just before dawn."

"Right. And there are checkpoints along the way where he is expected. If he doesn't arrive, military personnel will start heading for Progreso to investigate."

Cydya drummed a pencil on the tabletop. "I still have a lot of questions, Mr. Wallington. I hope you don't mind."

"Are you kidding? If I had a choice, I'd back away from this one. Too many variables. Too many people lost already. Too much evidence that these people will crush anyone in their way. By all means, let's hear your questions."

"When do you make your Pentagon contact?"

"My man knows this is a legitimate threat to the United States. We've agreed on a fairly new code system that has so far been used without detection. It's quick and can be communicated orally to

286

his scrambler phone. After I check on everything for Diego, and just before he arrives, I call the Pentagon."

Jordan raised his eyebrows. "And they send in the cavalry?"

Chuck smiled. "A ton of firepower will be nearby. The code name for the operation, in the event the cavalry might otherwise mistake you for the enemy, is 'Crimson Tide.'"

Cydya ran a hand through her hair. "The crimson tide on the Campeche Bank could be our blood."

Chuck shifted in his seat. "What would the late Bear Bryant and his boys have done if they'd known al-Qaeda was in their backyard?"

Cydya doodled. "What if Diego arrives early and you can't get away to make your call? Should you give one of us the information so we can make it?"

"I'm reluctant to put it on paper. If you were caught with it . . ."

She nodded.

Chuck pulled a note from his pocket. "I'm going early. I've booked you on a late morning flight. Both your weapons should be in Cydya's luggage, Jordan, just in case. I booked you under the Blanc alias, but you don't have any Blanc ID, do you?"

"No. And that reminds me: you wouldn't have an extra clip or two for a .45 automatic?"

"How many do you need?"

"Better give me two. I've got seven rounds left."

"Hope you don't need any of them. When you get there, see if you can find clothes that will allow you to blend in. If you look like foreigners nosing around the harbor, you may spend the night in jail."

Cydya stood. "Will we see you between the time we get there and when you're in the truck with Diego?"

"Not likely."

"So we won't know whether you made your call or if everything is all right."

"Nobody said it was going to be easy."

She shook her head. "It looks like suicide."

"Got any better ideas?"

Jordan saw fear in her eyes. Bravado would have worried him.

Finally she spoke. "I do get the feeling that we're going to be doing a lot of hanging around, waiting for action."

Jordan pursed his lips. "And when that action comes, we can only hope it's orchestrated by you."

Chuck sighed. "We worked together how many years? You know things rarely go by the book. If I can't call the Pentagon, if my cover is blown, someone still has to stop those warheads from leaving the ground in Mérida. That someone is you, and how you do it is up to you. It won't be easy, and it doesn't have to be sophisticated. We have no more help and no more time."

"What would you do, Chuck? Worst-case scenario."

"If the truck left the dock and headed toward the airport? I'd do whatever was necessary. Everything's out the window at that point. Shoot at it, jump in front of it, kill the driver, threaten to blow it up, blow it up, whatever. Once that truck pulls into the cargo bay of the jet and gets out over the Gulf of Mexico, al-Qaeda as good as has a beachhead on American soil."

Just before Chuck left for the airport, he raised another issue. "There's a problem almost as big as the operation, and, Jordan, you should know what it is from your poli-sci background."

"The U.S. may have to take overt military action, which they won't be able to hide from the press and the public."

"But they must do it without revealing that the MiGs are already in the States. Our government blockading a Mexican harbor where they've found nuclear warheads is one thing. Imagine the ramifications for U.S.–Mexico relations. But none of us will ever be able to tell a soul about the MiGs. If we somehow pull this off, it'll be the quietest, most anonymous thing we've ever done. People in four countries will disavow any knowledge of it."

• • •

Hours later, as Cydya and Jordan waited to board their flight, she looked pensive. "You realize that by this time tomorrow, they could be shipping us home in boxes?"

He felt uncomfortable around her. Despite her youthfulness, she had a depth and maturity not part of his memories. It was as if he were talking to the aunt or the mother of the girl of his dreams. He wondered how he would feel in Katrina's presence.

"Cydya, if this mission fails, they won't find enough pieces to identify either of us."

"Comforting. Two decades apart, a few hours to mend fences, and we exit as kamikazes."

Jordan wasn't a sentimentalist, but he found some macabre attraction to spending his last hours on earth with a woman he'd never really stopped loving. He had lost Rosemary and seen three friends die, all because a veteran agent trusted Chuck enough to tell his protégé the darkest secret in American history. Now death seemed a haven.

And yet, there was Katrina. Christa. Ken. Cydya. Whether he'd ever get an opportunity to say to his children what needed to be said was in God's hands now. But if he died without somehow impressing upon Cydya what she had meant to him, it would be no one's fault but his own.

"When I worshiped you in Indonesia, I thought you were too good for me."

"Oh, Jordan."

"Really. You would turn twenty-one while I was still eighteen. You'd been around." She laughed. "At least compared to me, you had. I saw you as an adult."

She stared out the window, watching baggage handlers. "You make me feel so old."

"That's my point. It's seeing you now that's such an education. Back then I hoped one day to grow up the way you had. But seeing you last night, I realized that you have grown up. You're a beautiful person, and at twenty, you were still a young girl."

She turned to face him. "There's nothing like the morning sun on the equator to expose every flaw. But not yours. No lines on the face. Wish I could say the same. I knew you wouldn't age. You were a youthful eighteen, and you look just as I imagined."

"Cydya, do you think you could ever trust me again?"

She didn't answer immediately, which cut him deeply. "Fair question. As I told you last night, I believed we were meant for each other, and I lost out. I was not meant for someone else."

"But I broke it off in the worst way."

"You were eighteen. Eventually I came to realize that the same wonder you brought to our relationship was what made you react the way you did. You were made that way."

291

"A scoundrel?"

"It was just that to you everything was black or white. Either we were in love or we weren't. Either I was interested in you or I wasn't. Something was either right or wrong. And if someone did something wrong, he paid for it."

"But I didn't mean to punish you. I know it must have looked that way, but I felt responsible. I had taken advantage of you. And the only appropriate penalty was to lose you."

Their flight was announced and they stood in line, whispering. "Don't misunderstand me, Jordan, but I need to clarify something in light of the fact that you are still mourning your wife. When I said I believed we were meant for each other and that I never stopped loving you, I'm aware that the 'you' I'm referring to does not exist anymore. I believed all that about the eighteen-year-old I was in love with. I still believe it was true about that Jordan Kirkwood. But I want to be careful not to imply that those feelings apply to the current Jordan Kirkwood." She tapped his chest. "You've lived longer since I saw you last than you had up till then. So despite that you're the father of my child, I don't really know you."

It was the kindest put-down he'd ever heard. "My question was whether you thought you could ever trust me again."

She took a deep breath. "If the forty-one-year-old is the same man he was at eighteen, I confess I'd be wary."

The line was hardly moving, the attendant carefully checking every boarding pass.

"I'd like to prove myself, Cydya."

"Well, I'm trusting you with my life tomorrow."

After an awkward silence, Jordan asked Cydya about her experience with weapons.

"I've fired three times in the line of duty."

"Ever kill anyone?"

"Almost, once. Wouldn't have made much difference. He was murdered later in prison."

"Yes, it would have. Believe me, it would have made a difference to you."

Jordan had come closer to telling her that he'd killed someone than he had ever come to telling Rosemary.

Finally they reached the gate. "Ms. LeMonde, is Mr. Blanc traveling with you?"

Jordan jumped in. "*Oui.* Problem?"

They were led to a small room off the main corridor where a chunky, dark man in a skinny tie leaned over the table and stared at Cydya with tiny, black eyes. "Miss LeMonde, in your suitcase we found a loaded .22-caliber Smith & Wesson and forty rounds of ammunition. We also found a Colt .45-caliber automatic, loaded with a partial clip of seven rounds and two additional full clips containing nine rounds each. Do you have a license to carry them?"

Cydya produced a document.

"Interpol. Customarily, you would have diplomatic immunity. And you should know that weapons must be unloaded for transport."

"My mistake."

"Further, especially in your position, you must know that firearms must be separately screened for transport."

"An oversight. I apologize."

"And you, Mr. Blanc, are you also with Interpol?"

Cydya raised a hand. "Excuse me, sir. Was there a problem with Monsieur Blanc's luggage?"

"No, ma'am."

"Then I suggest we concentrate on the problem at hand. I am in your country on official business and prefer to exercise my right to transport those weapons to Yucatán. I'll be happy to unload them if you prefer."

"What I prefer is irrelevant, as is your diplomatic privilege in this case. The government of Ecuador is cooperating with Mexico in not allowing any weapons to be flown out of our country into Mexico until further notice. No exceptions."

"But—"

"I am sorry, ma'am. You may file a grievance, or we will be happy to refund the cost of your flight."

"How will the weapons be returned to me?"

"We will ship them to whatever address you provide."

She snapped a business card on the table. "At your expense, I presume."

"I'm sorry, no."

On the plane, Cydya worried aloud about Wallington's guns. Jordan shook his head. "He'll have access to Diego's arsenal. You and I are going to have to find something on the black market. Anything reliable will be hundreds of dollars. How are you fixed?"

"Euros and pesos. Couple of hundred dollars' worth."

"Credit cards?"

"American Express."

"Perfect. What's the limit?"

"Ten thousand euros."

"A thousand in cash should be plenty, but we aren't going to have a lot of time."

They both slept during the flight and awoke to a blistering day in Mérida. Jordan felt gamy as he exited the plane, and they took a taxi all the way north to Progreso. They were deposited six blocks south of the harbor in front of a cheap hotel.

The place smelled like it looked. Drunks loitered in the lobby, where an ancient television carried a soundless soccer match. "Two rooms, top floor, two nights. American dollars."

The clerk, who had been leering at Cydya, lit up. "Two room. Two night. Two hundred dollar."

As they'd choreographed it, Jordan and Cydya

turned to leave. The clerk chirped. "One-fifty! One hundred!" Jordan turned and slapped the money on the counter.

Cydya had to be exhausted, and the weather was not unlike what they had endured in Indonesia half their lives ago. Her hair was moist and matted, her blouse wet in back. As the highest-ranking woman in the history of Interpol, she had to be used to nice things, comfortable accommodations, even luxuries. Yet Jordan heard not a word of complaint.

Cydya insisted they not wait to replace their weapons. He agreed. "You go class; I'll go trash."

A few minutes later Jordan met her in the hall. She looked way too good to be coming out of that dive and drew a lot of stares. Jordan looked right and left. "Modern buildings, maybe a hotel or two, to the west. Best bet for a bank. Get two thousand American. I'm going the other way, looking for a sombrero and some grubbies. Secondhand stuff so it looks like we've lived in it. What do you want?"

"Anything. Get a fix on my size."

He measured her with his eyes. "Don't mind if I do." That elicited a smile, and he wondered if he would ever see one from her again. "Back here in an hour. If you're late, I'll come looking for you. If I'm late, stay put."

He found a place that sold clothes so old and shabby that the prices were mere pesos each. Fat women in faded dresses milled about, children scampering around them. They picked through the stuff and haggled with the lone clerk. There was no cash register, just an oversize shoe box stuffed with bills and coins. Security came in the form of a German shepherd mix that slept at the foot of the counter.

Jordan started with shoes, trying a couple of pairs of all-fabric slip-ons. He picked through the women's shoes, not knowing where to begin. They were so cheap he chose three of different sizes, hoping to get lucky. He found khaki slacks and a top for Cydya. A deep burgundy corduroy beret topped it off.

For himself he chose work pants; a boxy, plain, oversize pullover shirt; and a sombrero that rode low on his forehead. He also grabbed two cloth shoulder bags and piled the stuff on the counter, causing the dog to open one eye. The clerk poked through the merchandise and said something about pesos.

Jordan held up a twenty.

The clerk beamed. "Ah, American dollar." He reached for it, but Jordan shook his head. "Nineteen." He shook again. "Eighteen." No. "Seventeen?" No. Jordan shook his head more slowly each time so as not to insult the man. Finally the clerk thrust out his palm. "Fifteen! That's it!" Jordan gave him sixteen, which brought a grateful grin.

He hurried back to his room and changed. He

didn't have enough cash for weapons yet, but he wanted to scout the possibilities anyway. He walked a mile south into a section where drunks and malcontents hung out. When he saw the store, he knew he had found at least the entrée to the type of weapons he wanted. In the window were a hundred knives, from daggers to switch-blades. An old Mexican with thick, black, horn-rimmed glasses smiled at Jordan as he admired the display.

Jordan stepped inside and looked at small-bore rifles and cheap handguns. Horn-rims spoke only Spanish, so Jordan made clear to him through hand signals that he was looking for two much bigger, much better handguns. The man shrugged. Jordan smiled. "American dollars."

The man smiled too. He handed Jordan a piece of paper and a pencil. Jordan carefully printed *.45*, *.38*, and *.357 Magnum*. For good measure, he also drew a hand grenade but wrote nothing next to it. The man went to the back and came out a few minutes later. He had crossed out *.45* and had written *$1,200* next to each of the other two guns. Next to the grenade he wrote *$150*.

Jordan crossed out the number and cut the prices in half and the grenade by two thirds. The man went in the back and returned, nodding and smiling. Jordan totaled the figures and wrote the new figure—$1,250. He took the man's wrist and pointed to five o'clock on his watch.

The man nodded, led him back to the door, and pointed upstairs, then back at his watch.

At the hotel, Jordan knocked on Cydya's door. "Got somethin' for ya." He showed her the clothes. "How'd you do?" She fanned out the large bills and he scooped them up. "Good work. You get your choice, a .357 Magnum or a .38."

She shrugged. "Both heavy and ugly. I've practiced more with a .38."

He told her of the arrangement and that he didn't want her to go with him. "Bad neighborhood."

"Oh yeah, I'm safer here alone." She picked through the clothes. "Lovely."

"Thought you'd like 'em. Just four hundred dollars at Saks."

"Jordan, I don't need to tell you that going upstairs at that place could be playing right into their hands. They play their cards right, they wind up with your money without coming across with the guns."

"We're on the same page."

"Be careful."

He skipped down the stairs, doing what he was born to do. No one in twenty years had ever told him to be careful. It was a good thing she had.

20

AT THE DOOR of the knife shop, Jordan stood in the shadows. He was not going upstairs, even if the owner accompanied him. He knew he was being watched and wondered how many on the street were aware of the gringo with hundreds of American dollars in his pocket.

Many slept in doorways—or were they not sleeping? The shop was closed for siesta, but Horn-rims had agreed to the appointment. Jordan kept an elbow clamped tightly over his shoulder bag. Five minutes. Then ten. He would give Horn-rims three more minutes.

Two men came up the street on the other side— one weaving, nearly falling; the other cold sober. They crossed midblock, the sober one falling in behind the drunk. As they passed, the drunk stumbled into Jordan, grabbing the strap of his shoulder bag as if to steady himself. As the loop slipped from Jordan's shoulder, the sober one joined the fracas.

Jordan ran his thumb up the strap and over his head so his neck was between the loop and the bag. He shot his fist past the face of the phony drunk and drew it back, elbowing him just above the nose. The man went down and didn't move.

Jordan saw terror in the eyes of the other and didn't want to disappoint him. He backed away, so Jordan rushed him and drove his foot into the man's knee. He helped up his partner and limped away. Jordan leaped around to face any surprise attackers but found just dozens of pairs of sleepy, curious eyes. Within seconds, Horn-rims appeared from upstairs.

He waved Jordan up, but Jordan shook his head and pointed to the ground. Horn-rims rubbed his fingers with his thumb. Jordan shook his head again and shaped his thumb and forefinger like a gun. Horn-rims went back inside and soon returned, holding open a bulging paper bag. Jordan pulled the .38 out just far enough to point into the chamber, signaling he needed ammunition. Horn-rims made the money sign again. Jordan flashed the bills. The man jogged upstairs a final time and returned with two boxes of bullets, one for each gun. After the transaction, the man extended his hand. Jordan ignored it.

Jordan and Cydya went for a walk just before dark. "Let's eat light and safe."

She sounded wistful. "I'm not even hungry. I won't sleep, either."

"Same here. Stay in your clothes and be ready to move."

They were within one street of the harbor. She stopped and looked between buildings. "It's really quite lovely, isn't it?" The sun sent orange and pink streaks across the water. The temperature dropped, but it was still humid. Jordan took Cydya's arm and led her north to the far right end of the harbor.

"I'll be up here. You'll be west about three hundred yards at the other end of where the ship will dock, Chuck's guessing sometime between four and five in the morning. Just before dawn, Diego will pull the truck to the ramp."

Cydya had picked up the pace. "They wouldn't lower the ramp until they were ready to go, would they?"

"Probably not."

"And they're definitely driving the truck off, not craning it?"

"I wouldn't crane a truck with that cargo, would you?"

She shook her head. "The lowering of the ramp should be our cue, then."

Jordan led her closer to where the ship would dock. "We'll have to play it by ear. I doubt we'll be able to see Diego or Chuck in the truck while it's on board. The ramp will probably be lowered as Diego is getting the truck in position, and that's when Chuck will make his move."

"How will we know?"

"There would be a delay. The ramp will come down, but the truck won't. Then I would expect some announcement from either Diego or Chuck with instructions for everybody. We'll stand by until he needs us."

They strolled within two hundred feet of the dock. "Jordan, what if Mr. Wallington isn't able to make his call? If he doesn't, the rest of this is meaningless. We can slow, stall, stop the truck, kill ourselves making sure the warheads are detonated here instead of in the States. But unless the Pentagon is notified, the only people who knew what was going on will be gone."

Jordan nodded. "If he can't make the call, it would make more sense to abort his plan of taking Diego hostage and just get in touch with the Pentagon as soon as he can."

"But if the truck pulls off that ship and toward the airport, what are we to assume? That Mr. Wallington has dumped the plan because we have no military backup?"

"The way it stands now, if the truck makes the ramp, our job is to stop it at all costs."

She turned to face him. "Then I'd better quit trying to second-guess Mr. Wallington. We'll have to assume he makes the call. If he doesn't, we're dead anyway."

They walked in silence toward the sunset, then south toward the hotel. Jordan stopped at a food cart and watched a man hand-making flour and corn tortillas with meat sauce. Jordan gave him American dollars and reached for his own tortilla. He held it directly over the flames for as long as he could stand it. That would take care of any bacteria. He dipped the steaming dough into the meat sauce and handed it to Cydya.

"Just what I needed."

"Me too." Jordan licked his fingers, praying this wasn't their last supper.

At her door, Jordan told Cydya he would knock at three thirty. "That should give us about six hours' rest, if not sleep. Ready?"

She gave a closed-mouth smile. "No. But I'll be there." He squeezed her shoulders, then waited until he heard her lock and chain the door before heading for his own room, two doors down.

Jordan arranged his room so he could simply rise at three twenty-five, fill his shoulder bag and pockets, and head to the communal bathroom. He stretched out on his back and put his hands behind his head. Looking at his watch, he told himself when to get up.

He hadn't realized how bone weary he was. His elbow ached from where he had coldcocked the drunk, but otherwise he felt fit. He ran the plan over and over in his mind, sending Cydya up the street at the west end of the harbor, making his approach from the east. How many people would be out and about that early in the morning?

His sleep was restless. He didn't dream as much as mix and match the images of the day. At two o'clock he bolted upright at a sound. He staggered to the door. There it was again. A shout, a thud, a door banging. He ripped at the chain lock and grabbed a pistol as he lurched into the hall.

Under the faint light of a single bulb he saw Cydya's follow-through as she karate-kicked a man over the railing. He landed with a hard flop halfway down the stairs and rolled slowly to the landing. Jordan bounded after him and held the barrel of the .357 to his temple. Bleary-eyed and reeking of booze, the man repeated a Spanish phrase over and over.

Jordan looked to Cydya. She was shaking her head. "He's saying, 'Wrong floor, wrong floor.'"

Jordan helped him up, guiding him to the room on that floor in the same spot as Cydya's. His key fit. When Jordan returned, Cydya was standing with her back to the wall, one hand across her stomach. He touched her shoulder. "You all right?"

"Scared me. Kept trying the doorknob and the key, and when they didn't work, he banged and hollered. When I peeked out past the chain, he kicked and the casing broke. I reacted instinctively."

"And wonderfully."

She shrugged. "You do what you have to do. Poor guy. If he hadn't been drunk, that tumble would have killed him."

"He won't even remember it in the morning."

"I won't sleep now. And look at this door." The casing was in splinters.

"Put your valuables in my room. I'll stretch out in here with my gun, and pity the next drunk who gets the wrong room."

"Don't be silly. You're not going to sleep either, are you?" He shook his head. "Then let's just talk. It may be the last chance we get."

He went back and gathered up his money and munitions. In her tiny room, she sat on the bed with her back to the wall and he sat on the floor, his back to the door.

Cydya made a clicking sound. "Do you remember one of the first things you ever said to me?"

"You mean the very first? At the airport in Jakarta? I was overwhelmed, I remember that. Thought your name was unusual, of course. What?"

"You said you felt grundy!" That made her laugh aloud. He nodded, smiling, and she laughed until tears came. At first she still smiled through her tears, but then she covered her face and great sobs wracked her body. Jordan stood awkwardly, not knowing whether she wanted to be comforted or left alone. He sat next to her and put his arm around her, holding her for half an hour until she seemed to doze. Then he stood carefully, laid her down, and returned to the floor by the door. He glanced at his watch before lowering his head to his chest and closing his eyes.

At three twenty-five his head popped up. He

licked his lips and stretched. Standing, he folded his arms and leaned over, touching his elbows to the floor with his legs straight. One in a thousand men could do it.

He bent over Cydya, put one hand on her head and the other on her shoulder. "Zero hour."

Her eyes were puffy and dark, but she forced a smile. Five minutes later, weapons in their shoulder bags, they tiptoed down the stairs. They walked four blocks to where they would part. He turned to her. "Remember, we're just on our way to work, whatever. Not tense, not interested, the type no one notices. Let's not get closer than a hundred yards from each other unless something's going down."

She turned toward her route. Jordan caught the elbow of her khaki top and turned her around. "Cydya. I've loved you all my life."

She wrapped her arms around his neck and whispered in his ear. "The next place we see each other might be in heaven. I have you to thank for that."

He chuckled as she pulled away. "For making sure you get there, or for getting you there early?"

Jordan watched until she turned. No one else was on the street. He wandered, forcing himself to relax, though every sense was raw, every fiber afire. He was glad they had come early. What a nightmare if the ship had already been docked when they arrived, the ramp down, the truck gone.

He meandered to the harbor road and casually looked west. Cydya sat on a bench along the bus route, almost as if napping. She looked small and fragile, but she had booted that drunk over the railing.

At four o'clock Jordan imagined the sky was lighter, but it was only wishful thinking. He also thought he saw lights on the horizon. He walked a quarter mile over the next several minutes, trying to will the clock to move.

This assignment had death written all over it. His wife was gone. His house was gone. His uncle's house, a refuge since he was a child, was gone. And what had he done to the only other woman he had ever loved? Run when she needed him the most. Now he might be leading her to her death.

Those *were* lights on the horizon. Faint, tiny, distant, but red and green and white against the sky. A great, ponderous ship, larger than usual for this part of the harbor, crept higher on the gray horizon, still miles from shore. The sky was changing now. Soon the horizon would glow with the lightest of pastels.

Jordan didn't know how to estimate the time of arrival of the ship. He reached the harbor road again while the ship was still at least a mile out, and he noticed a jeep pulling in near the dock. He could see a driver and three passengers. The driver emerged and began working at the gangplank, swinging it far over the dock, but leaving it suspended. Apparently he would lower it to the deck when the ship docked. He had some trouble with the gangplank but received neither help nor seemingly even interest from the other three in the jeep.

Jordan walked south three blocks and looked west at every intersection. As far as he could tell, no police or military personnel were in place to escort the truck. Obviously, Machala Diego thought his operation was the best-kept secret in Mexico.

Soon the ship appeared huge and clear against the dawn sky. Jordan heard the great engines and watched as the craft began maneuvering toward dock. This took several minutes, during which he also kept track of the men in the jeep. All four were now in the vehicle.

Finally the ship drew to within a hundred feet of the dock. Jordan wanted to head west on the harbor road, but not until he was sure the attention of the men in the jeep was fully directed toward the craft.

As the ship neared the moorings, a small crew appeared on deck and began securing lines. All four men emerged from the jeep. One was Chuck. Jordan transferred the .357 from his bag to his pocket and turned west on the harbor road.

Chuck walked strangely, hands behind his back. And Jordan suddenly recognized one of the others. Tall and dark and gangly—Felix. It couldn't be! Chuck had thought Felix would be waiting on the other end, in Alabama, protecting his identity. What a shock it must have been for both when they saw each other!

Jordan's mind raced. Had Chuck made his Pentagon contact? If he had, did Diego and Felix know? No way would they spare him after eliminating all the others. Felix must have really believed in Machala Diego to brazenly show up for the delivery.

The crew was on the bridge, their eyes on the foursome nearing the gangplank. All but Chuck had to be armed. The plan was out the window, and Jordan had no way of knowing whether Chuck had made his Pentagon connection. His priority now was to protect Chuck. If only he could somehow let him know he was there.

Within a hundred feet of the dock he could hear the truck engine. Someone from the crew drove the truck around from the cargo hold and left it idling in the middle of the ship near the ramp. The foursome from the gangplank boarded the ship, but only the short, slim, dark-haired one peeled off. That had to be Diego. He slid behind the wheel of the truck and slammed the door.

The other three—the driver of the jeep, Felix, and Chuck—moved past the truck and continued around the other side of the ship. Jordan had to get there. He wouldn't worry about the truck until the wide metal ramp was lowered to the dock.

He had to take the chance. With Diego in the truck and no one else on deck, he broke into a sprint across the gangplank, trying to stay low. The ship's engines and the idling truck covered the sound of his steps, but halfway across he felt the ship's engines shut down and the vibration of someone running behind him. Cydya.

He pointed to the right, intending to send her around the other side of the ship. He would go left and directly in front of the truck. He wouldn't deal with Diego unless forced to. He couldn't risk a shot at the truck. His best hope was that Diego would not see him until he passed directly in front of him. By then it would be too late to stop Jordan from getting around the other side to Chuck. If he and Cydya arrived at about the same time, they'd have a chance at saving Chuck's life.

From the bridge above him he heard the first cry. Military. Two Mexicans, both quickly removing weapons snapped in holsters at their sides. Jordan held out a hand to stop Cydya as she approached from behind. They stared up at the Mexicans, but now there was only one. He held his weapon in both hands, aiming for Jordan's head.

Jordan's voice was hoarse. "Amigo!"

But before the one on the bridge could answer, the second appeared at the ship end of the gang-plank.

Cydya kept her voice to a whisper. "Should we jump overboard?"

Jordan shook his head as the Mexican approached, weapon trained on them as well.

Jordan stole a glance at her. "Your weapon hidden?"

"They'll find it easily enough."

"Draw it."

"Are you crazy?"

"Easy, as if you're going to surrender it."

The cry from the bridge had stopped all activity. Diego sat in the truck, engine warming. With the ramp up, there was nowhere for him to go. The jeep driver, Felix, and Chuck had disappeared around the other side of the deck. Jordan was certain they wouldn't hesitate to use Chuck to get rid of him and Cydya.

The Mexican barked orders. Cydya translated. "He wants us to back slowly off the gangplank to shore."

"Play dumb. Draw your gun now. Carefully."

They both shrugged and tried to look puzzled in the faint light of dawn, but as their weapons came into view, both Mexicans shouted and raised their own. Cydya and Jordan dangled their handguns over their heads by their little fingers.

"Pray he moves forward to take them. I'll break his neck."

But the uniformed Mexican at the end of the gangplank wasn't buying. He signaled that they should throw their weapons overboard. Jordan talked calmly to Cydya. "Somehow we've got to get the one up there to come down here."

The other was growing impatient. He moved out onto the gangplank, twenty feet from them. He spit as he talked and looked ready to fire with any provocation.

Jordan called to him. "You know what's on this ship?"

He answered in Spanish. Cydya touched Jordan's arm. "He doesn't speak English."

The one above hollered in a thick accent. "What is on this ship does not concern us. What concerns us is that you are trying to get on. Throw your weapons overboard."

"We can't do that, amigo. What if they discharge? We know what is on this ship."

The door of the truck opened and Diego stuck his head out, screaming at the man in uniform above him. "Shoot them! Shoot them and be done with it!"

Jordan lowered his weapon and slid it along the gangplank to the soldier. Cydya, moving much more slowly, did the same. "We are unarmed now! Let us go!"

Diego was maniacal. "Shoot! Shoot!"

Jordan's eyes shifted between the two soldiers. Diego had no good sight line to them. If he and Cydya were to be dropped, the soldiers would have to do it. "Time to find out whether the soldiers know what's in the truck." He reached for

313

his grenade and pulled the pin. He held it out before the soldier, then waved it over his head so Diego could see it too.

"Shoot me and the whole harbor goes up. The whole peninsula and you with it!"

The soldier on the deck immediately dropped his weapon. Cydya started toward him. Jordan stuck his foot out to block her. "Wait! You, up there! Throw your weapon down." The gun clattered to the deck. "Now come down." The soldier ran down to join his partner. "I want you and the crew off this ship. Round 'em up and get 'em off. Now!"

Jordan stood with the pin in one hand and the lever clamped tight in the other. Cydya retrieved the weapons on the deck. Jordan began to shout. "Diego! Shut that truck off or I blow the ship!"

The engine sputtered and died. Jordan was surprised Diego hadn't called his bluff. The grenade was his last option. "Granger! If I hear a shot, a yell, a splash, anything, we're all going out together, you got it? Answer me! . . . You'd better grunt or something, Felix, or you'll regret it!"

Finally a mutter from the Southerner. "We're here."

"I want Chuck safe, and I want you and Diego and your people to surrender! Nothing less!"

The soldiers appeared at the end of the gangplank with six crewmen, terror in their eyes. The eight turned sideways and slowly crept past

Jordan onto the narrow gangplank. If Chuck had been freed, Jordan might have tried to lock them away somewhere. For now, he simply had to improve his odds.

He handed the grenade to Cydya. "Jordan! I've never used one of these."

"Just squeeze it."

Jordan manually raised the gangplank. The soldiers and crewmen onshore would immediately go for help, but an army wouldn't dare do any more than the two soldiers had done. Not as long as he and Cydya had a live grenade on board.

Jordan's bag was full of pistols now, and he followed Cydya toward the truck, where Diego sat behind the wheel.

"Weapon first, amigo! Then let's go find Granger and Wallington."

Diego tossed out an automatic. "More!" An Uzi clattered out. "Now you! Move!"

Diego stepped from the truck and spit in Jordan's face. Jordan could have dropped him where he stood, but controlling the boss until Chuck was safe was more important.

Diego slowly led them around the other side of the ship to where Chuck stood between the jeep driver and Felix Granger. They had bound Chuck's feet and were forcing him to lie on the deck.

"Tell them to cut him loose, Diego."

Diego cursed him in Spanish. Jordan turned to

Cydya. "This man wants to die." A door burst open behind Cydya, slamming into her back and popping the grenade from her hand. Diego and his people screamed and covered their heads, as did the one crewman who had stayed behind the door, waiting to ambush the intruders.

Jordan rushed the skittering grenade and kicked it overboard. Its explosion was a dull thud that barely rippled the water, and he knew Horn-rims had ripped him off. Diego leaped to his feet and raced around to the other side of the ship. Gunfire from Felix and the jeep driver drove Jordan and Cydya to cover.

They followed Diego, and the brave crewman followed them until a shot felled him. Jordan tossed a weapon to Cydya. She looked at him pleadingly. "Jordan! Chuck!"

"Diego's first!" He ran on alone.

Jordan saw flashing lights on the shore and heard the hydraulic ramp lowering as he sprinted toward the truck. Diego had set the lever in motion and was already behind the wheel again. The engine roared, the horn blared, and the head-lights came on. Still on the dead run, Jordan raised his weapon and pointed it at Diego. Ten feet from the vehicle and running at top speed, he saw the driver's door open and heard Diego screaming, "Don't shoot! Nuclear!"

Jordan veered directly toward the door. He leaped, throwing his feet out in front of him and smashing the door on Diego's body as he attempted to jump out. The door pinned Diego vertically, splitting his face and the back of his head. Jordan scrambled to his feet and charged the door again, this time giving it a flying kick with his left foot. He felt and heard tissue give way before Diego slid to the deck. Crushed ribs had torn through his heart.

Jordan ran so swiftly around to the other side of the ship that he slipped, tumbled, and rolled before bouncing back to his feet. The jeep driver held a gun to Chuck's head as Felix tugged at his feet. Finally the driver holstered his weapon and they bent over him, one at each end, and carried him toward the side of the ship.

Cydya crouched at the other end of the deck, both hands around her gun. Jordan pointed at her, then at the jeep driver. He raised his weapon toward Felix and they shot simultaneously. The driver grabbed for his gun as he went down. Cydya fired twice more.

Chuck had been dropped hard on the deck and was close to the edge. Felix, down and wounded, kicked at him, pushing him closer. Cydya screamed as Chuck flopped overboard. "Jordan!"

Jordan skidded to the side of the ship and put a final shot through Felix's heart. He hollered to Cydya. "Radio a Mayday and the code word!" He dove overboard.

Chuck struggled in the water and Jordan had

nothing with which to cut the ropes. He yanked the big man's head above the surface. Chuck sputtered. "Is Diego in the truck?"

"More likely he's in hell. Are we in this thing alone, or did you make your contact?"

They went under again, Jordan fighting to hang on to his friend. He yanked at the knots, but the rope was thick and slippery. Chuck stiffened and Jordan pushed him above the surface again.

Chuck sucked air. "Hands first!"

Jordan knew that was the best idea, because then Chuck could paddle to stay afloat while Jordan worked on the rope at his ankles. But the rope at his wrists was so tight it cut into his flesh.

Jordan bobbed him up so they could both get one more breath before he dived under to work the ropes off Chuck's feet. He pulled Chuck's shoes off, but the rope was still so tight that his socks came off when the rope did.

Chuck was able to kick, but keeping him upright with his hands behind his back was a chore. Jordan kicked and guided Chuck to the side of the ship. There he was able to pin him while working in earnest on the knots. Chuck kept shaking his head to clear the water from his face. "Those were good shoes!"

Finally he was loose and they rested, pressing against the side of the ship. Sirens sounded onshore and someone shouted through a bullhorn in Spanish.

"Cydya went looking for the radio, Chuck. She gonna be able to raise any help?"

Chuck stared into the distance. "That a good enough answer?"

Jordan turned to see a submarine surface and hear the scream of two jet fighters crisscrossing above the ship. A helicopter hovered, its searchlight scanning the gulf.

Jordan and Chuck waved and shouted. "Operation Crimson Tide!"

Cydya LeMonde was flown courtesy of the United States Air Force to Paris.

Jordan Kirkwood and Chuck Wallington were flown to Washington, where they were met at the airport by Jordan's daughter, Christa.

Christa offered to help her father look for a new home.

"I appreciate it, honey, and I may take you up on it when I get back. But first you and I are going to visit your brother. And then I'm going to France for a few days."

21

DURING THE THREE days it took Jordan to be debriefed at NSA headquarters, not to mention telling the whole story to Christa, he found himself agitated. The agency put him up in a nice hotel, and he understood the painstaking precision with which they had to mine his account for every detail. And Jordan loved getting time with Christa. They talked more than they had in years, perhaps ever.

The problem was, Jordan could not get hold of Cydya. Interpol reported that she was away from the office for "a time undetermined," and her cell phone immediately went to voice mail every time Jordan tried it. His was a secure phone that hid its identity, so neither Cydya nor anyone who might be hacking into her phone would know he had been calling. He comforted himself that the response from Interpol might be different if she were in danger.

Jordan's attempts to find a number for Katrina LeMonde were also futile. He couldn't wait to fly to Paris, though he had no idea where to start looking for either woman without trying the Ministry of Tourism, and he didn't want to do that.

Chatting with Christa over dinner one evening, Jordan found her unusually quiet. "Talk to me."

She shook her head. "I feel traumatized."

"Welcome to my world, princess."

"It's not just Mom. You're telling me I almost lost you, too. And I have a sister I never knew. Anything else I should know?"

"You want to meet her?"

"Of course! But I can't imagine how eager you must be."

"You have no idea."

"Dad, are you worried about Ken?"

"Should I be? You're free to go with me to see him in a couple of days, right?"

She nodded. "He was pretty angry."

"Tell me something I don't know. I felt like he understood, though. That he didn't still blame me or has forgiven me if he had."

"I don't think he's holding a grudge, but this isn't something you get over easily. Now you're going to add this news."

Jordan pushed his chair back and sighed. "You don't think he'll be curious about his sister?"

"Sure. But, Dad, you're not making any secret you're enamored with her mother."

"What? Me? Nah, I—uh—"

"I'm just saying . . ."

"I told you the whole truth, Christa. I deeply loved her once."

"That story carries some baggage Ken doesn't need right now. He's just lost his mother, and now when he hears you had a major secret all these years—"

"Katrina was a surprise to me too, you know."

"But what you had done . . ."

"Was before I met your mother."

"That's still quite a secret to keep all these years, especially from Mom."

321

"What good would telling her have done? And even if I had, I would not likely have told you kids—and neither would she."

Christa nodded but didn't look convinced.

To Jordan, Ken seemed nervous and distracted as he showed them around the vast Taube Tennis Center at Stanford University. No wonder. That afternoon he would compete in his first intrasquad matches against the best players at the university. But clearly something else was on his mind.

"I've got important things to tell you, Ken. I'll save it until after your matches, but if you've still got questions for me, frustrations, whatever, get them off your chest before you play."

Christa stepped close to Ken. "I can find somewhere else to be."

Ken shook his head. "This won't be any surprise to you."

He led his dad and sister to a set of bleachers, where they sat in the sun. Jordan shielded his eyes, but Ken sat staring at the ground. Jordan wondered if this would be a rehash of the anger Ken rightly felt over the loss of his mother. He put a hand on Ken's knee. "I know you're missing your mom the way I do."

Ken nodded, lips pressed together. When he finally spoke, it was so softly that Jordan had to lean in to hear him. "I miss both my parents, Dad."

"I'm right here."

Christa sighed. "Don't interrupt. I know what he means."

"I don't."

She held up a hand. "That's his whole point. Hear him out."

To Jordan, Ken sounded less angry than sad, and it pierced him. "What do you think of this facility, Dad?"

"What?"

"The tennis center. Impressive?"

"Of course. What are you getting at?"

"I was one of their top scholarship recruits."

"Your mom told me. I'm proud of you. It's why I'm here."

"Really?"

"Of course! What do you think?"

"I think I'm the only tennis prospect who came to one of the best teams in the country without his dad ever visiting the campus. My visits here, my meetings, all the discussions, everything, were all with Mom. A player's family is important to these people, so of course they asked where you were. Busy. Gone. Out of the country. Otherwise engaged. I felt like I was being dropped off at camp."

Naturally Jordan's absence had niggled at him over the years, but he had never remedied it— despite Rosemary's nudges. He hadn't known how to prioritize. He was valuable, important, needed. It wasn't that no one else could do his job, but few could. Something was always pressing. National security was always at stake.

Jordan wished he had an excuse that made sense, that would somehow exonerate him with his kids. But he knew nothing but an unequivocal apology would reach them, especially Ken. And even that might not do any good.

"I've been no kind of a father. I'd like the chance to fix that and—"

"How many times have you seen me play?"

"I don't remember."

"I do, Dad."

"Several, I think."

"Twice in high school. Twice."

"Oh, surely it was more than that."

"You think I wouldn't know? Mom may have kept you up to date on the others, but I remember both matches you were at. Once late in the regular season junior year and once early last year. That's it. Not the league championships, not the districts, not the sectionals, not the state finals."

"I knew you won, and I bragged about it to everybody. I'm sure they got tired of hear—"

Ken stood and shook his head. "You knew I won. I swept everything both years, had college scouts at every match, was considered the best player on the East Coast."

"I know. I was proud. I still am."

"That's not something you can fix, Dad. We can't get that back."

"Does that mean I shouldn't try? I want to start over, Ken."

"Your job's going to change? You quitting?"

"I'm considering it." The truth was, his resolve had waned in the afterglow of Crimson Tide.

"Well, that's something."

But like Christa a few days before, Ken didn't sound convinced.

That afternoon Ken dazzled on the courts, and Jordan could barely contain himself. He was introduced as the most promising freshman Stanford had welcomed in years, and the announcer listed his high school accomplishments. He showed a booming serve and agility and speed that rivaled the best upperclassmen. While they outlasted him and had the edge on him in nearly every match, Ken seemed the center of attention, and Jordan knew it would be only a matter of time before he was a star.

That's why Jordan was stunned at the conversation with the head coach late that afternoon in the man's office. "Ken is a fine young man and a stellar player, and he could enjoy a good run here. But he's not going to be a pro."

Jordan was taken aback that the man would say this in front of Ken, not to mention his sister and dad. He shot a glance at Ken, who appeared to have known this was coming. Jordan looked back at the coach and cocked his head. "I'm not following."

"He doesn't want it badly enough, Mr. Kirkwood. Do you, Ken?"

Ken shook his head. "I got a sniff of the life from the big tournaments and from teammates. I don't love it enough, Dad. And I'm not good enough."

"Who are you kidding? I know what I saw today."

The coach gestured with both hands. "It has to become an obsession. Ken's not obsessed with it."

"But look at what your future could be!"

Ken shrugged. "Tell you the truth, Dad, I'm not happy with economics either. I'd really like to study criminology."

"Follow in my footsteps?"

Jordan saw Ken and the coach catch each other's eyes. "What?"

"That would be just a coincidence, Dad. I never knew what you did for a living until recently. And I'm not entirely sure now."

"What're you telling me? You're going to give up your scholarship, quit tennis, switch majors?"

"Might even leave here. Stanford doesn't offer a criminology major."

The coach stood. "I recommend Cal State Fresno or San Diego State at Imperial Valley."

"You're *encouraging* this?"

"You bet I am. I'd love to have Ken here a long time. I think he could help our program. We've made an investment in him. But if it's not his passion, there are plenty of other prospects we can gamble on."

Jordan sat back and sighed. The air crackled with unspoken truth, and he was grateful no one said it aloud. The sad fact was that he didn't know his own son. Didn't know him at all.

That night at dinner Jordan waited for the opportunity to tell Ken all that had happened since his mother's funeral. But everything was off-kilter now. He felt lost, confused. "Did I do the wrong thing, coming to see you play?"

"Hardly. I only wish you'd done that before."

"I know, okay? We've been through this. I was a bad father, and I'm trying to fix that. Is it too late?"

Ken looked down. "No, I appreciate it. But showing up for stuff doesn't even begin to let you know who I am, what I'm about, what I want."

"Clearly."

Christa put a hand on Ken's arm. "Let him up. He's trying."

Ken looked cloudy, but he nodded. "So Christa tells me you've had some kind of adventure since I saw you last."

"It's really involved. But I want to talk about what you want to talk about. Dropping tennis, transferring, changing majors . . ."

"All that's just in the thinking stages. I want to hear what happened."

· · ·

Jordan drove Ken and Christa back to his hotel room, agonizing over how to tell the story and dreading what his son would think—not so much of the danger he had faced, but of the family he never knew he had.

Ken stretched out on the bed, while Christa sat at the desk and Jordan in a recliner. "You going to fall asleep on me, Ken?"

Ken lay with his hands behind his head. "Depends on how good a storyteller you are."

"You understand I must swear you to secrecy. I'm telling you the kinds of things I never even told your mother."

Christa snorted. "Especially the good parts."

Ken sat up and scooted to the edge of the bed, planting his feet on the floor. "There are good parts?"

It took Jordan just less than an hour to tell his entire history with Cydya and how they had been united again recently. He was careful to generalize about Operation Crimson Tide, as he had with Christa, but he included how dangerous it had been and how close he had come to death. Jordan saved the news of Katrina until the end, and in spite of himself, he found his voice thick and quavery as he told Ken about a sister he had yet to meet.

Ken sat staring and rocking, as if speechless. Was he judging his father for a youthful indiscretion, angry with him for never telling his mother? Jordan was tempted to quiz him, to ask what he was thinking. But he thought better of it and left the boy with his musings.

When Ken finally spoke, he surprised Jordan. "This is the first time I've ever seen you cry, Dad."

"Are you sure? My profession necessitates that I remain as unemotional as possible in the heat of the moment, but I was emotional when your mom and I got married and when you kids were born, when you started school, all that."

Ken shrugged. "Never seen it; that's all."

"Okay, so I'll try to remember not to hide my emotions from you too. But surely you have questions."

"Yeah, I have a question. Are you even going to try to parent me?"

"Sorry?"

"No opinions on my tennis future, my changing majors, maybe changing schools?"

"Ken! I asked if you wanted to talk about that and you said it was just in the formative stage. I trust your judgment and your coach's. Selfishly I wish you'd stay with the tennis because you're so good. But what do I know? I just like bragging about you. But you have to do what you have to do. You need a career that gets you up in the morning. If you don't like what you're doing, you'll never be any good at it."

"Thanks. I didn't know you cared."

"Well, I don't appreciate the sarcasm."

Ken stood and faced Christa, raising his brows and shrugging before moving to the window. Jordan knew the view—just a parking lot. But Ken studied it as if it were something special. He spoke with his back to his father. "At best you've been a spectator in my life, and not a good one."

"Are you going to keep beating me up over it? I don't know what else to do but try again."

Ken turned but still wouldn't look at Jordan. "Look, it's obvious you can't wait to get to France—I hope as much to see your daughter as to hook up with your old girlfriend. I guess I just wish you were that eager to see me."

Jordan didn't want to argue. Ken was clearly speaking emotionally, so there would be no reasoning with him. "I'm not the gushy type, Ken. But maybe I can work myself up to tell you how much you mean to me, how much I love you, how much I want to see you, how much I miss you."

"That would be something anyway."

"As for why I'm going to France, of course it's to see Katrina."

Christa held up a hand. "That was my question too. You didn't hold anything back talking about Cydya. Now are you saying you're not enamored with her?"

"Hon, we're different people. It'd been years

since we'd even seen each other. It's not like we have a relationship."

Ken and Christa spoke at once, but she fell silent and let him take over. "You only have a daughter together. That sounds like a relationship to me."

Jordan had been careful not to tell them that in many ways he had never stopped loving Cydya. He didn't want to be disingenuous, but nothing would be served by talking about that to kids who had so recently lost their mother.

Christa stood and embraced her father. "I'm exhausted, and you and Ken need a little alone time."

"You don't have to go."

"Yes, I do."

Alone with Ken, Jordan felt overwhelmed with the need to be understood. "Please hear me out."

"I've got to get back to the dorm, Dad. Talk to me on the way."

Jordan was grateful he could concentrate on driving and not have to face Ken. As he drove, he spoke earnestly and as honestly as he knew how. "Yes, I need to meet my daughter. And no, I haven't ruled out anything related to Cydya."

"You haven't."

"Why would I? Why should I?"

"Because you haven't even grieved Mom yet, that's why."

"Don't you dare, Ken. You have no idea what this has been like for me."

"I don't? I lost her too, you know."

"I'm not disparaging your own pain, but don't jump to conclusions about what it's been like for me."

"Sorry."

"You don't sound sorry."

"Well, I'm dubious, but you're right. I shouldn't assume I know."

"Thanks. I loved your mother deeply and was loyal and faithful to her from the day we fell in love."

"That's good to know."

They didn't speak again until Jordan pulled into the parking lot of Ken's dorm. They got out of the car and stood awkwardly on the sidewalk. Jordan put a hand on Ken's shoulder. He had never been physical with the kids. "Are we all right?"

Ken embraced him and held tight. "Of course, but I have to know, Dad. Am I going to have to get used to another woman in your life?"

"My priority in France is meeting your sister. You want to meet her eventually, right?"

"Of course."

"And I promise you that any future with Cydya will be appropriate, dignified, and with you and Christa fully informed all the way."

Ken pulled away. "Sounds like a done deal."

"Trust me, it's not. There's a lot of pain in our

past and a beautiful young woman in our future. But the fact is, I *am* still grieving your mom, and I will be for a long, long time."

In truth, much as Jordan thought he may have connected with Ken on a different level than ever before, he couldn't wait to get back on the phone, trying to locate Cydya or Katrina. By now it was late, but Jordan knew he wouldn't sleep anyway. He ran through his mind the Interpol personnel he might know in the more than 175 member countries.

Jordan knew that the International Criminal Police Organization was not to be mistaken for some sort of global police force. Rather, it serves as more of a clearinghouse for law enforcement agencies around the world, giving them access to each other's databases and intelligence. It has no agents of its own but rather coordinates the work of police agencies in each country.

But as Jordan was dozing in the lounge waiting for his return flight to Maryland, his phone beeped. "Mr. Kirkwood? This is Katrina, Cydya LeMonde's daughter."

22

"YOU'RE IN AMERICAN intelligence?" The voice was Katrina's, but it sounded so much like Cydya it made Jordan hold his breath.

"I am."

"And you met her on a recent case?"

"Uh, actually, we've known each other for some time. She told me a lot about you."

"Really? Anyway, she wanted me to tell you she's in Athens on her way to see me."

"And where are you?"

Katrina hesitated. "Izmir. That's in—"

"Turkey, yeah. So she's coming there?"

"No, see, I'm a tour guide. I'm going to meet her in Istanbul tomorrow when my current assignment is over and my group heads for the airport."

"Any idea what time her flight leaves Athens?"

"Noon, but, Mr. Kirkwood, she's afraid of being followed, so . . ."

"I'll keep that in mind."

"No, the thing is, she'd rather you meet her in the city tomorrow afternoon, at two."

"Sure, I can do that. Where?"

"The Kapali Carsi. Do you know it? It's the great covered—"

"Market, of course. The bazaar. That's only, what, ten miles or so east of Atatürk International?"

"Eight-point-six."

"My, you really are a tour guide, aren't you?"

Jordan expected a chuckle, something. But Katrina sounded flat. "Comes with the territory."

"Katrina, is something wrong? Anything I can help with?"

"Mother clearly thinks so."

"What? That something's wrong, or that I can help?"

"Both."

"Anything you can tell me?"

"I'll leave that to her."

Jordan was trying to read an attitude but couldn't. "Are either of you in imminent danger?"

"I don't think so."

"Will you be there too, Katrina? I'd love to meet you."

"Well, I'd like to meet you too, sir, but this is more than a social meeting. I think she's hoping the three of us might get together in the evening for dinner."

"I'd like that."

"Mm-hm."

Clearly Katrina had on her mind some picture bigger than meeting a friend of her mother's. Jordan hoped that whatever the trouble was, it could be dealt with quickly and they could get on to the news that would affect both their futures.

"My recollection is that the bazaar has hundreds of shops."

Finally a chuckle, making Katrina sound more than ever like Cydya. "A lot of the tourist guide-books say four thousand or so, but naturally I know the truth. It's fewer than fifteen hundred, but nonetheless impressive. You want my whole pitch? More than a quarter million visitors a day, fifty-eight covered streets, more than five hundred fifty years old."

"Impressive. So where am I to meet your m—"

"You know there are eleven gates."

"Well, I knew there were several."

"Enter through the Mahmutpasa Gate, follow Aynacilar Street past the police station and go left. Cross Aga Street and look for a silver shop with a proprietor spelled E-N-D-E-R but pronounced End-*air*. That's the silver section, Mr. Kirkwood, so be sure you get the right shop."

Jordan changed his destination to Istanbul and slept soundly on the flight. During his waking moments the irony was not lost on him that while he was using his French alias, he was also tempted to wear a disguise and originally planned to meet an old love in an airport.

He endured a sleepless night at the Ritz-Carlton, then spent the morning trying to busy himself. Waiting had always been the worst part of his job. And despite the life-and-death situations in which he had found himself, nothing compared to reuniting with Cydya, finding out what was going on, and finally getting to meet his daughter. He had no idea what Cydya was up to, why she was rendezvousing with Katrina, or what she was afraid of.

Jordan wandered the streets, window-shopping, people-watching, and following stray dogs to the harbor. He enjoyed just gazing and had long considered Istanbul one of the most beautiful cities in the world. The skyline with its towers and mosques and minarets, the bridges, the fishermen . . . Jordan made a point to go through Sultanahmet Park, where the famed ancient Blue Mosque and Hagia Sophia give way to the stunning four courtyards of the Topkapi Palace.

Finally, late in the morning, feeling zombie-ized by jet lag, he made the fifteen-minute walk to the Grand Bazaar. A cab would have been faster, but he was in no hurry. And a taxi would have to let him off several blocks from the bazaar anyway to avoid the ridiculous traffic.

Farther to the west he came to the grand covered market, one of busiest and most bizarre bazaars in the world. Rather than enter the gate Katrina had suggested, Jordan walked outside the sprawling complex and entered through the southwestern Beyazit Gate that led to the main way, Kalpakcilarbasi Street, famous for its jewelry stores.

The place swarmed with tourists and locals, and Jordan was fascinated by the shopkeepers' ability to guess where people were from. "U.S.? Brit? *Français?*"

One smiled broadly as Jordan passed. "Hey, American! Spend your money here!"

Every shop he passed had a spotter who tried to entice the passersby.

"Is it my turn?"

"Many specials!"

"Lowest prices!"

"Almost free today."

With time to kill, and loving the colors and aromas, Jordan set out to find one of the tiny restaurants that would offer local cuisine, specifically eggplant dips and a mixture of nuts and seeds. On the way, however, he succumbed to the tempting simit cart, offering a sesame seed–covered circle of bread that looked like a combination pretzel and bagel, and tasted much like just that.

As he munched, Jordan wandered through the various sections and districts, avoiding eye contact with the purveyors of leather, antiques, copperware, fabric, carpets, and the like. He was struck by ornate blue tiles in the ceramic and souvenir area and could barely shake the owner. "Just looking."

"Look here!"

With an eye on his watch, Jordan snaked his way to the northeast and the silver section sur-rounding the police station. He didn't know which shop would be Ender's, but he narrowed it to a few and loitered where he could see if Cydya showed up. But as the clock moved closer to two, he wondered if she was already there waiting.

As he approached, Jordan was suddenly struck with a memory that made his legs feel heavy and slowed him. The last time he had agreed to a clandestine meeting in a tradesman's shop, it had been in the Old City in Frankfurt. Shortly he had lost the love of his life, and a dear friend had wound up dead. Did it make sense to follow the same pattern with the mother of a daughter he had not yet met? Obviously Cydya trusted this Ender. And it was way too late to change plans.

"The finest silver work in Turkey, sir!"

Jordan spoke with a French accent. "I'm looking for Ender, *s'il vous plaît.*"

The shopkeeper shrugged and pointed across the way. "He's good too."

Ender proved to be trim, dark-haired, and middle-aged. He was quietly showing a couple a beautiful candelabra. "I do the work myself, right here."

"When do you find the time?" The woman sounded Scottish.

"When traffic is light and I have help." Ender spoke earnestly but quietly and was quick to smile.

The couple told him they would be back, and unlike so many other shopkeepers, he did not protest or try to detain them. Jordan approached as

Ender placed the piece back in the window. "Lovely, isn't it?"

"*Ouah!* It's spectacular, monsieur."

"You'd like to see it?"

"*Non merci.* I'm looking for *ma amie.*"

"Aah, Mr. Blanc?"

"*Ouais.*"

"Here for the beautiful Mademoiselle LeMonde."

"*Oui.*"

"She has not yet arrived. Follow, please."

Ender led Jordan through the tiny shop to a back room hardly bigger than a phone booth. The place was crowded with raw goods and tools. Could the man have really fashioned such a magnificent piece in this minuscule chamber?

Ender smiled and pointed to one of two chairs, the one that sat before his workbench. Jordan climbed into it, ducking under a lamp. He felt conspicuous, looking up at Ender, who remained standing. "I am the reason her daughter is a guide."

"Is that so?"

Ender nodded. "I was a guide for many years. But when my wife and I started a family, I wanted to be home more."

"And clearly you're an artisan."

"You are too kind. I come from a long line . . ."

"And you met Katrina how?"

"She was a college student on tour. Very bright.

Good with languages. Curious. Full of questions. I tried to discourage her, telling her the life of a guide can be long, hard, and lonely, despite all the people. She would not be dissuaded. I believe she will teach one day, but for now . . ."

"And you already knew Cydya, or—?"

"No. Katrina introduced us. I spoke so much of them that my wife insisted I invite them home. And she fell in love with them too. You?"

"Me? Oh, I knew Cydya in a former life."

"And did you fall in love with her?"

Jordan started. Did Ender mean in the way he himself had become smitten with Cydya and her daughter? "As a matter of fact, I did. Of course. Who wouldn't?"

"Indeed. And Katrina?"

"I have yet to meet her."

"You will love her, too."

I already do. How could I not? "No doubt."

"Ender?"

The voice was clearly Cydya's, and Jordan banged his head on the lamp, standing.

Ender hurried out and Cydya met him in the doorway between the shop and the work area. "Back here with your friend, dear."

Cydya and Ender alternated cheek kisses, and while Ender was smiling broadly, Cydya looked grim and harried. She pulled from Ender's embrace and rushed to Jordan. "Oh, thank God you made it." She set her things down and grabbed both his hands. "Ender, if you would excuse us . . ."

"Certainly. My place is yours for as long as you need it."

"Thank you for coming, Jordan."

"Of course. You knew I'd come."

"I knew you would if Katrina got my message and you got hers."

"She reached me by phone."

"You didn't tell her anything, did you?"

Jordan shook his head.

"Save that for when you meet her face-to-face."

Jordan moved Ender's chair so it faced the other, and they sat. "What's up, Cyd?"

"Hopefully nothing, but I have to be sure. I don't want Katrina involved in the kind of work you and I do . . . well you, anyway. I'm pretty much a pencil pusher."

"You were more than that in Operation Crimson—"

"If I ever find myself on the front lines again, it'll be too soon. I love what Katrina is doing, but I worry about her. And I don't know if she's imagining things or whether there's anything to this . . ."

"Just tell me."

"I don't know what to say, how to characterize it. She leads various tours, you know, for universities, tour companies, religious organizations. I told you she's one of the youngest in the business, but she's already getting raves. People ask for her."

"I'm not surprised."

"You've never even met her."

"I know her parents."

"Stop. Anyway, she's analytical and observant to the point of compulsion."

Jordan cocked his head. "Good qualities for a guide, no?"

"Maybe it's made her paranoid; I don't know."

"Spill it, Cydya."

"She's done this Turkey route several times, and this time, in Izmir, she saw something she'd never seen before. Katrina is fascinated by the local mosques. You know, there are these spectacular ones here in the big city, tourist attractions. She leads tours through them like all the guides do. But along the way, when her bus is rolling through the country past the villages, she likes to point out how some little enclaves seem to have an abnormal number of mosques."

Jordan shrugged. "Muslim country. What's the big deal?"

"I'm not sure. I know they have to pray five times a day and that they can pray in any clean place, but that a mosque is preferred."

"Lots of mosques in a village is not an indication of factions, as many churches in a small town would hint at in the States. The Muslims don't have to go far to pray is all."

"Fine. But during Katrina's time as a guide, she has seen many mosques, big and small, in cities and in hamlets. She has made impromptu stops and allowed her tour groups to watch as mosques are being built, their minarets rising."

"But?"

"But outside Izmir, in a small village with several mosques already, one is being built that is off-limits to the curious."

"Okay . . ."

"Seriously off-limits. Walls, gates, tarpaulins, signs."

"So it's a particularly beautiful structure, and they want to unveil it all at once to admiring observers."

Cydya sighed. "That was my conclusion. It was not Katrina's. Her mantra is always that nothing is as it seems. No, she had to rent a scooter. Once her tour group had settled in for dinner at a nice Izmir hotel, she ventured back out."

"To get a closer look."

"Exactly. She even tracked down the imam in charge of the new structure. Was he proud of the soon-to-be-finished holy place? He didn't even want to talk about it. He demanded to know why she was interested. Katrina told him the truth—that she wanted to be able to explain the secrecy to her tour groups and that she was looking forward to one day seeing the finished product."

"Still couldn't draw him out?"

Cydya shook her head. "He became suddenly jovial and talkative, but about everything except what she wanted to know. He walked her back to her scooter and urged her not to insert herself into private religious matters. She was aware of being watched, Jordan, and on her way out of town, another man tentatively waved at her. Being in public in broad daylight, she stopped. The man turned out to be the imam of the mosque nearest the new one, and he was eager to know what she had learned."

"And she told him she had learned nothing."

"Right. And he said, 'The man you talked to is no imam. He is a warmonger, full of hate and treachery. There is no reason to build a house of prayer in secret. Unless one has evil designs.'"

Cydya fell silent, and Jordan rubbed his eyes. "I don't know. Sounds like she got herself in the middle of some local religious politics, doesn't it?"

"It does if that was all there was to it. You haven't heard the rest."

"Don't tell me she went back."

"After dark."

"And she got caught nosing around."

"Almost. She was smart enough to walk her scooter while she investigated, and when armed guards lit out after her, she jumped on and sped away."

"Did they get a good look at her?"

Cydya nodded. "Enough to put it together if the so-called imam remembered their conversation."

"She had told him too much."

"Did she ever. That's my fear. That he can track her down with little trouble."

"And why would he do that?"

"Because of what she saw."

"I'll bite. What did she see?"

"I'll save that for her to tell you."

"C'mon, Cydya. Katrina told me she was leaving it for *you* to tell."

"I set up the story. You need to hear it from the eyewitness."

Cydya told Jordan that after her Interpol debriefing about Operation Crimson Tide, she had asked for a two-week leave of absence and had spent a few days alone in the south of France before hearing from Katrina. "I had a feeling you would come looking for me, and I had a lot of thinking to do."

"I was that obvious?"

She nodded. "I'm flattered, Jordan, but you know you're being very premature."

"I have no illusions."

"Of course you do. And so do I. Can we be adults about this and not be coy? You think I'm not also curious about whether we could rekindle a fire whose ashes went gray years ago?"

Jordan put a hand over hers. "That's more encouragement than I expected."

"I just don't want to dance around this. To be frank, I'm afraid it's way too early to be encouraging. I know you deeply loved your wife, and you have a lot more grieving to do. I don't want to get in the way of that, and I won't."

"You sound like my kids. They think I haven't mourned Rosemary yet."

"Of course you have, but the loss may be fresher than you realize. It simply hasn't been that long."

"How do I know when the process is over?"

"There's a question for the ages. Everybody knows the conventions—that you shouldn't even think about another relationship for a year."

"Just for propriety's sake, you mean? I've never cared about that."

"For the sake of our children, Jordan. Yours and ours. I know these are unique circumstances and that we would start from a place that most couples wouldn't. We had something once, and now you feel free to pursue it. But the last thing I want is you on the rebound."

"Is that even the proper term in this case?"

"Maybe not, but you know what I mean."

"So we wait a year; is that what you're saying?"

"Maybe more."

"Please don't say that, Cyd. We're not kids anymore."

She stood and seemed to study the silver and the jewelry on the crowded shelves. "How will we know when you've really processed your loss?"

"That's what I'm asking you. What if I do give it a year and you aren't convinced?"

"It would take me longer than that, Jordan."

"How do you know?"

"You forget I've been through this. You think I didn't grieve my loss, that I didn't mourn you?"

"It was like a death?"

"Of course it was! You were dead to me, weren't you? My grief was mixed with anger because I thought you knew about Katrina and still ignored me—"

"Which wasn't—"

"—the case; sure, I know that now. But imagine my pain. I lost the man of my dreams, blamed myself for a moment of weakness, and then hated you for turning your back on me and our child. Maybe that made it harder and longer for me, but to tell you the truth, it was years before you weren't the first thing on my mind when I awoke in the morning or the last thing on my mind when I fell asleep at night."

"I'm sorry."

"I know, Jordan. Really. I don't need any more apologies. I just want us both to be wise and sure and do this right. I could not bear another misfire."

"And so what are you saying? We don't see each

other for at least a year, and you're making no promises even after that?"

"Your kids need you. All three of them. It's not like I could keep you from getting to know Katrina. But she lives in Athens."

"And you don't want to see me if I come to see her? How far can it be?"

"Our tour guide tells me we are a little over thirteen hundred miles apart by air and a little more than eighteen hundred miles by car. But it's not a matter of not wanting to, Jordan. I'm not playing hard to get. I'm trying to be an adult about this."

"I hear you."

"Do you?"

He nodded. "I don't like what I'm hearing, but I'm listening. I've got fences to mend in the States too, of course."

"Our kids need to meet one of these days too, you know."

Cydya left to check in at Katrina's hotel, agreeing that the two of them would meet Jordan at the Beyti Restaurant near Atatürk at six o'clock.

Why did everything have to always be so complicated? On the one hand, Jordan was deflated, despite knowing that Cydya's counsel on their relationship was only wise and prudent and necessary. On the other, he selfishly wanted to pursue her as soon as possible. This was all superseded by his eagerness to meet Katrina. He was surprised by an overwhelming paternal need to be sure she was safe. He wanted to get to the bottom of whatever it was she had discovered at the mosque outside Izmir.

Most of all, Jordan longed to tell Katrina who he really was.

Again, the issue now was time to kill. If he knew more about the matter outside Izmir, perhaps he could have initiated some action. Short of that he would wander the Great Bazaar looking for the perfect gift. As he left the shop, Ender nodded and waved while dealing with a customer.

If anything, during the time he had spent with Cydya, the crowds in the vast market had increased. Some corridors found him shoulder-to-shoulder with people from every tribe and nation. He loved the aroma of the spices when he moseyed near that district, but that was hardly what he was looking for for his daughter.

Jewelry. It would have to be jewelry. What would appeal to a young woman? From the picture Cydya had shown him, Katrina had her mother's lovely olive complexion. He quickened his step and moved back to the gold shops. Everything and nothing caught his eye. After nearly two hours of wandering, he made his way back to where he had started, in the silver district. Silver would work. It would look beautiful next to her skin.

Even more striking would be something inlaid

with turquoise. Rings, bracelets, earrings, necklaces, brooches, pendants abounded in the windows of every silver shop. But it had to be just right. Jordan found himself in Ender's aisle and waited his turn to approach.

"A necklace with turquoise would work for a woman with Cydya's coloring, would it not?"

"It would be stunning, sir. If I may say so, it would be as stunning as the sudden loss of your French accent. You are an American."

"Guilty."

"There is no need to apologize for caution. We must all be careful. But your special lady friend trusts me, and so may you. Now let us see what we have for the lovely Cydya."

"It's actually for Katrina."

"How nice."

"Price is no object. It must be exquisite."

"Oh, you drive a hard bargain, Mr. Blanc."

"Kirkwood. Jordan Kirkwood."

"Well, Mr. Kirkwood, we are looking in the wrong place. Let me show you something in the back."

Jordan followed him to his workbench, where Ender stretched and reached a high shelf, bringing down a corrugated cardboard box with several loose pieces. He pulled from it a delicate chain and a flat one-and-a-half-inch-square piece of silver inlaid with a dazzling wafer of turquoise of the lightest hue, the color of a summer sky.

Jordan gasped and shook his head. "Wow."

"All it needs is a connecting piece for the chain and a little polishing. I can have it for you in the morning."

"Sorry, too late. I need it for dinner tonight at six. And I want it engraved."

Ender's smile froze and he hesitated. He carefully laid the piece and the chain on his workbench and discreetly scribbled on a scrap of paper, showing it to Jordan. He was amused by Ender's apparent need to announce the price this way, when no one else was around. He was not amused by the price, but he would have paid double.

"I can have it by five? We're having dinner near the airport."

"Tell me you're going to Beyti!"

"Of course. Where else?"

"I will personally deliver this to your hotel. Where are you staying?"

"The Ritz."

"And how would you like it engraved?"

Jordan borrowed the pencil and paper and wrote carefully. Ender studied the plain block letters under his work lamp. "Ah, Mr. Kirkwood! And you told me you had never met her."

"I have not."

"Congratulations, sir. And be assured, your secret is safe with me."

Jordan phoned the restaurant on his way back to the hotel, making a reservation for six o'clock and requesting a secluded table. He showered and shaved and pulled on his most understated and comfortable outfit.

About fifteen minutes before he was to leave, he was surprised and delighted to answer a knock and find that Ender himself was making the delivery. The necklace was more brilliant than he could have hoped. He thanked Ender profusely and tried to press upon him a tip.

"Entirely unnecessary, sir. I only wish I could be there tonight."

23

AS THE SUN dipped, the temperature didn't, so Jordan laid his sport coat across the backseat of the taxi. He waited until he was inside the modern three-story restaurant, named for its founder and original chef, Beyti Güler. Chuck Wallington had introduced Jordan to the place more than fifteen years before. He had been there half a dozen times since, enjoying the Ottoman Turkish decor and the succulent lamb, pork, and beef.

He was greeted by name and led to one of the eleven various-sized compartments, a favorite that looked out over the terrace. A corner table apart from the rest suited him perfectly. Jordan set the slender necklace box under his napkin and told his host of the guests he was expecting.

"I assume you will recommend the Beyti kebap special and urge your friends to go easy on the preliminaries."

Jordan smiled and nodded, remembering when he had ignored such advice to the detriment of his comfort. It wasn't that the main dish itself was so filling; it consisted of roast lamb wrapped in lamb fat. The problem was that the servings just kept coming. He guessed that both Cydya and Katrina would want to sample everything.

Jordan sat with his back to the wall and his eyes on the door, feeling like a high schooler on a first date. He kept trying to convince himself that whatever danger Katrina might be in or whatever suspicion she had about what was going on at the mosque construction site had to take precedence over his excitement. He was not succeeding.

Should he have ordered flowers for the table? It would have been a nice touch, but too much. He couldn't appear to be trying too hard. Most of all, Jordan wanted the news to remain a surprise until he chose to reveal it.

Jordan knew enough about Cydya to know they would not be late, and as the zero hour approached, he found himself more nervous than he had been in any crisis on the job. Would he be able to calm himself, to communicate without fumbling or stuttering?

When the table host approached with the two women, Jordan forced himself to rise slowly. He pulled the ladies' chairs out and followed the Turkish custom by double-cheek-kissing both, allowing Cydya to make the introductions. When they sat, he stared at Katrina. "Your picture doesn't do you justice."

She blushed. "Thank you."

He wasn't kidding. He would have recognized her anywhere, even without having seen her picture. She was the essence of her mother from the Jakarta days. But behind her luminescent eyes, Jordan saw fear and what he judged an eagerness to get down to business. They ordered their drinks and Jordan cleared his throat. "Would you mind if I asked the blessing?"

Katrina flinched and shot her mother a double take. "You didn't tell me he was a believer."

"She didn't? Maybe she didn't know."

"Of course I knew, Jordan. Now stop it."

"She told me *you* were, Katrina, or I wouldn't have suggested saying grace."

"Well, please do, Mr. Kirkwood."

Katrina had followed Jordan's advice and only nibbled at her dinner roll. "I can't believe we're sitting here in this beautiful place when I need to make sense of what I saw."

"Is this your first time here?"

"It is, but it won't be my last. Some of the groups I bring want to spend this kind of money on a special dinner. Most don't. But anyway . . ."

"Yes, go ahead, Katrina. Your mother tells me you're worried about something you saw."

"I'll tell you what troubles me, Mr. Kirkwood—" Jordan did not ask her to call him by his first name, hoping that by the end of the night she would be calling him Dad—"is Turkish-American relations. If I'm right about my fears, this could be a serious blow."

"You study such things, do you?"

"I did, and as a guide for many internationals, I like to keep up. You know only about ten percent of Turkey's general populace have a favorable opinion of the U.S.?"

"We're not exactly popular among Muslims these days, let alone vastly Muslim countries."

Katrina glanced at her mother. "It didn't help when the U.S. House tried to pass a bill condemning what the Ottomans did to the Armenians nearly a hundred years ago."

"My, you do know your history. Genocide is reprehensible, but I wondered about that bill too. I mean, after all this time . . ."

"Well, there was the U.S. arms embargo in the seventies. But Turkey knew they needed you at the end of the Cold War and they supported your war on terror. The U.S. needs Turkey to remain an ally. They were both charter members of the U.N. and NATO, and don't you have an air base here?"

Jordan nodded. "Incirlik near Adana. It's the

Turks' 10th Air Wing of the 2nd Air Force Command, but there are something like five thousand staffers there total, including our 39th Air Base Wing."

Katrina looked impressed. "Talk about knowing your stuff. I assume the U.S. knows how strategic that installation is."

"Of course." With his napkin in his lap, the necklace box lay conspicuously on the table.

"Please eat, Mr. Kirkwood. I can tell you what I think I saw, and you can decide what I should do about it."

Cydya stopped midbite. "You're not going to do anything about it. If there's anything to what you told me, it's not an Interpol matter either. It will either fall to Jordan or he will know who to take it to."

"Oh, Mother . . ."

Jordan cut his meat. "Start from the beginning, Katrina. Please."

Katrina rehearsed what Jordan had heard already from Cydya.

Chewing, Jordan held up a hand and sat back. "Could this imam identify you? How much does he know?"

Katrina pressed her lips together and shook her head. "More than he should, of course. I went into it thinking that honesty was the best policy. I told him I was a guide, but I didn't tell him who I worked for."

Cydya turned her attention to Jordan. "I was thrilled when Katrina became a tour guide. I know it's not easy, and I'm proud of her, being so young and all. But I will not be able to function if I have to worry about her safety. I swear, I'll—"

"Put that to rest, Cydya. Whatever this turns out to be, we'll somehow get word to the imam and whoever his people are that the beautiful young tour guide is not worth the effort."

"I'd rather you communicate that she's an untouchable."

"The result will be the same. I would caution you, though, Katrina, that it's not wise—"

"Got it. I know. Sorry to interrupt, but I learned my lesson."

"Good. Continue."

Despite the three of them raving about the delicious food, it was clear Katrina had lost interest in eating. "I don't think the ornate minaret I saw is really a minaret."

Jordan found himself as ravenous as ever. Truth was, he wanted to get to the bottom of this conversation so he could begin the one he wanted. "Because?"

"I'm no construction expert, but I had to know why so much secrecy around the erection of a prayer tower. I saw extensive wiring, way-too-involved a base, and what looked like lead and concrete circular walls. And a hole had been dug for another."

"The electronics couldn't be for the PA system that announces the prayer times?"

"Mr. Kirkwood, that minaret looked to me like a silo. A missile silo. And that hole next to it for a second? Come on. A tiny mosque in a tiny village with *two* minarets?"

Jordan stole a glance at Cydya's knowing look and lost his appetite too. "What are the odds?"

Katrina shook her head. "How would I know that?"

"That's not what he means, honey. He's wondering how likely it is that he could be involved in two straight nuclear threats."

Jordan sat shaking his head. "Anybody still hungry?"

"Hardly."

"No."

Jordan flagged down the waiter and asked for the bill, assuring him everything was perfect but that they were stuffed. When the waiter left to get the check, Jordan pulled his secure international cell phone from his pocket. "Would you excuse me for a few moments? Find us a nice spot on the terrace."

When the women were gone, Jordan paid the bill and checked his watch. They had talked and eaten for more than an hour, and it was nearly seven thirty in Turkey. Roughly lunchtime on the East Coast of the U.S. As he had done with every crisis he had faced his entire adult life, Jordan called Chuck Wallington. He filled him in as quickly as possible.

The initial response was silence, and Jordan wondered if he had lost the connection. Finally he heard the old man. "You have a penchant for stepping in it, don't you, Kirkwood?"

"I guess. You know my priorities here."

"Well, I hope your top priority is the security of the United States."

"Goes without saying, but there's a personal component."

"Does she know yet?"

"Soon."

"Wish I was a fly on the wall."

"You're not the first who's said something like that today. But I'm not even going to let Cydya in on that conversation. Anyway, this silo thing won't wait. Department of Defense has to know immediately, right?"

" 'Course. Why bring me into it?"

"Habit."

"Keep me posted, but go to the top. And don't dawdle."

Jordan slipped the necklace box into his pocket and moved outside, gesturing to Cydya and Katrina that he would be a few moments. He found a secluded spot surrounded by foliage and placed his call, giving the NSA operator his top-level security clearance code and asking to be patched through to DIRNSA, director of the NSA.

The top man's secretary informed Jordan that DIRNSA was in an uninterruptible meeting with the president of the United States. Jordan was tempted to insist that he be connected with the Oval Office, but in the unlikely event Katrina had misinterpreted what she saw, he couldn't risk it.

"Who's taking top-level security calls from the field?"

"Let me check. Um, the D/DIRNSA, sir."

Great. Blake Bauer. All Jordan needed. "Guess I have no choice."

He thought he heard a snicker, as if DIRNSA's secretary empathized. "I'll put you through."

"Kirkwood? You know this line is restricted to emergencies from the field."

"Affirmative."

"I don't know where you are, but you're not officially in the field, are you?"

"On temporary leave, Blake."

"Then if you need to talk to me, call me on a standard line."

"What, you think I'm new at this? I know the protocols and that I'm willing to talk to you should tell you something. How about we put aside our personal issues and you hear me out for the sake of the security of the country."

"All right, but this had better be good."

When Jordan finished his rehearsal of the facts as he knew them, Blake Bauer was uncharacteristically silent. Usually he responded immediately, bloviating about all he would have to do to remedy the situation.

"Taking notes, Kirkwood. Bear with me."

"Take your time."

"Time is something we don't have."

"That's what I thought, Blake. A worthy call, then?"

"Yeah, sorry. And listen, I thought you did remarkably well with your Crimson Tide debriefing."

Jordan hesitated. What was this? "Don't start complimenting me after all these years. You'll confuse me."

Blake Bauer chuckled. "Let me just say I agree with DIRNSA that we don't want to lose you."

"Oh, so that's—"

"And this call is one of the reasons why."

Shameless. Jordan realized that if he somehow decided not to leave the agency, Bauer would take the credit. "Let's keep in mind the urgency of this, eh?"

"Right, right. I'll get to the DOD and involve DIRNSA as soon as he's available. Meanwhile you and yours stay away from Izmir, hear?"

"Just know I'm here if you need me."

"I imagine Defense will start with space and air surveillance, then ground troops. Izmir is not that far from Adana and Incirlik."

"About five hundred miles, Blake. And about six hundred from Tel Aviv."

"Hadn't thought of that."

"That's why they pay me the big bucks."

Bauer actually laughed. Was it possible he was human, after all? "Thanks, Jordan. You should probably stay in Istanbul until somebody gets back to you."

Normally those would be fighting words and Jordan would head straight for Izmir to insert himself into the middle of the action. But he didn't need any more reason to stay in Istanbul than the young woman waiting for him on the terrace with her mother. He was sworn to protect the security of the United States, but he would die for one of his own children. Jordan would keep Katrina far from Izmir until he knew the situation was stabilized.

When he rejoined Cydya and Katrina, Cydya looked jittery, Katrina curious. He filled them in on his phone calls. "Believe me, if something nefarious is going on, U.S. intelligence and Defense will ferret it out and deal with it. You did the right thing, Katrina."

Cydya put a hand on Jordan's arm. "And when it's all said and done, she will be safe?"

"Truth is, she was a little reckless."

Katrina snorted. "I know."

"But, yes. We'll keep an eye on you, and we'll root out this faction, and there won't be anyone left looking for revenge on a snitch."

"*Snitch* seems like such a tame word for me if I really protected the world from some danger."

"You're better with words than I am. Actually, you may prove to be a heroine."

"I like that better."

"Hey, Katrina, could I get a few moments with just you? There are things I'd like to discuss."

She looked at her mother, who nodded. Katrina shrugged. "Sure."

"Let's take a walk. We'll be back soon, Cyd."

As they strolled the upscale neighborhood, occasionally deafened by planes landing at Atatürk, Katrina seemed to study Jordan. "You seem very familiar with my mom. How far do you go back?"

"Many years."

"How many?"

"Since before you were born."

"Where did you meet?"

"Peace Corps."

Katrina stopped and blanched. "Mr. Kirkwood, did you know my father?"

"I did. I do."

"Would you tell my mother that I'm of age, old enough to meet him? I have some questions for him. Like how he could have ignored me my whole life."

"That's what I wanted to talk to you about. He was unaware of you."

"Mom told me that recently, but how can that be? And if it's true, why can't I meet him?"

"It had to do with mail he never saw."

"You know him well enough to know that?"

Jordan nodded. "He's been so eager to meet you, he couldn't stand it."

Katrina found a bench at a bus stop and sat. "I need you to be very careful what you say to me, Mr. Kirkwood. This person who claims to have known nothing of me has dominated my thoughts since I was old enough to figure things out."

"I can only imagine."

"Know what it's like to not have a father?"

Jordan shook his head.

"I mean, other kids had dads who were gone. Separated. Divorced. Dead. But at least they knew where they were. Mom never even showed me a picture. I can't complain about her as a mother. I never wanted for anything—except a father, or at least to know."

"You're trembling, Katrina."

She folded her arms across her middle and rocked. "I want to meet him and he wants to meet me. Can you make that happen?"

"Yes, ma'am, I can. I brought a gift for you from him."

"You did not."

Jordan pulled the box from his pocket and handed it to her. She was shuddering so much that she could barely grasp it. "I saw this on the table in the restaurant. This is really from my dad?"

Jordan nodded. "Open it."

Katrina set the box in her lap and removed the

lid with fingers she could barely control. She drew in a breath when the turquoise caught the light from a nearby lamppost. "It's gorgeous."

Jordan sat next to her, his shoulder barely touching hers. She pulled it from the box and let the chain dangle as she studied it. Finally she turned it over, tilting the piece toward the light and squinting. She read aloud. " 'With delinquent love from your father. J.K.' " She looked up at him. "J.K.?"

Jordan nodded, fighting tears, and reached for the necklace. He fastened it around her neck and she collapsed into his arms, sobbing.

They held each other for a long time.

"You need to know you have a half sister and a half brother."

She pulled back and stared into his eyes. "Seriously? Something else I always wanted. Tell me all about them."

"I've got a lot to tell you, sweetheart, but let's not make your mother wait, hm?"

When they reached Cydya, walking with arms around each other's waists, she stood smiling to embrace them. They spent till midnight sharing life stories and planning a meeting between Katrina and Christa and Ken.

Six days later, Jordan was interrupted during an afternoon of shopping with Cydya and Katrina by a secure text message from Chuck Wallington.

DOD CONFIRMED INAPPROPRIATE HEAT
SIGNATURES FROM YOUR MOSQUE'S
MINARET VIA SATELLITE IMAGING.
TURKISH INTELLIGENCE AND NATO
GROUND FORCES STORMED THE SITE
YESTERDAY AND CAPTURED THE PHONY
IMAM ALONG WITH DOCUMENTATION ON
HOW TO ATTACH A NUCLEAR WARHEAD TO
A SCUD MISSILE. DATA ONSITE
SUGGESTS THE RADICALS WERE
PLANNING TO TARGET INCIRLIK AIR
BASE AND TEL AVIV. YOU DIDN'T HEAR
THIS FROM ME, BUT KATRINA LEMONDE
IS GOING TO QUIETLY RECEIVE A
PRESIDENTIAL MEDAL OF FREEDOM.
WELL DONE.

When Jordan put his phone away, Katrina
looked up from a piece of fabric she was scruti-
nizing. "What was that about?"

"Let's just say your future as a tour guide is
secure."

Cydya surprised him by taking his hand. "What
do you think of inviting Ken and Christa to France
next semester? I'd like for us all to meet."

Center Point Publishing
600 Brooks Road ● PO Box 1
Thorndike ME 04986-0001 USA

(207) 568-3717

US & Canada:
1 800 929-9108
www.centerpointlargeprint.com

DATE DUE

JW			